HUNTED

THE SACRIFICE

BOOK ONE

ABOUT THE AUTHOR

Donna Collins was born at home in Romford, Essex, England. Five minutes later, she was one-hundred-per cent a bookworm. Her favourite novel, Enid Blyton's *The Children of Cherry Tree Farm*, was a gift from her parents and now the most worn book on her bookshelf.

It was this book, and her love for 70's and 80's TV shows such as *Hart to Hart*, *Charlie's Angels*, *Hunter*, and *Dempsey and Makepeace*, that lured Donna to the dark side of mystery and thriller writing. Since then, Donna has racked up many favourite authors, including Paula Gosling (*A Running Duck* is the second most worn book on her bookshelf), Jonathan Kellerman, Patricia Cornwell, and A.J. Quinnell.

Although Donna loves to write, she also loves crime - and her career proves it. Having founded her school magazine, her professional career includes not only working at OK! Magazine but also for Essex Police, Ormiston Prison Services, and Essex Offender Services. With publishing credits for freelance and commissioned magazine articles under her belt, Donna has now turned her

attention and imagination to what she is best at –
storytelling.

In her spare time (what spare time?), Donna loves
anything scary that will get her adrenaline
pumping, including storm chasing, fright nights,
zombie-infested shopping malls, and séance panic
rooms - with her all-time goal involving the open
sea, a cage, and a whole heap of great white sharks.
Donna also proudly boasts finishing the 2010
London Marathon, but you'll have to ask nicely if
you want her to tell you where she was placed and
who overtook her.

The Sacrifice is the first in the Hunted Thriller
series.

Contact

admin@donnacollins.co.uk
www.donnacollins.co.uk
Facebook /DonnaCollinsUK
Instagram @DonnaCollinsUK

Also by Donna Collins

<u>The Hunted Series</u>

Resurrection

The Undoing

<u>The Jason Wade Series</u>

Dead in the Water

HUNTED: THE SACRIFICE

Donna Collins

Willow Books

AUTHOR'S NOTE

I love the south-west of England.

Needless to say, the majority of this book is set across Devon and Cornwall. Most of the places are real and some, although real, have a little of my imagination thrown in for good measure. It's up to you to decide which aspects are true and which are false. For instance, it is true that James Hamilton's residence is in Readymoney Cove in Fowey and based on the location of a house that Daphne de Maurier lived in for a year? And, it is true that if you walk towards the woods, there is a path that leads to the ruins that were once St Catherine's Castle?

I would also like to thank the following people who helped make this book happen.

Jackie Elliff – Your artistic skills never fail to amaze me.

Will Terran – For your great imagination.

Kristen Lamb – For teaching me the ways of the WANA Warrior, and for taking me to pick a fight at the Bonsai Gardens.

Megan and Jamie – For bearing with me

For Dad

My Rock. My Inspiration. My Hero.

CHAPTER ONE

TWO WEEKS AGO
Amalfi Cathedral, Campania. Italy.

The climbing harness cut into his groin.

Roman shifted position, tried to ignore the dull ache as best he could, and listened.

For forty-five sodding minutes he'd been hanging in the darkened caverns beneath the cathedral, listening.

He pulled back his cap, ruffled his hair, and scratched his lobe. These earphones irked the shit out of him. Water droplets fell from the ceiling and splashed into the water fifteen metres below. At first the tiny splashes had absorbed his attention, each droplet falling exactly ten seconds apart. The bright light on his diver's watch had timed the first twelve. After that, he'd grown bored and released the button. Now the noise just aggravated the hell out of him. The crowd in the room above shuffled across the floor, and Roman listened until the group exited through the north door. Time: quarter past seven. Time to rock and roll. He slid the headphones around his neck, hooked the listening device onto his belt, and pulled the additional ropes he'd secured to the ceiling to haul himself out of harm's way. From his pocket he drew a pen-like detonator. He had exactly six minutes and forty-two seconds until the next tour arrived.

Turning his face, he pressed the detonator. Pre-placed explosive wire fizzed to life, and debris rained down upon him. Light exploded in the air and ignited the damp, chiselled cavern, and only when visibility died did he turn back. The pungent aroma of sulphur hit the back of his throat, a taste he'd come to love, and he slipped the detonator back into its holster and released the rope until he hung underneath the weakened section of the ceiling. Taking a deep breath, he raised his palms and pushed upwards, his arms shaking under the weight. The destabilised rock broke free and, with one last heave, flipped over onto the floor above him.

Roman pushed the goggles up onto his head, loosened the harness around his waist, and pulled himself up through the small hole. Now perched on his arse, he illuminated his watch and glanced around the narrow sarcophagus he'd just broken into. Cobwebs, dirt, and the skeletal bones of St Andrew - wrapped in eroding cloth and crushed beneath the overturned concrete slab. Roman felt the underside of the coffin roof. Not jagged rock as before, but the cold smoothness of a more impressive, expensive stone. He placed his hands flat in the centre and slid it to one side. The onyx marble made a high-pitched squeal as it glided surprisingly easily apart, and Roman wondered how many dogs had heard. Once open, he popped his head out and gave the room a quick once-over. It was empty, as it should be, and he checked his watch again. Three minutes fifty-eight seconds remaining. Damn, he was fast.

On the opposite side of the room, an old, oversized timber frame shrouded a wooden door. Ignoring several priceless antiques and treasures, Roman hurried towards it. Reaching over his shoulder for his backpack, he pulled out a bundle of material. Once unrolled, he removed four Plasticine pads and stuck them to the wall above the frame, each approximately a foot apart. Across them, he ran a metre-long length of wire and jammed each piece of clay with a small explosive. Then, he backed away from the door and took shelter behind a thick marble pillar.

With the detonator in his hand again, he pressed the button. The wall above the door ripped apart and plaster and brick tumbled to the floor, sending a cloud of white debris gusting across the immaculately kept room. Roman raced back towards the door, stumbling across the minefield of broken limestone and concrete. Clearing the fog of dust from his view, he saw the wooden frame lying among the rubble. It could have been mistaken as part of a railway sleeper. Luckily, it wasn't nearly as heavy as one. He dragged it back to the sarcophagus, tilted it upwards, and dropped it through the hole. It hit the shallow sewer below with more of a thunderous crash than a splash, and by the time the echo died, he'd already climbed back into the crypt.

The hall door burst open and a herd of security men charged the room. Any sound the coffin made as Roman reset the lid was drowned out by the disorganised shouting of panicked guards. Another thirty seconds before the dust settled and his footprints around the crypt would be swallowed up by every Keystone Cop who scampered around up there. Roman reattached his harness, lowered himself down through the hole until water touched his feet, and then unhooked himself.

Taking his baseball cap from his rucksack, he pulled it onto his head. The timber weighed heavily on his shoulder as he broke into a light run through the shallow sewer and towards the open sea.

WEDNESDAY – PRESENT DAY
Pendennis Port, Cornwall. England.

Roman saw the old man – or at least saw his blacked-out Mercedes waiting at the docks.

As he approached, the old timer got out, his grey hair combed over to cover the bald patch on top of his head, and his two-piece suit no longer able to hide the hunch across his shoulders.

Roman held out a hand but the old man crossed his arms, clearly discouraging any attempt to connect.

"Do you have it?"

Roman glanced over his shoulder and motioned towards the wooden crate being winched off the boat.

"Good. As before, I will need to verify the contents before payment."

Roman blocked the pensioner's path. "And as I said before, I need to know where the blood is."

"And, as I also said before, we are still working on that." The old man turned towards his car. A burly gentleman emerged and raised an aluminium case into view. "Now. The contents?"

Roman stood aside.

A thin, almost anorexic-looking woman got out of the Mercedes and scurried over to the crate. She waited while a second, hefty-looking gentleman prised the lid off the box, and then examined the contents, her spindle-like fingers whisking through the straw packaging like a dog digging for its bone. It wasn't until she gave a thumbs up that the old man signalled for the briefcase to be handed over.

"Expenses for your next trip are also in there," he said.

Roman took the case. "Thank you. I'll have the third piece back here day after tomorrow."

"Don't be late, Mr. Holbrook. I have much depending on this arrangement of ours."

"*We* have much depending on it." Roman looked the old man in the eye. "And I expect to hear some news about the blood then, as well."

"You will know as soon as I do."

Roman leaned in closer to the old man. "I hope you're not thinking about shafting me."

"Shafting you?" The old man chuckled. "Do I have to remind you of what's at stake? This arrangement between us will fall apart if we don't work together."

"From where I'm standing, it feels like I'm the only one doing the work."

The old man's eyes narrowed. "Have you forgotten what I am capable of doing to you?"

"Don't threaten me, old man. You can't kill me."

The old man glanced at Roman's hand. Immediately, Roman's little finger snapped outwards to the side.

A suppressed groan left Roman's lips. He felt his face redden, cracked his finger back in place, and hoped his short-lived vulnerability had been overlooked. "Thought you'd have learned some new tricks by now."

"Likewise."

Roman didn't need to look at his finger. He felt it realign with the knuckle. It was seconds from being fully healed. To prove the point, Roman raised his hand. "I could take your life like that." He clicked his fingers.

The old man smiled. "Then why don't you?"

Roman clenched his fist.

The old man grinned. "We need each other, Mr. Holbrook. Whether you like it or not."

Roman relaxed his hand and stretched his fingers. He wanted to tell the old man to go fuck himself.

"Remember, Mr. Holbrook. We want the same thing, you and I. I will soon have the blood."

"Yeah, yeah, and I will soon have the wood."

The old man headed back towards the car. After the skinny woman had gotten in, he climbed in alongside her. It was only after the car pulled away from the docks that Roman let out the frustrated breath he'd been holding. *Shit.* When exactly had he become the old man's bitch? He slung his rucksack over his shoulder, picked up the briefcase, and headed towards the Aston parked in the far corner of the docks.

He knew one thing for sure: the old man had no intention of handing over the blood. So Roman would just have to find it for himself.

CHAPTER TWO

Doctor Bob Marino moved like a little boy trying to make it to the toilet on time.

He swiped the stack of disposable surgical gloves and cardboard kidney dishes to the floor and patted the cleared surface, unable to hide the expectation of what the next few minutes would bring.

Eliza Hamilton stepped forward, and Bob's expression turned to one of pure excitement. He handed her a plastic champagne flute and topped it to the brim with a wine Eliza had never heard of, then gulped back the contents of his own glass and offered a strawberry from a supermarket punnet.

"Happy birthday, Eliza," he said, re-topping her glass. "How's it feel hitting the big three-O?"

Eliza took a strawberry and seductively bit it in half. "Officially, it's not my birthday for another fifty-four minutes."

Bob was a handsome guy, although older than her by about fifteen years. He put down his glass, along with the punnet, and grinned like a cat ready to pounce on its prey. His arm slipped around her waist and he gently pushed her into a secluded corner of the supply cupboard.

"I still have a patient to see before I can leave tonight." Eliza glanced towards the door, her feeble attempts to stop him going unheard.

"But I can't hold back any longer."

"Someone could come in and find us."

A satisfied grin crept across his face. "C'mon. You've got five more minutes."

This tryst between the two of them was supposed to happen back at her place later, where she had a bed, and candles, and romantic music. Not now, in a cramped cupboard surrounded by bottles of liquid soap and a bin of used syringes. But Bob was gorgeous and had that Doctor Kildare thing down to a tee, and like some teenager with a school crush, Eliza felt extremely flattered at his persistence in trying to get her into bed. Okay, so it was true he'd slept with almost every nurse in the hospital, but Eliza hadn't had sex in seventeen months – not that she was counting – and my God for once did she need to just let her hair down and live a little. It was this latter point that made it very hard to say no to Bob now. Well, that, and the staff gossip that ranked Bob's sexual performance second to none. Oh God, was she actually going to go through with this and have some rushed, sneaky shag in a dingy hospital supply cupboard?

Heck, yes.

Bob eyed her, and his cocky smile widened. "We can do it all over again back at your place later. This can be the test drive."

His blue eyes sparkled, and although Eliza knew it had more to do with his bout of autumn hay fever and less to do with his Italian heritage, she couldn't help but feel aroused.

"And," he pressed against her, his erection evident, "whatever we fail to discuss tonight, we could continue over breakfast tomorrow."

A full night of sleazy, sordid, hot, sticky sex. Guaranteed. Finally, that little red number from Victoria's Secret would see some action. Oh, tonight would quench her yearning needs. Tonight, *50 Shades* and the vibrator had the evening off.

Bob manoeuvred his thigh between her legs and gently tugged open the collar of her uniform. The stiffness in his trousers couldn't be ignored.

"What about my rounds?"

"The patients can wait. Half the buggers are so drugged up they don't even know what day of the week it is." He ran his index finger along the edge of her bra and his eyes lowered to her bust.

A shiver tickled the length of Eliza's spine.

He cupped her breast. "Oh, Eliza, I want you so much."

I want you, too. But maybe play a little harder to get. "Bob, I don't think I can. Not like this."

"You're right." He took her champagne glass and lifted her onto the counter.

"No, I mean I think I should finish my rounds and we continue this back at my place like we planned."

"Yeah, yeah, we will do all that. After. This won't take long." He hooked up the hem of her skirt, then fiddled with the buckle on his belt. "I need to unload before I burst."

Unload?

"Rub it, baby. Tell me how much you need it."

Unload?

Less than a second. That's all it took for her fantasy to disappear in a puff of smoke. Goodbye, hot sex siren. Hello again, workaholic nurse...albeit now a seemingly naive one with moist knickers. "I'm not a sperm bank," she said.

Bob nuzzled into her neck. "Mmm, I know. Now, spread 'em. Daddy needs in."

His aftershave wafted beneath her nostrils, and for a moment she wondered if she'd heard him correctly. Regardless of how much she needed this rendezvous, she had standards, and this sleazy tryst had just plummeted to a whole new level she didn't appreciate. She slapped his hand from her breast.

"I'll be real quick, I promise," Bob said, reaching for it again. "I can only release with you, baby."

The tip of his warm tongue teased her neck. His lips covered her skin. Was he actually giving her a love bite? Eliza grabbed a scuff of his hair and yanked his head back.

A puzzled look clouded his eyes. "What's wrong?"

She jumped down off the counter and straightened her uniform. The bastard had undone her bra. When the hell had that happened? "I'm sorry, but I have to go check on a patient."

"I don't understand. Is it something I said?"

Eliza stifled a laugh. He was almost funny. "No, no. I just feel like..." *Bridget Jones...?* "Daddy will have to release somewhere else tonight."

"And what am I supposed to do with that?" Bob looked down at his erect penis.

"You have an imagination. Use it."

He smiled. "You have a mouth?"

"I have many things, all of which are off limits to that thing tonight."

"But I won't be able to leave this cupboard until it's deflated. You could at least give me a hand."

"Tell you what, Bob, you give yourself a hand. I'm going to finish my rounds."

Bob's lips tightened. "At least stay and watch."

"You're unbelievable." Eliza started towards the door.

"And you're a tease." Bob snatched the half-eaten strawberry from her hand.

The self-professed Adonis of a man stood before her, dick in one hand, half-eaten strawberry in the other. Eliza bit her lip and killed the smile trying to blossom. "Goodnight, Bob."

The corridor outside was empty, and Eliza thanked God for small mercies. She fumbled for the back of her bra through her uniform. Bugger, she couldn't re-fix the clasp. Bloody Bob. She crossed the corridor and entered Jason Devlin's room, the last patient on her rounds. Drawn curtains blocked any moonlight, and other than the small television set that glowed in the corner, the room was dark.

Eliza switched off the set.

The bed squeaked as the patient stirred, and a bedside lamp illuminated the room.

"Sorry, Jason. Did I wake you?"

Jason, his elevated leg in plaster, struggled to sit up. "I was awake."

"Here, let me help you."

The bruised face he'd arrived with ten days earlier had lightened to a yellowish-green, and the swelling around his jaw had almost disappeared. "You're an angel. What would I do without you?"

Eliza blushed. *If only he'd seen me minutes earlier.*

"I can't wait to get into my own bed and have a decent night's sleep."

"Well, you'll be out of here tomorrow." She poured him a glass of water. "Be a while before you're on your bike again, though."

"Be a while before I have a bike to ride again. I hear it's a crumpled mess."

Eliza smiled sympathetically, and plumped his cushion until he looked a little more comfortable. "Is there anything else I can get you before I leave for the night?"

"You could turn the television back on."

Eliza closed the door behind her at the same time Bob exited the storeroom. He tucked his shirt into his trousers, threw her a look that would turn a person to stone, and marched towards her.

"Here. Seeing as I bought these for you, you may as well have them." He took her hand and plonked the punnet of strawberries on it. The plastic edge sliced the side of her palm and tiny blood dots pricked into view. If Bob noticed, he didn't show an ounce of concern. "Enjoy."

Eliza wiped the blood away and watched Bob swagger off along the corridor. Now she was glad she'd neglected to tell him his zipper was still undone.

Outside, the night had cooled significantly from the surprisingly warm October day. Eliza pulled the collar of her coat tight around her neck, wishing her car hadn't chosen this day to break down, and headed out towards the street. A night bus passed, and she yelled for the driver's attention. The bus didn't stop, and two teenage youths mooned her from the upper back window.

Then, rain began to fall.

Searching her bag proved fruitless for an umbrella, and Eliza turned back towards the hospital. The thought of going back in there evaporated when she clocked Bob through the main doors in hot pursuit of the pretty receptionist. As much as Eliza detested the rain, being wet was a small price to pay to retain what little dignity she had left. *Happy birthday to me.*

She turned up the collar on her coat and began the long walk towards the taxi rank.

Looe Station was small, like its village, and at this time of year the derelict platform was only manned for a few hours a day. Hardly any trains stopped and hardly anyone used it, with the business entrepreneurs preferring to drive to nearby towns. Outside the station, on top of the bridge, a tiny wooden hut served as the village's main taxi rank. Eliza walked up and pushed on the door. No light escaped past the mesh-covered window, and when she glanced down and spotted a padlock securing the door, it confirmed her worst fear.

"Damn it." She reached for her phone, her fingers hovering over the buttons. She had no idea what the nearest cab number was.

A blanket of darkness swept across her. She stared up at the sky, catching a brief glance of the moon before the clouds regrouped and blocked it again. Not the usual silvery white moon one would expect to see, and not the copper red of a lunar eclipse. This moon was dark, with a halo of green light glowing around it. Eliza had never seen the moon look like this before, and its haunting appearance unnerved her.

A train sped beneath the bridge and pulled her from her thoughts. It continued through the station before disappearing into a tunnel of trees and leaving a whirlwind of fallen leaves and foliage to settle on the track. Eliza glanced once more at the sky, but the moon had completely disappeared behind the clouds. She wanted nothing more than the comfort of her own home, a hot bath, and a bottle of wine. Catching a train suddenly seemed her only logical option. She made her way back across the bridge, where a rusty handrail aided her down some iron steps to the station, and headed for the pebble-dashed shelter at the far end of the platform. Screwed to its wall was an information board. If nothing else, she could check the timetable and at least stay dry while she waited for the next train.

One surviving Victorian streetlamp flickered midway along the platform, the glow just touching upon the information board. Rain streaked down the scratched Perspex, and no matter how hard Eliza tried, the jumble of departure times was impossible to decipher. The lack of information meant she could be waiting hours for a train – maybe even until morning. She lowered her head in defeat.

She had no choice but to return to the hospital.

Beyond the streetlamp, in the shadows, a tall figure stood in the shadows – a man, Eliza instantly presumed. She paused, unsure for a moment whether she should feel threatened at her obvious vulnerability, or indeed safer at the prospect of having another person nearby to help her. Seconds ticked by. The figure didn't move, nor did it offer conversation. Instead, it remained still, and watched her. The hairs on the back of Eliza's neck pricked to life, and she pushed her wet, auburn hair from her face in the hope her body language would convey some kind of confidence. It certainly didn't instil any inner strength. Her heartbeat accelerated, and she found herself backing away.

The figure stepped forward and followed her. Slowly at first, its feet not walking but floating inches above the ground. An ice-cold breeze, the kind only felt on the wintriest of days, surrounded Eliza, and when she exhaled, her breath frosted the air.

Then the figure surged towards her.

The nearer it got, the blurrier its shape became, until it resembled no more than a dark cloud. A Shadow, which engulfed Eliza like a tidal wave would a ship. Finger-like claws grabbed her hand, and chilblains immediately pained her fingertips. Eliza parted her lips to scream but the Shadow invaded her mouth, darting to the back of her throat and down into her stomach. Now inside her, it slammed her back against the shelter. In an instant, Eliza's battle against the attack turned to one against suffocation. She kicked and fought the force that smothered her, but its fingers dug deeper against her arms, pinning her harder against the wall. Eliza's chest burned, and her lungs felt ready to explode. Realisation dawned. This thing wasn't letting go until it had sucked the last pocket of air from her dying body. Again, she tried to punch free but her weakened arms were no longer a threat.

Through the Shadow's haze, the streetlight had become no more than a small, orange dot in front of her. Convulsions shook her body, but the orange light called to her. Was this Heaven trying to guide her from this pain? *No. I am not ready to go.* In the distance she heard the bulb shatter, and the orange dot vanished completely from sight.

Tiny shards of glass rained down upon her, and as quickly as it had attacked, the Shadow retreated from her throat and evaporated from sight. Eliza slumped to her knees, her legs unable to hold her up unaided. Tears streamed the sides of her face, and spluttered coughs choked her with every shot of night air she desperately sucked in.

Beside the broken streetlamp, she saw a shape running down the station steps. For a second she froze.

The shape came closer and Eliza scrambled to her feet. "Somebody help me!"

The shape drew closer, its humanlike qualities mimicking that from before. Eliza's soul filled with dread. But even with the lack of light and the torrential rain beating down upon her, she started to notice the differences. The first shadowy shape had floated. When this Shadow moved towards her, she heard footsteps echo on the wet platform.

Eliza retreated further and the human shape slowed, each step now gradual, until a man stood only feet from her. He paused, the rim of his baseball cap shadowing his face and leaving only a stubbled chin visible. Without uttering a word, he reached for her hand. The swift movement caught Eliza off guard. She tried to pull free, but the man held tight.

"Goddamn. You're one of them, aren't you?" the man said.

His question confused Eliza, and she could only gaze at him.

"Can't you speak?"

But Eliza had no words. Her mind raced over the events of the last ten minutes in an attempt to decipher what was happening to her now. A slight movement caught her attention and she turned from him. Ice-cold air returned around her and the man released her hand, his face not revealing even the smallest glimmer of surprise. Several Shadows crept forward from the darkened corners of the platform, stretching out across the floor to touch and caress each other until their edges morphed into one, taking on an almost human look.

"Go. Now," the man said, pushing Eliza towards the stairs.

Eliza ran, but the Shadow blocked her path. Its spindly fingers grabbed her waist and spun her until the tips of her shoes wavered on the edge of the platform.

Then, the grip let go.

The man lunged towards her, his arms outstretched, but Eliza tumbled off the platform edge. Her skull whacked the train tracks and a sickening crack, like that of a whip, reverberated inside her head. A gurgled cry left her throat. Acute pain burned behind her eyes, and with shaking fingers she fumbled through her blood-soaked hair and tried to reach the source of her injury. When she found the swelling lump, she retched.

A cold grip entwined her waist and flipped her onto her front. Eliza's face hit the dirt, and the Shadow swept down her legs and tightened around her ankles. Before Eliza could kick free, the Shadow dragged her backwards along the tracks. Eliza screamed for help, clawing at the loose gravel, the shingle fracturing and splintering her short but manicured fingernails. The man jumped onto the tracks, his rust-coloured Timberlands landing on the railway line some metres away and charged her way. He leapt over her and the grasp around her ankles loosened, leaving Eliza lying motionless, listening to her own erratic breathing. She lifted her head. Matted hair fell across her eyes. She tried to move but collapsed again. Darkness blurred her vision, and only the whine of the approaching train told her she was still alive...for now.

Water splashed Eliza's face.

She partially opened her eyes, blinking away further onslaught from the rain, and looked at the man staring down at her. "Am I dead?"

For a moment, he didn't answer. He wiped some of the water droplets from her cheek and gazed at her, his blue eyes radiating concern. Then, his face hardened. "Why? Do you want to be?"

Did she want to be? Did his response mean that she was? "Where am I?"

She tried to sit up, but pain exploded behind her eyes. The man pressed her back against the ground, that look of concern returning. He reached for her face, and again Eliza felt his warm fingers brush her cheek. Like magic, she felt a calm sweep over her. *Where am I? The hospital cupboard?* No, she'd left the hospital. *Where did I go?* She couldn't remember. "The train—"

"The train's been and gone," the man said, his fingers lingering against her skin.

"Did it hit me?" Eliza tried again to sit up, but the man held her still.

"Relax. You're not on the tracks, you're on the platform." He seemed to realise he still touched her face, and cleared his throat. "You're one of them, aren't you?"

One of who?

"Jesus Christ. I thought you were a myth." The man leaned back. He seemed unsure what to do next. "As long as they can smell your blood, they will come for you again."

They? They who? What was he talking about? That Shadow thing?

Eliza sat upright, her eyes searching every inch of the platform.

"It's gone." Again, the man lowered her back to the floor. "Do you know what you are?"

What is he talking about? "N..Nurse?"

The man sat back, pulled a cigarette from inside his jacket pocket, and lit it. The match flicked from his hand and landed somewhere in the darkness.

Eliza tried to focus on him, but he'd become a blur. "Who are you?"

He stared at her, seemingly apprehensive to answer. Finally, he puffed on his cigarette and said, "Roman."

Dizziness took hold. Blurred shapes swarmed inside Eliza's head. Only the orange glow of the cigarette stood out like a beacon in the darkness. Somewhere in the distance she heard voices. Maybe male, she couldn't be certain. Eliza closed her eyes. Good, more help was on the way.

"Fuck." A hand clasped the side of her face and then Roman's voice was in her ear. "You're okay for now. But when daylight fades and it gets dark again, they'll be back. Stay in the light."

Without uttering another word, Roman stood. "And get your head stitched up. They know the scent of your blood now." Seconds passed, and then he turned and headed towards the train tracks. *He's leaving me?*

Up on the bridge, panicked echoes of conversation floated down as the two males hurried by. Eliza lifted her head. Tried to call out for help, but the words stuck in her throat. Pain reignited behind her eyes and she collapsed back on the platform.

She lay there, cold and alone, not knowing what to do.

Billy.

She fumbled inside her coat pocket, felt the smoothness of her phone, and for the first time in a long while, wished she didn't have a touch screen. Pulling it out, the bright screen blinded her. She squinted, touched what she thought was the green receiver icon, and prayed.

CHAPTER THREE

THURSDAY

Roman Holbrook needed to take a piss.

He stirred and jolted upright. His head protested the sudden movement, and immediately he massaged his temples until the pounding subsided and he was able to think more clearly.

Moonlight filtered through the open curtains, bringing a blue haze to an otherwise sparse and dismal bedroom. Only four items of furniture lived in this room: a small, paint-chipped side table covered in woodworm, which was probably the reason the previous tenants had left it behind; a single bed, complete with stained and sagging mattress; and a television – not a modern flat-screen, but a 1970s box with a metal coat hanger jammed into its top. It balanced on a broken stool, which wobbled whenever there was nearby movement. Apart from the TV, the room wasn't dissimilar to the one he'd shared with Jane many years before.

He closed his eyes at the mere thought of her. She hadn't visited his memories in such a long time, but here she was, her skin pale and smooth, her lips longing for his touch. He savoured her image, happy to lie with her until the day death came for him – as he'd wished it to so many times in the past. But slowly Jane drifted away from him, leaving nothing but a foul taste in his mouth, and an overwhelming guilt that would no doubt consume him for the rest of the day.

The phone rang and Roman, hung-over as he was, reflexively answered it before the second ring. He tried to swallow, but his tongue scraped across his dry palate.

The old man spoke, his voice cold and controlled. "Where were you last night?"

"Out getting pissed."

"Would the drinking establishment happen to be in the vicinity of the train station?"

"Not to my knowledge."

"When you left, did you happen to follow two of my men to the station?"

"You have a hard-on for the trains first thing in the morning, don't ya?"

The old man chuckled. "Knocking them unconscious was a little excessive."

"Like I said, I don't know what you're talking about." Roman yawned. "Is that the Q and A session done with?"

"Don't push me, Mr. Holbrook. My patience is wearing thin as it is. Now, when do you leave for Paris?"

"Later today. Why? You gonna miss me?"

The line went dead, leaving Roman listening to nothing but a dial tone and the feeling he was still one step behind whatever the old git was planning. *That old fuck-head.* Roman replaced the receiver and lay back against the pillow. Thought about the girl's bag he'd found on the train tracks. The bag that now lay on his kitchen table.

Christ, he felt like shit.

A soft voice groaned beside him, but he didn't look at her. He didn't need to. She'd be blonde, married or engaged to be and, with a little persuading, up for anything. She slid her arm across his chest, a small diamond ring on her wedding finger from a man obviously too tight to buy her anything decent. No wonder these girls were so easy to pick up. On the bedside table sat a Smirnoff bottle, still open, and almost empty. He shook his head in disbelief, remembered the first drink and, at a push, vaguely remembered the second. The amount of nights he'd gone to bed drunk, he'd have thought he'd be immune to bloody hangovers by now. He rubbed crusty flakes of sleep from his eyes and yawned again. His bladder felt ready to explode.

His overnight visitor nuzzled in closer to him. *Shit.* He really needed to send these one-nighters home in a cab before he passed out.

Beside the bottle sat the clock. Five-twenty a.m. Fuck sake, no wonder he couldn't wake up. He'd only just gone to bed. But he couldn't, nor did he want to, go back to sleep with this girl beside him. She'd wake in the morning and expect breakfast, then push for conversation and finally finish with the grand finale of more sex. Whereas he was never hungry in the morning, definitely wouldn't want to shag her while sober, and as for talking? He did very little of that on a good day.

The ache in his groin intensified his need for the toilet, so he gently removed his overnight guest's arm and whipped his legs out of bed. His left foot landed on the threadbare carpet, his right on a carton of leftover chicken chow mein. The foil container crumpled beneath his weight, and oyster sauce shot between his toes. Glazed carrots and strands of noodles clung to the bottom of his foot, and when he shook it, shards of Chinese food spiralled in all directions, hitting everything in sight, including his crumpled navy linen suit.

When the hell did I buy Chinese? He gazed up at the water-stained ceiling for help. He bloody hated Thursdays.

Ten minutes later, and without time to shave, Roman was ready to be anywhere but here. With a chocolate digestive gripped between his lips, he tucked the crumpled shirt he'd found at the bottom of his wash basket into his jeans and headed to the kitchen, fastening tight his belt buckle as he went. He filled a glass with tap water, waited for the bubbles to clear, and then gulped it down, hoping to wash away the filthy taste at the back of his throat. It didn't. He needed something stronger.

A box of cigarettes lay beside the briefcase on the work surface, and Roman pulled one out. The young girl from his bed appeared in the doorway, wrapped only in the bed sheet, hair on end, mascara smeared halfway down her face. She smiled, and scratched beneath her left breast.

Classy.

The girl yawned and stretched, letting the sheet fall to the floor, revealing she wore no clothes whatsoever. "What's for breakfast?"

And there it is. Roman casually slipped his hand into the pocket of his jeans, finding an old tissue and the Zippo lighter he'd misplaced the month before. He lit the cigarette and took a long drag, holding the smoke at the back of his throat until it burned, and then exhaled. Grey-blue smog polluted the air, forming the perfect line, but it still wasn't enough to kill the bad taste in his mouth. He dunked the cigarette out in his glass of water, took a beer from the fridge, and headed to the front door. Remembered the briefcase of money on the table, and grabbed Eliza's bag and the cigarette box along with it. "I want you gone by the time I get back."

CHAPTER FOUR

Sunshine blazed through the hospital window, its rays warming the right side of Eliza's face.

She shielded her eyes and turned away. Her perspective on the room, which was identical to every other room she frequented when on her rounds, seemed different now she was the patient.

Her brother, Billy, turned from the window. Usually dapper, he looked disorganised and sloppy this morning. "Hey, you're awake." He came to her and planted a kiss on her forehead. "I'd wish you happy birthday, but under the circumstances..."

"How long have I been here?"

"A couple of hours." His police hat lay on the side table, his car keys nestled inside. He looked like he hadn't slept in days.

"When can I leave?"

"Not yet." He settled beside her. Tiny red veins coloured the whites of his eyes, and Eliza guessed her first diagnosis had been right: Billy couldn't have had any shuteye at all in the last twenty-four hours. "The doctor wants to keep you in, make sure you're okay."

"But I feel fine."

"Three stitches say otherwise." Billy squeezed her hand and gave a reassuring, if not condescending, smile.

Eliza slipped her hand free. "It's too bright in here."

Billy's eyes narrowed, but he got up and lowered the blinds, dimming the morning sun. "Is that better?" he said. His posh boarding school accent sounded misplaced while he was dressed as a police officer.

Eliza nodded, and prayed he'd stay where he was. Her head ached, sickness churned in the pit of her stomach, and the last thing she wanted was to deal with her brother and his quest to find out what had happened to her.

He must have sensed her feelings, because he remained by the window. He pulled the clip-on tie from his collar and struggled to unbutton the top of his shirt. "Uniform has way too much starch in it. I don't have to hang it up when I take if off at night, it just stands in the wardrobe like a dressmaker's dummy."

A slight smile creased the corners of Eliza's mouth. Billy, the Eton boy born with a silver spoon in his mouth who only seemed happy when he had something to moan about.

"So, how are you?"

"My head hurts."

"That's not what I meant."

"I know. But I'm not discussing Dad with you, Billy." Eliza sat up and felt her head, the ache intensifying even under her light touch. Billy was right: there was a huge lump there.

"You know, you scared the bejesus out of me last night," he said. "What on earth were you doing at the train station so late?"

Eliza thought back to the night before, trying to make sense of the muddled mess inside her head. She recalled Bob in the supply cupboard, which seemed more than ironic because that whole episode was the one thing she desperately wanted to forget. "I was waiting for a train. I left work and missed the bus."

"You should have called me."

"You are not my taxi service."

"I am if the alternative is you walking the streets late at night."

"You're treating me like a child."

"I'm treating you like a sister."

Sister? It seemed an age since they'd shared the sibling thing. It felt nice hearing him say it. "Always looking out for me, eh?"

Billy smiled. "Maybe just making up for lost time."

"You didn't choose to go to boarding school."

"Don't go there, Eliza."

She couldn't help herself. "But it's time you call a truce with Dad."

"Please. Don't start that up again."

"Start what? Every time I look at Dad I see you and remember."

"Remember what? How he sent me there because..." Billy paused. He stared at her and it was a moment before the fire in his eyes died. "Would you like me to say I made a mistake?"

"If you meant it?"

Billy sighed.

"Why can't you let it go? Mum died."

Billy huffed. "Mum was murdered."

"Seriously, Billy. It's been years. You need to let it go. It's destroying you."

"No, it isn't."

"Look at you! Your clothes, your hair. You're falling apart."

"Hey, I look like this because, thanks to you, I've had no sleep."

Eliza relaxed back against the pillow. They were going around in circles, just like always. "It's not healthy."

"I knew the truth. So did dad. That's why I was sent away."

"How many times do I have to say it? Dad did not kill our mother."

"I saw it with my own eyes."

Eliza shook her head. "You were just a boy."

Billy turned back to the window. "I'm going to prove it."

Eliza watched him. His shoulders rose with every heavy breath he inhaled. She loved her brother to death. Would do anything for him. But, their mother's death was slowly destroying him and there was nothing she could do about it. "I can't take any more of this."

"Any more of what? Our relationship is fine. The only time we argue is when you mention Dad."

"Because you're stopping us from being a real family."

"He stopped us, the moment he killed our mother and sent me away."

For a second, Billy's shoulders slumped and his eyes glazed. He looked ready to say something else, seemed to think better of it, and swiped his notebook from the table with little enthusiasm. "Tell me what happened last night."

Eliza paused. She wanted to console Billy. She wanted to be close again like they had been when they were kids.

"Well?"

"Billy, don't be like this."

"Be like what? We believe different things."

"We don't."

"Oh, so you no longer think the sun shines out of Dad's backside?"

Eliza turned away. She wasn't going to get anywhere with Billy now he was in this mood. She repositioned herself against the pillow. Nothing about last night made sense, and if she struggled to believe it herself, how would Billy react? "I slipped and hit my head on the tracks."

"Your injuries are from more than just a fall. You kept mumbling about a man in the shadows."

Eliza nodded. She flexed a cramp from her fingers. "He helped me."

"Off the lines? Why didn't he stick around? Why didn't he call for help?"

Eliza didn't know why. She wasn't even sure whether this man existed or was a figment of her imagination. She shrugged and reached for the water jug beside her, but Billy intervened. He filled a plastic cup and handed it to her.

"What did he look like, this man? Do you know him?"

Eliza sipped the water, which even at room temperature still managed to refresh her mouth. "Timberlands. Rust-coloured I think. And a hat, a baseball cap that hid his face."

"Have you seen him before?"

"No."

"And this wasn't the man who mugged you?"

"Mugged me?" Eliza handed back the cup. "Stop it. I fell. That's all, and now I just want to go home."

Billy's eye twitched. He was nervous about something. He caught her staring and closed his notebook. "Dad's on his way."

"What? You called him?"

"No. George did."

Eliza slumped back against the cushion.

"Hey, I don't like it either, but George is my sergeant and he pulled rank."

The room whirled before her and she closed her eyes, allowing the darkness to clear her mind. Images flickered across her memory like a flipbook. She remembered seeing the lamppost and hearing the sound of the bulb exploding; the feeling that she'd somehow done it even though she couldn't possibly have.

Billy felt her forehead. "Are you okay? Do you need me to get a doctor?"

"I'm fine. Just tired." Her father was the last person she wanted to see – especially while Billy was there. "You'd better go if he's on his way."

"Screw him. You're my little sister. How about I go fetch us a coffee?"

Eliza shook her head. Having Billy nearby gave her the confidence to deal with her father, but the awkwardness between them was just too much to handle.

The hospital door swung open. Her father, a handsome man by any standard, sauntered into the room. Hitting fifty, not one lock of his dark-brown hair had turned grey, and he looked as young as any forty-year-old she knew. Only a hint of crow's feet betrayed he may be older than one first assumed.

He ignored Billy completely, and went straight to his daughter's bedside. "So it is true."

Eliza tried to interject, but her father was having none of it. Once he started on one of his lectures, there was no stopping him.

"You have a car for a reason, Eliza."

"I thought you were in Geneva?"

"Landed an hour ago." He looked her over. "I was informed you were mugged."

Billy cleared his throat and stepped forward. "She slipped and banged her head. Has a couple of stitches and a concussion, nothing more. She'll be fine."

James glared at him. "When you have a medical degree, son, then I'll listen to your prognosis. Until then, I suggest you get on with what the good people of Looe pay you for: directing traffic and visiting primary schools."

"Well, *Dad*. I still have an hour before my shift starts."

"Then I suggest you use it to have a shower and smarten yourself up. Or is this the level of professionalism our police force aspires to these days?"

Billy stepped forward. "Hey—"

"Billy, it's alright," Eliza intervened.

Billy took a deep breath, and it was several seconds before the annoyance in his eyes died. His rigid lips hardly moved when he next addressed Eliza. "I'll phone you later. Maybe do Curry Thursday here tonight?" He grabbed his hat off the side table and opened the door.

"I'm sorry," he mouthed before closing it behind him.

"There was no need for that." Eliza glared at her father. "Billy found me last night. He's here as my brother."

"Trust me. He is only here to cause more trouble." Her father turned to her, clearly irate. He tugged at the sleeves of his casual yet no doubt expensive sweater, and folded his arms. "You've had a traumatic night, and I have to be outside in ten minutes to open the new wing. The amount of money I've thrown at this hospital, it's about time it increased in size and joined the twenty-first century. Now, the car's outside the main entrance—"

"Doctors want to keep me in overnight."

"What do they know? I'll talk to them. Arrange for you to be taken to the car. As soon as I've finished, we'll get you home."

"My home?"

A trying sigh escaped her father's lips. His jaw tightened, and impatience hardened his eyes. His whole face seemed to take on a new dimension. Then it simmered, and he was once again in control.

"Dad, we've had this conversation a thousand times. I have my own place now. You even agreed."

"That was before your safety was put at risk." He lowered his head and clasped the bridge of his nose. Deep furrows creased his brow, and Eliza wasn't sure if he was in pain or if she'd really tested his patience this time. He walked around the bed and stood by the window with his back towards her.

"You okay?"

He took a pillbox from his pocket and swallowed two tablets. "Your shenanigans cause me nothing but bloody headaches." He crossed his arms. It was nothing more than an elaborate display to show his disappointment in her – something she'd seen him do a hundred times before to staff and colleagues.

After a moment's silence, his stance softened and he let out another long sigh, although this one seemed more from relief.

"I don't wish to cause you pain, but I am old enough to make my own decisions now, Dad."

The stiffness returned to his shoulders. He glanced towards her, his cheeks burning red like they did every time her strive for independence aggravated him. The veins in his neck swelled, and Eliza prepared herself for his retaliation. She bit her lip, suddenly worried she wouldn't be strong enough to stand her ground.

"I will not argue over this, Eliza. You're hurt and need care, so like it or not, you are coming home with me. You can have your independence back when the doctor says you're fit enough."

Eliza wanted to argue, but she honestly didn't know what else to add. That today she'd turned thirty – something her father had obviously forgotten? Or that she was way too old to be controlled by him any longer? The weight of his glare bore down upon her. She wanted to reach for her necklace, but then he'd know she was nervous and take it as a sign of her weakness and his victory.

He paused, then forced an unconvincing, "You know I love you?"

Eliza's hands trembled. She clasped the bed sheet, scrunching it between her fingers.

Her father clapped his hands together, and rubbed them like he was trying to start a fire. "Good. Then it's settled."

There was a gentle tap at the door and her father's male assistant popped his head in. He was a very good-looking guy, but so far up her father's arse that at times Eliza was surprised he didn't vanish up there altogether. "They're ready for you, Mr. Hamilton."

"Ah, just the person." Her father pulled on the cuffs of his shirt, his silver cufflinks emerging from beneath his jumper sleeve. "My daughter will be accompanying me home. Arrange for her to be taken out to my car."

The assistant straightened and nodded, and for a moment Eliza wondered if he was about to salute. "Right away, sir." He backed out, bowing as he went.

Eliza relaxed against the pillow, defeated. Her head hurt, and she no longer had the energy to argue.

Her father watched, as if to bask in his triumph and remind her who was boss. "We'll have an hour together at home, then I am off to Switzerland. I'll be back tomorrow evening." Then he also left the room.

Wow, she got to have a whole hour with her father. He *must* be worried about her health. When she realised she'd started to stroke her hand she gazed towards the window and thought back to the previous night. Had the lamppost's bulb broken because she'd wanted it to? Or had she imagined it all in the blur of the attack? She looked at the vase of flowers beside her bed. "Move," she muttered. The flowers stayed where they were, and she was glad she was alone and nobody had seen her.

The wheelchair squeaked like a supermarket shopping trolley, attracting the unwanted attention of both staff and passing visitors.

Several openly gawked, one even smirked, and just when Eliza didn't think things could get any worse, she saw Doctor Dick. He leaned over the reception desk and reached for a pen, using the opportunity to cop an eyeful down the young receptionist's blouse. He stood back, a satisfied twinkle in his eyes, and waved the pen (his ogle alibi), before scribbling on his clipboard. When he looked up, he saw Eliza. She wasn't certain, but for a brief moment she thought she saw him lick his lips.

"Crap." Eliza gripped the wheels of the chair and tried to stop it continuing forward.

"Hey, hey, hey. What're ya doing?" the orderly said, his Jamaican accent thick and heavy.

"It's okay, I can walk from here."

"No can do. 'Ospital policy states I 'ave to wheel de patient in da chair." He forced the wheelchair forward.

The rubber chafed Eliza's palms, and she let go. Bob sauntered towards her, the top button of his shirt undone. He winked and overextended his grin. Did he mistake her agitation at having to speak to him after last night's fiasco for that of excitement? *Crap, I think he does.* Eliza pressed harder on the wheels, but the orderly ignored her protest and continued to push her closer to the randy doctor.

Bob stood in front of her, looking way too smug. He glanced towards the orderly. "It's okay, I can take it from here."

"No, the orderly needs to push me. It's hospital policy... right?" Eliza twisted in her seat.

"Hey, you jus' need to be transported in da chair. Makes no difference who by."

Bob disappeared behind her and the chair started to move towards the exit again, albeit at a much slower pace. "So, what happened to you last night?"

"I don't wish to talk about it."

"I heard you can't, that you've got amnesia. Have you forgotten everything that happened last night?"

Oh God, please don't go there. "Such as?"

Eliza heard the smile in his voice as he spoke. "We hooked up. A kind of...pre-birthday celebration."

Bob leaned down, and murmured, "Man, you were so hot. I could come over tonight. Finish what we started?"

"I thought you finished yourself off?"

His warm breath left her ear. "You do remember? So what the hell am I doing wasting my time?"

The wheelchair quickened its pace, only to come to an abrupt halt at the main entrance and launch Eliza onto her feet. Darkness spotted her vision and for a moment the corridor blurred. She held her position and waited for her head to clear, then walked unsteadily to the exit.

Outside, the fresh air seemed to agree with her. Her head cleared a little, and her senses sharpened enough to see the small gathering of local reporters and onlookers watching the unmistakable figure of her father on the far side of the car park. Eliza couldn't hear what he said, nor did she care. All of her life she'd listened as he manipulated the press, and from where she stood now it looked as if his over-rehearsed performance was, as usual, delivered with perfection and pure conviction. She turned away and walked to the black limousine that blocked the ambulance entrance. The driver leaned against the bonnet, totally engrossed in the grotty tabloid he held, and didn't hear her approach. She'd only met him once before, but it was obvious when he finally glanced up that he had no idea who she was.

"Daddy said to take me home," Eliza said, hoping that would clear things up. When it became apparent he was having some trouble digesting her request, she held out her hand. "I'm James Hamilton's daughter, Eliza."

Flustered, the driver scrunched the paper under his arm and shook her hand. "Miss Hamilton. I wasn't informed you'd be joining us today. Your father shouldn't be too long."

"Haven't you been updated? You're just taking me home now."

The driver seemed a little unsure. He glanced at the podium.

"Another car is coming for Daddy."

"Oh, of course." And without any further hesitation, the driver immediately opened the rear door. Probably for the last time, as the poor soul would be sacked for sure when her father found out she'd duped him.

"Miss Hamilton, what a pleasure," a familiar voice called out.

Eliza froze. It was Davis, her father's long-time aide. She contemplated jumping into the car and getting the hell out of Dodge before he cottoned on to what she was doing. She had much affection for Davis. He had, after all, been around more than her own father had while she was growing up, and after the death of her mother, she didn't know what she would have done without him. But his loyalty always fell at her father's feet. If Davis caught the slightest whiff that Eliza planned to go home, her cunning scheme would be foiled before the limo had time to reach the car-park exit.

Instead, she put on a brave face, turned, and took him into a gentle hug. "Hello, Davis. It's good to see you."

His grey hair was thinning, and his back slightly hunched under the toll of age and waiting hand over foot on her father. Regardless, he seemed genuinely happy to see her.

"How have you been, Miss? It's been lonely at the house these past few months since you moved out."

"I'm only a few miles down the road."

Davis nodded, unconvinced. He faced the driver, who waited by the open door. "Are you going somewhere?"

"Home," Eliza said.

"Without your father?"

"Daddy said I could take the limo."

"Really? Are you sure?"

"Uh huh, as I wasn't feeling too well."

An awkward silence fell between them and Eliza knew it was only a matter of time before Davis checked with his employer.

"Well, I must go. Feeling awful an' all." She half-hugged the old man again, this time only briefly, and climbed into the back of the car. "Tell Daddy I'll see him later."

CHAPTER FIVE

Roman didn't like being questioned.

Not by his mother, not by his brother, and especially not by somebody who, at this moment in time, held him over a barrel by his nuts. No. Roman needed a back-up plan.

He sat back and tried to admire the view.

The waitress placed the pint glass on a beer mat, and smiled a smile that probably earned her extra tips with the other punters. Roman declined to leave one. Music pounded from the speakers, each beat blasting vibrations to the ends of his fingers and toes. With music this loud, body language was the only way to communicate, and this waitress spoke volumes. She turned from him and walked her long legs back to her station. Twenty-first-century girls sure didn't have any qualms about showing off their bodies, unlike the ones he'd grown up with.

Roman picked up his glass. On the napkin, scrawled in black biro, was her phone number. The waitress leaned on the bar and flicked her hair. *Here it comes*, Roman thought. Sure enough, she glanced over her shoulder, her tight T-shirt stretching across her breasts, and her skirt struggling to cover her pert bum. As no other girls in the club caught his eye, Roman raised his glass. Although not really his taste, she was still more appealing than the one he'd left standing naked in his kitchen.

Around him, girls smooched on the stage, their silky bodies gyrating to the dulcet tones that caressed the room, curling the metal poles like constrictors around their prey. A leopard-print bikini top fell by a dancer's feet, and she gracefully wrapped her slender legs around a pole and arched her body backwards until her head touched the floor. In true implant style, her breasts didn't move. A man reached forward and tucked some of the club's dance dollars into the elastic of her G-string. She smiled, seductively licking her finger, and trailed it down the middle of her toned stomach. A little too eagerly, the man tucked in further cash.

Sucker. Roman turned away. Fancy paying for it when they'd give it up for free. He gulped down a mouthful of beer, and checked his watch. The windowless club was dim, subtly conning customers into believing that time inside the place stood still. But outside, morning had arrived, and in another hour or so the club would close. Until then, Roman decided to drink while he thought of a plan to ensure his end of the deal with the old man came through.

On the table in front of him lay Eliza's bag. Scattered around it were her driving licence, a parking fine, some makeup, and a letter from a solicitor regarding her recent house inheritance. He looked at the letter again – more so at the address. She didn't live too far from here. Roman turned back to the stage, but didn't watch the dancing girl. His mind was on Eliza...Or what he assumed the old man thought she was.

He drained the remains of his drink and whistled to the waitress to bring him another beer. She did, a tray balanced skillfully on her hand as she wiggled her backside between the tables, her shoulders pinned so far back Roman swore her breasts would rip right through her T-shirt. She tucked her hair behind her ear and smiled.

Roman didn't return it.

She was so hot for him, she made this whole scenario way too easy. If Roman had a conscience, he may feel sorry for her. But he didn't have a conscience, at least not where she or any other female was concerned. Easy or not, she was still a lay, something he could use to release all the damn tension that old man had brought him. He needed to gain control. Something he knew wouldn't happen without a fight, no matter what the old fucker threatened. Roman had been stupid handing over the two pieces of wood the daft old git was so obsessed with – though, knowing what that wood represented, Roman could understand the obsession. Shit. He really had to do something about his weakness for money. So now, the old man had most of the wood as well as the blood. And Roman had nothing other than a sour taste in his mouth.

The waitress placed a second beer on his table. Roman studied her more carefully. Her face was quite thin as far as faces went, and she had a dimple in the middle of her chin. He turned away, his focus once again on what he stood to lose if his deal with the old man went south. Was Roman barking up the wrong tree with Eliza? Probably. But what if he wasn't? What if Eliza was the answer? What if her blood was the key into Heaven? And Roman had let her slip right through his fingers.

The tension in his neck worsened. He reached for the shot glass that remained on the waitress's tray, and downed it in one. "You got five minutes?"

"Now?"

"Yes. Now." Christ, did he really have to spell it out?

"My break isn't for another hour."

"Forget it then." Roman scanned the room for his second choice, the girl in the corner by the cigarette machine. Damn, he'd need another beer if he was going to do her. He got up to leave. Standing, he towered over the tiny waitress. From this vantage point, he saw the black roots that separated her bleached hair from her scalp.

The waitress grabbed his arm. "I could say I need the toilet. Get Charlene to cover?"

"Whatever. Just do it quick. I'll meet you out back."

The waitress put the tray down on a nearby table and sashayed over to the bar, where she spoke to another employee. The woman, much older and looking like she'd been around the block more than a few times, turned and studied him. If Roman had thought about it sooner, he could have mentioned having the girl by the cigarette machine join them. Maybe another time. A double act would definitely distract him long enough to get this building irritation out of his head. The waitress pointed out back and then disappeared through a door to the side of the bar. Her legs were nice, he'd definitely give her that.

Roman pushed open the door and morning light flooded the dingy club, highlighting the cigarette-burned carpet and peeling wallpaper. He pulled his baseball cap down over his face to shield his eyes from the brightness, and stepped out onto the pavement. An OPEN sign hung above the club door, the pink glow emphasising the black painted brickwork stained with dried urine. The empty streets showed little sign of life, and his footsteps echoed along the side alley. His neck ached, and his back felt as stiff as a board. The sooner that waitress had her hands on him, the better he'd be.

He found her waiting beside a stack of bottle crates in the very far corner. She spotted him and pounced, her tongue warm and wet as it slithered across his neck. Her mouth found his ear and she nibbled at his lobe. Roman closed his eyes and tried to enjoy the sensation, but he couldn't shake the fact that he was about to be shafted on this damn deal.

The waitress unbuttoned his shirt, quick, like an expert. She trailed her hands over his skin and down to his belt, loosening the buckle. The buttons on his jeans popped: one, two, three, four, five. Roman didn't move. His mind was elsewhere. He needed something, anything, to give him the power back. The wood he was collecting in Paris maybe?

The waitress took his hands and placed them on her breasts. "Do you like?"

They felt weighty, like two bags of water. At any other time Roman would have ripped off her top and had her nipples in his mouth. So why not now? He tried to focus, grabbed the waitress's hair, and pulled her close. Her cheap perfume and the stench of cigarette smoke clung to her clothes and assaulted his nostrils. His lips found hers, and a disgusting taste of cherry lip balm invaded his mouth. Her hand moved down towards his waist and slid beneath the elastic of his boxers. Roman pulled it back out, and without uttering a word, he seized her by the thighs, slammed her against the brick wall, and forced himself between her legs. He ripped her panties to one side and fumbled inside his jeans. The waitress tried to kiss him, but he turned his head, entering her hard and fast, wondering if she'd be able to take it. Her delighted squeal confirmed she could.

Roman pounded harder, and the waitresses' squeal morphed into a much deeper, pleasurable groan. Her arms curled his neck.

"Don't," Roman said.

The waitress removed them. A smile cocked one side of her mouth, and she stretched the neckline of her T-shirt down over her left breast. She was bra-less. She licked her finger and teased her already erect nipple. The look in her eyes was one of a cat bringing a dead mouse to its owner.

"Put it away. That ain't what I came for."

The waitress pouted, obviously hurt by Roman's comment. Roman didn't care. His only mission was to get a load off, and then maybe he would be able to think more clearly.

Any rejection the waitress felt quickly dissolved, and soon her groans filled his head once more. Roman tried to block her out, but the more he did, the more Eliza Hamilton dominated his thoughts.

He stopped, and withdrew from the waitress.

"What's wrong?"

Roman buttoned his trousers. "You're what's wrong."

"I can do it better."

Roman re-buckled his belt. "You're not the girl I need." He fastened his shirt and, without saying another word, he turned and left the alley. He had a plan.

CHAPTER SIX

Autumn had arrived in the Cornish village of Polperro, bringing with it freakishly warm weather.

Normally, waves would be crashing against the cliff rocks, causing the ocean spray to soak anything within a fifteen-metre reach. Cafés and craft shops would be all but closed in preparation for the winter season, and the harbour would be desolate. However, as the limousine crawled around the cobbled streets, what Eliza saw was a hive of activity. Tourists trudged the rickety streets and quaint antique shops in a desperate bid to take home a reminder of their last-minute getaway. Children walked with ice cream cones while others played on the beach, their parents keeping a watchful eye as they soaked up the rays outside the local inn and enjoyed a much-needed beer. It reminded her of good times before Billy had been sent away. They'd been close then. Inseparable. Billy had looked out for her. Protected her when their parents argued. But he'd returned from boarding school a different person. Unhappy. Frustrated. And with a growing resentment towards their father.

The limousine rounded the narrow lanes and finally pulled to a stop directly in front of Eliza's house. The driver hurried to open her door and Eliza clasped his hand, accepting his offer to help her from the car. For a moment, she let the welcoming breeze caress her weary body. Her neighbour, a tall, thick-set man known only as Mr. McKenzie, swept imaginary dirt from his front path. As a child, after Billy had left, Eliza had spent many nights and the occasional school holiday with her gran. During those times, she'd watch Mr. McKenzie return home from work, sometimes with his black and yellow uniform still clean, and sometimes with it covered in smoke and soot. It was those days, after he'd been fighting fires, that he'd sweep his garden.

Mrs. McKenzie appeared with a cup of coffee, her bright-pink lipstick dazzling in the sunlight. She patted her husband's shoulder and he stopped sweeping, looking relieved at the opportunity to take a break. He took the mug from her and they exchanged a few words while Mrs. McKenzie straightened his collar. Then she disappeared back inside their house.

Watching the two of them made Eliza feel eight years old again, and a small smile curled the corners of her lips, thankful that some things never changed. Mr. McKenzie looked up and waved, but before Eliza could return the gesture, he'd already returned to sweeping the brick-red path. Eliza's hand remained poised mid-wave. Embarrassed, she patted her hair and faked straightening it.

"Is there anything else I can do for you, Miss Hamilton?" the driver said.

"No, thank you. You can go."

Eliza watched the young lad get back into the car. She felt like the worst person in the world. Guilt that he'd probably be out of a job by tonight resurfaced, and she called after him to apologise, but the limo was halfway down the road and out of earshot. Eliza stared down at her shoes, scuffed and covered in dirt; her clothes, grimy and covered in blood. The limo driver drifted from her thoughts, and now all she wanted was a much-needed bath.

"Eliza?" It was the sing-song voice of Mrs. McKenzie.

Eliza sighed. She really didn't feel up for a conversation.

"Hello, sweetheart," the lady cooed from across the narrow lane.

Eliza waved even though she knew it would encourage a visit.

Mrs. McKenzie was by her side in ten short, tottering strides. She motioned towards the disappearing limousine. "He seemed a nice strapping young man. A friend of yours?"

Eliza made a mental note to call her father and beg he not sack the driver. "Not really, no."

"How are you feeling? I heard about last night. Are you okay?"

How on earth did Mrs. McKenzie know about last night already?

"And so soon after your grandmother's passing. She was a lovely lady. We sure will miss her."

Eliza tried to answer but Mrs. McKenzie cut her off, something she frequently did. She patted her platinum-blonde Dolly Parton wig, seemingly to check the pink flower still held its place, and motioned towards the foil-covered bowl she clasped to her voluptuous bosom. "This ought to cheer you up."

She leaned in closer, the frilly, low-cut blouse purposefully accentuating her assets, and the sweet smell of her perfume bringing a tear to Eliza's eye. "It's Stargazy Pie."

"Oh. That's nice of you." Eliza had never heard of Stargazy Pie, but accepted the dish. She balanced it in one hand, reached under the front mat for the door key, and slipped it into the lock.

Mrs. McKenzie noticed. "Lost your keys?"

"Lost my bag." Mrs. McKenzie would keep her talking all morning if she didn't cut her off now. "You'll have to excuse me but I was just going to have a lie down—"

Mrs. McKenzie waved a dismissive hand. "Here, let me." She seized the key and opened the door and, without invitation, barged into the hallway.

Eliza paused, and took a deep breath to hide the irritation. *Just count to ten.* She'd reached three when Mrs. McKenzie spoke again.

"I see you still haven't finished packing up your grandmother's things yet?"

Eliza peeked around the door. It wasn't all that bad… Packing boxes piled five high and tilting like Pisa. She squeezed past her neighbour, bashing her shin against the bottom box. The cardboard tower swayed, and before she could stop it, the boxes of wrapped ceramics tumbled across the floor like broken Lego. Eliza rubbed her leg and hitched up the hem of her soiled uniform. A small bruise had already turned her skin a darkened shade of pink.

"Oh dear. I guess that's a few less boxes you need to worry about," Mrs. McKenzie began. "Still, your grandmother had an awful lot of clutter. Never liked to throw anything out, that one."

Eliza bit her lip and watched her neighbour's intrusive stare scan the rest of the knickknacks and photos that remained on show.

"I'm surprised you're not staying with your father until the house is sorted – especially after the traumatic evening you had last night."

"How do you know about that?"

Mrs. McKenzie cocked her head to one side. "I bumped into Agnes. She hears and sees everything, that one."

Her red varnished nails curled around the dish Eliza held, and seized it. "Tell you what, I'll just pop this in your refrigerator, dear." She disappeared into the kitchen.

Eliza didn't bother to move from the doorway. She didn't want Mrs. McKenzie in her kitchen, or in her refrigerator for that matter, but the woman was going to do what she wanted. Best let her see the refrigerator was almost bare and be done with it.

Eliza rubbed her knee again, the newly formed bruise turning purple before her eyes. She blew on it, hoping it would somehow mask the ache. It didn't. "Actually, I really need to get out of these clothes and take a bath."

"I won't keep you long, my dear..."

Eliza let her mind drift. The red light on the answer machine flashed impatiently, and Eliza hit play. Mrs. McKenzie continued to rabbit on in the kitchen, and it didn't seem to matter that Eliza no longer listened. The machine beeped and announced a message had been left little more than an hour earlier. Then Billy's voice stating her father had called him and he was super angry. He finished saying he'd pop by later tonight to check on her.

Eliza's stomach knotted. No doubt he'd bring a curry and a bottle of wine, and a million more reasons she should believe him about dad.

She loved her brother more than anything, but that was something she just could not stomach. Not tonight.

CHAPTER SEVEN

Tiredness had come and gone.

Eliza stood at the kitchen door, the ceramic mug hot in her hands, and blew on the liquid. Circles rippled across the surface, but she didn't attempt to drink any of the steaming tea. Mrs. McKenzie had jabbered on about food and packing boxes for over forty minutes before Eliza finally had to ask her to leave, and by the time the bath had filled with water, Eliza had fallen asleep on the bed. She woke to find the tub overflowing, and water fast on its way towards the landing. She thought about just leaving it there and letting Billy mop it up when he arrived. He was trying to get her on side after all, and by his reckoning this would have scored him some major brownie points and earned him another shot at convincing her of Dad's murderous crimes. Instead Eliza spent most of the afternoon cleaning up, and then left a message for Billy at the station saying she was tired and not to come round.

Outside, the afternoon sky had turned gloomy and dark, and torrential rain beat down upon slate rooftops and gushed into the gutter. It was a dramatic change from the earlier heatwave the South of England had experienced, and one the forecasters definitely hadn't seen coming. At first, Eliza welcomed the change in weather. In her garden, the flowers had looked wilted as they sat in the dehydrated earth, and a good downpour was just what the ground needed. But now, saturated mud and excess water slid down from the hills and puddled the patio, bringing with it a whole heap of new problems.

The musical tones of the wind chime sung in the air. Eliza loved to hear the breeze dance its way through the metal pipes. Her grandmother used to say the sound of the wind chime denoted the arrival of bad spirits and other diabolical evils. Eliza reinterpreted that to be a warning against heinous men. The memory brought a smile to Eliza's lips, but the movement caused the dull ache at the back of her head to intensify. She grabbed two aspirin from the counter, popped them into her mouth, and lifted the mug to her lips. Its warmth moistened the tip of her nose and scalded her tongue, and she jerked the mug away. Tea sloshed over the edge, splashing across her hand and covering her white T-shirt.

"Shit." She slammed the mug down on the counter. The handle broke away and the sharp ceramic sliced her thumb. "Shit. Shit."

Blood seeped from the slit at a slow pace. The cut wasn't deep, but it stung like hell. She grabbed the tea towel, dabbed at her hand, and then at her T-shirt. But the more she wiped the mark dry, the more prominent the stain became. It was official. Eliza had become her grandmother. Whether gravy from a Sunday roast or chocolate from an ice cream flake, as far back as Eliza could remember, her gran always had one blemish or another dried into her clothes.

Giving up, Eliza threw the towel over the back of the chair. The rain showed little sign of easing, and as thunder grumbled across the ocean, the promise of a storm seemed evident. Eliza checked her watch, wishing she would feel tired again so she could catch an early night, but sleep was nowhere in sight. She rinsed out the handle-less cup and sat it on the drainer, staring at it for a moment. Memories from the previous evening emerged. Had she really broken that light bulb using the power of her mind? She stared harder at the cup, for what reason she wasn't quite sure. To move it? To prove to herself that last night wasn't a freak event? That she hadn't imagined it?

She stared until the back of her eyes hurt.

The cup didn't move.

What was she doing? Trying to reerot a scene from a Stephen King novel? Stress. That was what was wrong with her. And it was all Billy's fault. Then again, her father's suffocating hold around her life was also sending her a little nuts. Maybe moving out of his house and into her grandma's wasn't far enough. Maybe she had to put miles between herself and the two men in her life, rather than just streets.

Lightning flashed across the sky, followed moments later by the rumble of thunder. The kitchen light extinguished, leaving nothing but natural light streaming through the kitchen window, but even that grew bleaker by the second. Day turned to night before her eyes and she hesitated, unnerved and willing her eyes to hurry and adjust. Outside, the early arrival of the moon eclipsed the sun, the same halo of green she'd seen the night before orbing it. Rusty hinges creaked and groaned, and the back door slammed shut. On the wall behind, she just made out the door hook swinging from side to side.

Eliza stood rooted to the spot, the coldness of the floor now evident under her bare feet. Outside, the metal rods on the wind chime smashed together, losing all of their serenity. Lightning flared in the sky, briefly illuminating the kitchen before plunging it back into an even gloomier darkness. Gradually, the outline of familiar appliances began to materialise: the fridge, the sink, the oven. Eliza's hand slid across the cold granite work-top and searched for a glass jar. Power cuts were frequent in Polperro, and her gran kept boxes of matches everywhere. Inside the jar, Eliza found the long-stemmed variety used to light the hob. One strike and the head fizzed to life, the smell of sulphur lingering in the air long after the flame had calmed. It was a smell Eliza loathed.

The match burned down quicker than she liked, and she reached in to the cupboard beneath the sink, lighting a candle just as the flame singed her fingers.

An eruption of thunder followed, bellowing its way through the murky sky, and it was a few seconds before the sound of the rain could be heard once again.

Rain streamed from the brim of Roman's baseball cap and flowed down his black overcoat. He was drenched, and could no longer see the suede of his Timberlands for soggy mud.

Lightning flashed across the sky, and for a brief moment both he and the inside of Eliza's kitchen were visible. He'd seen the entire show. When the match burned her, he'd nearly laughed out loud. Eliza certainly wasn't what he expected. In fact, he wondered why he bothered wasting any more time here at all. This girl wasn't a Mind Mover. The old man had gotten it wrong thinking her blood was the key. She'd shown no strength or power while being attacked on the station platform, and she certainly didn't display any here now. And yet the Shadow came for her. *Why?*

More to the point, why did Roman remain watching her?

He refused to believe it was because of guilt. He needed a conscience to feel guilt, and he'd shed that curse years ago. And it definitely wasn't pity. Roman was the first to admit that apart from his beloved Jane, he had zero respect for women. And this girl didn't resemble his Jane at all. Their looks, their mannerisms, every attribute was as far from one another as could be. Yet, every time he so much as thought of Eliza's fate and the part he was to play in it, Jane appeared to him, and guilt – no, not guilt, this alien feeling that he was doing wrong, reared its ugly head. He needed to get his mind back in the game. Eliza was weak. But there was something else, something inside him that found her clumsy, half-witted behaviour oddly familiar and attractive. There was a stirring in his groin and, surprised, he shifted position.

Fuck this.

Roman took one last drag on his cigarette, readjusted his deflating manhood, and threw the butt on the floor. It hit the patio and bounced into a puddle, the ember glowing for a second before it fizzled out. He glanced back into the dark kitchen. He couldn't ignore the feeling in his gut that this girl was important. The Shadow had failed in its quest to kill her last night, but if she was a Mind Mover and it caught the scent of her blood in the future, it would come for her again, more ferocious than ever, and not stop until it had obliterated her bloodline. If the Shadow killed her, Roman didn't stand a chance of opening Heaven's Gateway and reuniting with his Jane again. Preserving his own future overruled any sense of guilt... or whatever the fuck it was he felt. He pulled off his hat and tilted his head back towards the sky. Rain splashed against his face and he closed his eyes, letting the cool water refresh and invigorate him. He ruffled his hair, challenging the early evening breeze to un-clutter his mind.

He needed leverage.

He needed Eliza.

No woman could resist that sweet-arse charm of his. He'd be in Eliza's house within two minutes and, with the pretense of dinner, have her in his car within five. The chloroform in his pocket would stop her from giving him any grief and, within half an hour, he'd have her tied up in the cabin and be negotiating with the old man. He almost felt sorry for the poor girl.

A burst of lightning brightened the room, and for a split second Eliza's surroundings became visible. The lightning dispersed as quickly as it had arrived, but it was enough for Eliza to see her way to the fuse box.

The doorbell chimed and Eliza's shoulders tensed. *Please, not Mrs. McKenzie again.*

She hopped off the table and limped into the hall, avoiding the packing boxes as she went. Thunder boomed through the sky, and the hairs on the back of her neck spiked. She paused at the front door, and her fingers dropped from the handle. She leaned forward and pressed her eye to the peephole, seeing the silhouette of a man, head bowed, his baseball cap protecting his face from the torrential downpour – and from Eliza's vision. The stone floor felt cold as she quickly hurried back into the kitchen. She rounded the table, not really knowing what she was looking for. Midway, she paused and slid a knife from a wooden block. It was small. No bigger than a potato peeler. *Great, if I wanted a toothpick.* She lowered the knife to the counter and grabbed a large carving knife. Perfect.

She turned back to the door.

CHAPTER EIGHT

The doorbell rang again, this time followed by an abundance of hammering.

Eliza's stomach tightened. She reached for the door chain and slid it into the latch. "Who's there?"

"I have your bag."

A long sigh escaped Eliza's lips, and the familiar tingle returned to the pit of her stomach. She opened the door and immediately rain blew through the five-inch gap the chain allowed and hit her in the face.

There he was, the man from last night. Hat held tight to his head, his totally inadequate jacket wet through. He held out her bag. His head tilted away from her, the rim of his cap still shadowing the majority of his face.

She wanted to say thank you, to invite him in out of the rain, to find out who the hell he was and if he could shed some light on what had happened the night before. Instead, she stood there and, under the low light from the flame, watched the raindrops trail his jawline and drip from his chin.

The man shifted feet and looked up. "Aren't you going to invite me in?" He held out his hand.

Eliza didn't shake it. "You're from last night. Robert?...Raymond?..."

"Roman. Roman Holbrook." What little light the nearby lamppost put out curled beneath the rim of his hat and lit his face. Wet eyelashes shaped his blue eyes, and when he spoke again she saw a faint scar curved one side of his mouth. "I also wanted to make sure you were okay."

"Do you know what happened last night?"

Roman lowered his hand. "I assumed you were being mugged."

"That was no mugging."

"Well, I don't know what else to tell you other than I'm getting soaked out here." He smiled and his blue eyes almost sparkled.

Eliza eyed him. Was he telling the truth? Was last night simply a mugging? "Why did you leave me?"

"I chased after the mugger. Got your bag." He held out her black tote again. "By the time I got back, you were gone."

"You ran off across the train tracks. I saw you."

"Because that's the way the attacker went."

Eliza looked at the bag. It was far too big to fit through the narrow opening.

An awkward silence ensued. The man flicked up his collar, seemed to check his coat pocket, and glanced over his shoulder at the narrow lane behind him. For a split second he seemed tense or nervous, Eliza wasn't sure which.

"Why didn't you take my bag to the police?"

His brashness returned. "Would you prefer that? Because I can take it there right now."

When Eliza didn't respond, Roman turned from the door. He was halfway down the pathway when he stopped. "You know what, screw this. I thought I was doing you a favour bringing it here."

He walked back to the door and dropped the bag on the doorstep. "Everything's in there." One last lingering stare, then he turned and walked away.

Eliza glanced down at her bag sitting on the doorstep, the rain trickling down the leather. Against her better judgement, she closed the door and slid the chain from the latch. When she reopened it Roman had made it as far as her front gate.

"Thank you." Eliza picked up the bag.

Roman turned. "Does that thank you come with the offer of coffee?"

Eliza felt the knot in her stomach tighten further. A strange man in her house. What would her grandmother say? "Sure."

Roman checked his watch and smiled. His swagger was evident even when he jogged the few feet back to her house. He entered the hallway and Eliza closed the door.

"Why is it so dark in here?"

"I'm on some kind of power-saving mission. Doing my bit for global warming?" The comment had sounded humorous inside her head.

Roman didn't appear to appreciate her joke. He reached for her bag, his hand brushing against hers. An unexpected excitement fluttered inside Eliza's stomach. Roman froze, as though he felt it too. He stared at her, his blue eyes looking just as surprised under the glow of candlelight. Then, he abruptly turned away and dropped the bag into the corner behind the front door.

Eliza waited for him to speak. When he didn't, she said, "So, no coffee, but I have tea?"

"Tea's good."

She was aware he'd followed her through to the kitchen. He remained quiet while she felt her way to the sink and filled the kettle with water. "I have strange memories of last night."

"Probably just shock."

"Did you get a good look at the attacker? Because if you did, I'd appreciate you speaking to the police." She refused to let his silence discourage her. "Maybe give them a description."

"It was dark. I saw nothing that would help."

"Anything would help, no matter how little."

"I saw nothing."

"Not even when you got my bag back?"

"The guy dropped it." Legs scraped the floor as Roman pulled a chair out from under the table. He sat down. "Was long gone by the time I reached it."

"But you saw it was a guy?"

"Figure of speech. Could just as well have been a woman."

Eliza sat the kettle on its heating element. "What do you think I am?"

"Is that a trick question?"

"No. You asked if I was one of them."

"One of what?"

Eliza eyed him. "You always answer a question with a question?"

"I'm not sure what the hell you want me to say?"

"I just want some answers."

"To what? You hit your head and things are a little muddled. It will pass."

"You're saying I'm imagining you telling me to get to the light. Or that you said *they* would come for me again."

"Yes. I am."

"I don't think—"

Roman gave an exaggerated sigh. "That tea ain't gonna make itself."

Eliza turned back to the kettle and hit the switch. *Crap.* "I have no electric."

"There's a pub down the road, right?"

"Yeah."

"Good." Roman stood. "I'll drive."

He disappeared into the hallway.

Eliza stayed put.

A moment later, he reappeared in the kitchen doorway. "Something wrong?"

"Yeah. I have no idea who you are."

"Sure you do. We met last night when I saved your life."

"A night that you can't remember."

"No. I remember it all. I said I didn't know who attacked you."

"But you fought with him. You must remember something."

Roman sighed. "Look, it was dark. I saw you being attacked and I stepped in to help."

"And I am thankful for that."

"Good. You can prove it by buying me a pint." Roman disappeared back into the hallway.

This time, Eliza followed. She paused in the kitchen doorway. Roman had already opened the front door. Common sense screamed for her not to go with him. To wait until he stepped outside and then slam the door shut behind him. Curiosity, though? Curiosity was a dangerous thing when she wanted to know what the hell had happened the night before.

She picked up her house key from the small table. Roman remained by the door. For all she knew, he could be the one who attacked her. He wasn't, though. Deep down, she knew that. He'd arrived later, after someone or something had tried to choke her. Still, she wasn't stupid, and she wasn't getting in the car with him. Not until he told her the truth at least.

She grabbed her coat, which lay over a packing box. "I'll go, but we have to walk there."

"Trust issues?" Roman glanced back at the rain pelting from the sky. "Do you at least have an umbrella?"

Eliza took one from the coat stand. Cream and trimmed with baby pink frills.

Roman sighed. "I'd rather get wet and catch pneumonia."

"Pneumonia it is then."

The temperature dropped. Eliza's breath frosted the icy atmosphere.

Roman saw it too. His face hardened. "Get to the light."

Fear paralysed Eliza. She stared until the whiteness of her breath had faded. That thing was back.

Frantic, she raced back into the house. She didn't know, nor did she care, what the hell that thing was. She sensed something charging after her, close at her heels. Locked in the memory of last night, she could make sense of nothing. Something grabbed her arms. She screamed, her warm breath turning ice-white.

"Stop fighting me," she heard a voice say. Someone she knew, but through the panic she couldn't place it. "Get to the fucking light."

Eliza gazed at the man before her. Saw it was Roman and gave up struggling. He urged her back to the front door and this time she went willingly. "What the hell is it?"

They made the doorstep. Rain immediately pelted her face, her clothes. "Tell me. It's the thing from last night, isn't it?"

Something grabbed her shoulders. The pressure dug deep and ripped her free from Roman's grip. She catapulted backwards into the hallway, landing in a heap at the bottom of the stairs.

Eliza got to her knees, but Roman was nowhere to be seen. Through the open door, she saw him some twenty yards away, lying flat on his back on her lawn. When he moved, she felt relieved.

"Get out here," he said, rushing back up the path towards her.

A gust of wind tore through the hallway. The front door slammed, and Roman was gone from view.

Around her, book covers flew open, their pages ferociously ripped from the spines. Together with loose photographs and other papers, they rose into the air and whirled in circles above her head.

Eliza heard Roman on the other side of the door, shouting her name and hammering to get in. She clambered across the hallway, scrambling to her feet as she went. The wind attacked and tried to push her back, but she reached for the door and grabbed the latch. Roman's hammering intensified and Eliza screamed back when the door refused to open.

Behind her, a stack of boxes tumbled like a building in an earthquake. Eliza raised her arms, protecting her face from spiralling debris. Above, Shadows crawled down the walls. The coat stand toppled and crashed, its wooden hooks splintering free.

The wind howled louder and louder. She heard Roman pound against the door and again she screamed for help, but her cry was no more than a muffle buried beneath a windstorm of noise. All around her, Shadows descended along the walls. But unlike any other shadows she'd ever seen, these rolled across the floor like an ocean mist, where they merged in the centre of the room and embraced each other, entwining as lovers would, growing until just one shape floated before her; the same shadowy figure that had attacked her at the station.

Eliza raced across the hall. The Shadow swept closer, its claw-like fingers stretched out and reaching for her. It curled her legs and swiped them out from under her. Eliza fell on to her back and the Shadow was upon her, gripping her arms and legs, holding her down so she couldn't move. She tried to scream, but her efforts were thwarted. The Shadow seeped into her mouth and down her throat, the ice-cold air drying everything it touched. Eliza gagged, wanting to cough, needing to breathe. She thrashed from side to side, convulsing at the lack of air in her lungs, but she couldn't escape the force that held her captive. The dense outline of the ceiling lightshade swung in the gale above her, and the sensation she'd felt the night before whirled inside her head. She stared at the shade, her eyes straining so hard she thought they would pop from their sockets. Faster and faster the shade swung, until Eliza's eyelids grew so heavy it became too much of an effort to keep them open. Then, the light bulb exploded. Glass particles fell like snow, and the

Shadow retreated from her mouth as suddenly as it had arrived. Renewed air rushed into Eliza's lungs and burned her throat, and through blurred vision she watched the Shadow retreat to the corner of the room and fade into the darkness.

Glass shattered somewhere in the living room. The wind in the hallway died and the temperature warmed, and no more did her breath frost the air. She lay on the floor, her knees drawn to her chest like a child too terrified to move, and just concentrated on drawing air back into her lungs. Had she just done it again? Had that glass smashed because she'd wanted it too?

Something rushed through from the living room and dashed to her side. Hands gripped her shoulders. "Are you hurt?"

She turned to face the voice beside her, and saw Roman. He didn't make eye contact. Instead, he frantically checked and rechecked the room, his gaze darting into every nook and cranny. When Eliza tried to speak, to warn him, the words scratched across her throat like sandpaper. She swallowed, which hurt even more, and had no choice but to remain quiet and hope this man was here to get her the hell out of the house.

Roman took her in his arms and lifted her from the floor, and she let him. She couldn't have been more than a foot or two from the ground when her breath frosted white again. She looked up at Roman to warn him, but the look in his eyes told her he already knew.

The Shadow swelled behind him. His eyes widened and, still holding Eliza, he got to one knee. The Shadow swooped upon them, knocking Eliza from

Roman's arms. Roman reached for her a second time, but the Shadow yanked him backwards and thrust him into the corner of the room. Eliza crawled to her knees. The front door was only metres from her. If she could just get outside...

CHAPTER NINE

The Shadow hauled Eliza's arms behind her and dragged her across the floor into the living room.

The door began to close, and through the gap Eliza saw Roman launch a flying kick towards it. The sole of his boot connected and wood splintered in every direction, smashing the door open with such force that it whacked the glass cabinet and toppled what she hadn't packed of her grandmother's decorative plates and ornaments. The Shadow released Eliza's hands and floated towards the ceiling, where it circled her like a predator would its prey. Everyone remained still, watching, waiting to see who would make the first move.

"You must be bleeding? That's the only way it could have found you." Roman was back at her side, his fingers feeling across her scalp. He touched her stitches. "There's no blood."

Now he frantically checked her everywhere. His hands clasped hers, as if remembering. "That fucking cup of tea."

The Shadow descended across her grandmother's furniture, overturning every item it touched. Pictures fell from the walls and shattered across the wooden floorboards. Two candlesticks flew from the mantle, followed by an array of photo frames and old china knickknacks that hadn't been moved in years. The mahogany antique clock, a gift to her gran from her grandfather, tumbled forward.

Roman pulled Eliza to her feet. The streetlight glowed across his jawline. When he spoke, his cheeks hollowed and his nose crinkled slightly. "Get outside to the light, and wait for me there."

The Shadow continued its descent across the fireplace. The safety guard toppled, as did the brass pokers. They clashed together and hit the stone surround. A side table overturned, and her gran's favourite vase smashed across the floor, spilling tap water and freshly cut marigolds everywhere.

"Go." Roman urged her towards the door.

The Shadow moved towards them, now swollen to twice its original size, and Eliza ran. A high-pitched scream vibrated across the room, and Eliza covered her ears. Only when she reached the door did she allow herself a stolen glance over her shoulder.

"Hurry, I can't hold it for long," Roman said, clinging to the black mist.

Eliza raced into the hallway, her only mission to get to the front door and run like she'd never run before. In the living room, she heard what was left of the furniture topple and smash. Could she really leave this man to die? She reached the doorstep and was halfway down the garden path when she stopped. A familiar feeling tingled inside her. The last fourteen hours had raised so many questions, especially what she herself had done, and this man seemed to either be part of it, or somehow know the answers. Could she really run from him and risk never finding out? Yes. She wanted to run. And run as fast as she could. She wanted to charge on through the gate and flee down the road, but the lure to go back inside grew more urgent. Why she had to help this man, she didn't know and couldn't understand. She just knew that if she wanted to find out what was happening to her, she needed him alive.

By the time Eliza got back to the living room, the Shadow no longer fought for freedom. Instead, it had turned on Roman and coiled his legs like a boa constrictor. In retaliation, Roman thrashed from side to side, his arms punching through the dark mist, his legs trying to kick free. He needed Eliza's help, yet she didn't know what to do. Pain itched the tips of her fingers. The Shadow crawled up Roman's legs and curled his waist, trapping his arms against his sides.

Roman's eyes met with hers, and anger replaced his first look of disbelief at seeing her again. "Get to the light."

The Shadow wrapped Eliza's ankle and worked its way up her calf. Within seconds it had encased the lower half of her body, and both she and the man who'd tried to save her were trapped.

Glass from the window lay crushed around Eliza's feet. Red-hot pulses cramped her hand and she flexed her fingers. Tremors began to rumble across the broken shards, and one of the larger pieces flew up from the floor and into her palm. Eliza stared down at it. An instant earlier she'd wanted it, and now here she stood, holding it.

The Shadow rolled up around her waist, and with the glass gripped in her hand, she stabbed down towards her stomach, slicing through the dark mist and cutting her own skin. The Shadow released her, its shriek perforating the air and eclipsing her own anguished cries of pain. Eliza covered her ears, now free to run again. However, the Shadow hadn't let go of Roman, and now held tighter than ever.

Jagged glass jutted out around the window frame, and the familiar sensation Eliza felt in her hand burned inside her head. Images whirled like a movie reel playing over and over, shooting glass across the room towards the Shadow, one direct hit after another. And then it started to happen for real. Small fragments at first, each one snapping free from the wood and hurling across the room. Piece by piece, they cut through the Shadow like a samurai sword through silk. Eliza heard the man grunt as they stabbed him, but she couldn't stop further glass from flying through the air towards him. Larger shards broke loose and followed, and an ear-splitting scream finally drowned out Roman's agonising groans. Then, as had happened with Eliza, the Shadow released him.

Roman seized his chance and grabbed the Shadow in a bear-like hug. Unlike the pieces of glass, which had cut right through the dark mist, Roman trapped it, whipping it one way then the other, as though the two were dancing a frenzied waltz. The Shadow bulged and thrashed, morphing from one shape to another. A deafening screech, one more of anger than despair, cut through the gloom. Roman locked his fingers and held tight, and with one last ear-piercing shrill, the Shadow weakened and vanished from sight.

Roman stood panting, then glanced down at his slashed shirt and pulled a shard of glass from his shoulder. Another piece from his stomach.

"Shit." He threw the pieces to the floor and surveyed the room. The crescent-shaped scar circled the corner of his mouth, his stubble unable to disguise it. "Hell if I'm cleaning up this mess."

He brushed down his coat. "Why didn't you run when I told you to?"

"Because you needed help."

Roman rubbed the back of his tattooed hand across his chin, and when he tipped his hat, vigilant blue eyes stared at her. He hatched a nonchalant smile. "Well, one thing's for sure, I was totally wrong about you."

"You know why I can do the things I do?"

He smiled again. "I do."

Eliza waited for him to elaborate.

Instead, he took her hand and turned for the hallway. "Come on, we need to get out of here before it comes back."

"Before what comes back? What is that thing?"

But the Shadow had returned, floating up from the floor behind him.

The cocky expression fell from Roman's face and he sighed, looking more put out than worried. He turned to face his threat. The Shadow moved quicker. It tossed him across the room, and what was left of the display cabinet smashed under his impact. Roman fell to the floor, unrecognisable pieces of smashed Dresden and Wedgwood showering him, and the Shadow engulfed him again, dragging him from the living room and out into the hallway.

Eliza raced after them, stopping in the doorway and staring at the glass, willing it to fly across the room to save him again. The Shadow hovered mid-air for what seemed like minutes. Then, as if certain Eliza was no threat, it swooped down and mercilessly coiled Roman's neck.

In the blink of an eye, Eliza heard a sickening crack.

The Shadow held Roman, but he no longer kicked or fought the attack. Instead, his head lolled to one side and his blue eyes drained of life. The Shadow dropped him and Roman hit the floor, landing face down, one leg sprawled to the side, the other bent at the knee. Eliza scrambled to his broken body. She shook him and rolled him onto his back, but his eyes were closed and his lifeless body showed no signs of waking. She buried her head against his jacket and listened for a heartbeat; felt his wrist for a pulse, then his neck.

She found none.

Anger bubbled in the pit of her stomach, and the sensation inside her head returned, causing hot jolts to spike through her whole body. In the kitchen, cutlery and appliances started to clang together. In the living room, the already-broken furniture shook and rumbled. Eliza sensed the Shadow circling above her, and the vengeful feeling inside her intensified.

She should run, she knew that. But anger stopped her.

Pain burned behind her eyes, and electrifying spasms cramped her arms. In the living room, furniture crashed together. In the kitchen, drawers opened and fell to the floor. Spontaneously, items flew into the air and darted from both rooms. Knives slashed through the dark mist above her and embedded in the walls. Pots and pans and splintered chair legs also charged to the centre of the hall, every item piercing the Shadow before crashing into the far walls to create a noise louder than thunder itself. The room whirled around Eliza, and another high-pitched scream wailed from the Shadow, the sound of its pain cut short only when finally it exploded into a ball of dust.

The light in the kitchen brightened. Eliza collapsed to the floor, drained of energy and unable to focus. Ash rained down upon her like snow at Christmas, and although she knew Roman lay only feet away, she could barely see him through the haze of powder that had once been the Shadow. She reached out and felt his jacket.

Then, slowly, her eyes closed and she passed out.

CHAPTER TEN

Eliza felt as if she were soaring high into the sky.

A breeze swept across her face, and she partially opened her eyes. The kitchen ceiling moved by in a blur, and somewhere in the distance the front door bashed open and Billy's voice called out her name. Then the floating sensation abruptly ended, and she rapidly descended to the cold, hard surface of the kitchen floor. She heard the back door open, followed by the sound of footsteps rushing through from the hallway.

An urgent hand gripped her shoulders and shook her. "Eliza?"

Eliza fully opened her eyes. Billy stared down at her, his two-day-old stubble still unshaven, his brow creased with confusion and worry. He pulled her close, and as much as she wanted to stay comforted in his arms when he embraced her, she pushed him away. "Where am I?"

"In your kitchen."

Sure enough, as she scanned the room, she found herself lying on the tiled floor surrounded by a clutter of emptied drawers. Cutlery, crockery, the toaster, her microwave oven; every item either bashed and dented or completely destroyed.

"What the hell happened?" Billy said. "Who did this?"

Eliza scrambled to her feet, shrugging Billy away when he tried to hold her still. "There's a man in the hallway. He needs help."

"What man? There's no man out there."

Eliza reached the doorway. As with the kitchen, the hall looked as though a tornado had rattled through. Broken pieces once belonging to beautiful tables and clocks, and every other item her grandmother had cherished, lay trashed across the floor. "Where is he?" Eliza rushed into the lounge, easily the worst of the three rooms.

"Eliza," Billy said. "Tell me what the hell happened here."

Eliza turned to him. She knew the next three words about to leave her lips would sound utterly ridiculous. Even she didn't completely understand what had happened. Regardless, she said them anyway. "I did it."

Billy paused for a moment, and Eliza could only imagine what thoughts raced through his mind. He rubbed the back of his neck, seemingly to take time to digest the explanation she'd offered. Either that, or he was deciding what nut home to put her in. He shuffled closer and pushed strands of hair from her face. "You are not making any sense. You couldn't have done this."

"Billy, I don't understand it either, but there was a man lying right there in the middle of my hallway." She pointed towards the rug, now covered with her gran's broken possessions...but no body. "I need to find him."

"You need a hospital."

"But he has the answers."

"Is this the same man you say was at the train station last night?"

"Yes, but—"

"What are you not telling me? Who is this man?"

"I don't know. On my life, I'd never seen him before last night."

"Then how did he know where you lived?"

"He brought my bag back."

"And then what? He destroyed your house?"

"I told you, I did it."

Billy scoffed and clicked the side button on his radio, muttering something about a 10-33 and 10-52.

"I'm telling you the truth," Eliza said.

Billy turned back to her. "Why should I believe you when all you're doing is lying to me?"

"I'm not lying." Eliza blinked back the tears. "Please find him, Billy. Prove I'm not insane."

Billy stared at her, and for a full minute he did not blink. Then his shoulders relaxed, his eyes softened, and he took out his notepad. "Give me his description again."

CHAPTER ELEVEN

Roman made it out just in time.

He looked back towards Eliza's house, nestled in the hills some thirty yards up the small, gravelled lane. The front door was still open – as, he assumed, was the back, after he'd rushed out when he heard the cop arrive. Damn it. He'd had Eliza in his arms, and had been so close to escaping with her. He reached into his pocket for a cigarette and cursed when he saw the box was empty. He sighed and took a moment for his head to clear. The situation hadn't changed. He still needed to get the girl; other than the wood, which remained in Paris, his kidnapping plan still appeared to be the only viable option against the old man double-crossing him.

He crushed the cigarette pack in his hand and threw it to the ground. The short walk back towards Eliza's house felt as though he was walking to his death. A strange feeling stirred in the pit of his stomach, and no matter how much he tried, he couldn't shake it. He needed time to think. He needed time to plan. He needed time to kill this fucking feeling of guilt.

Rain had slowed to little more than a drizzle, but the steady stream of rainwater that gushed along the gutter was as ferocious as ever. He reached Eliza's house and took shelter underneath the old oak tree opposite. Through the open door, he saw Eliza sitting on the stairs. She seemed okay. At least she was awake now.

A light breeze brushed against the remaining leaves, and water dripped onto his hat and down the back of his neck. His lightweight coat was useless, and he pulled the hood of his jumper over his baseball cap. The tree hadn't provided the adequate cover he'd first anticipated. *Freakin' rain*.

An engine revved somewhere down the hill, and two headlights pierced the darkness like the eyes of a cat. Roman lowered the rim of his cap and ducked further behind the oak's trunk. The ground squelched beneath his feet, but he remained still and waited for the ambulance to park before he looked out again. Two paramedics ran inside, and it was a while before they emerged and helped Eliza into the back of the van. The cop leaned in and said something to her, and then the ambulance took off down the lane. The cop watched them leave, checked his watch, and then disappeared back inside the house.

Neighbours had gathered. Roman stepped out from behind the tree, confident of blending in. With the sun now completely eclipsed, the lack of light made it hard to see, but under the nearby lamp he saw lumps of mud clinging around the sides of his boots. He let out a sigh, and lowered his head. The water in the gutter gushed past and, seeing no other option, he stepped in and cleaned his shoes.

CHAPTER TWELVE

James hung up the phone and reached for his whiskey.

He could feel the pressure building in the back of his head, but he pushed the pain aside. For now.

A cigar smouldered in a nearby ashtray, but he no longer wanted it. Around him, books filled the shelves of several floor-to-ceiling bookcases: horror novels, Cornish history, legal paraphernalia, the UK taxing system. Photographs hung in a designed order across the wall: childhood holidays, Eliza's university graduation, himself with Richard Branson and the Prime Minister. James smiled. He was a very powerful man, and he liked everyone to know it.

He turned to the window and sipped his drink. In daylight, the waters of Fowey Estuary lapped against his private jetty. Tonight, though, the darkness outside caused the window to mirror his reflection. He hadn't slept in twenty hours, which on any other day didn't cause a problem. But tonight, his eyes fought to remain open.

His daughter was back in hospital. He didn't know whether to be alarmed or relieved. He did know one thing, though: this time, Eliza was coming home to his house, where he could keep a closer eye on her and properly protect her.

He rubbed his temples. The pain in his head wasn't dulling. He took another sip of his drink, but didn't swallow. Instead, the liquid rolled across his tongue until its burning sensation refreshed the inside of his mouth. When he finally gulped it back, it was warm and had lost its potent taste. He heard movement behind him but didn't turn. He didn't need to. He could see his butler's reflection in the window. "She's back in hospital, Davis." He swirled the remainder of the drink around his glass and turned to face the old man.

"Would you like me to get the car ready for you?"

"Is the plane ready?"

"Yes, sir, but I meant would you like the car to take you to the hospital?"

James downed his drink and reached for the decanter. It only slightly numbed the pain but, at this stage, he'd take whatever was offered. "No. She's safe for the time being, and that little stunt of hers earlier has delayed my business meeting enough already. Just make sure she stays there until I return."

At last, pain ripped open inside his head. His first reaction was to scream for his painkillers. Instead, he filled his glass and gulped back another whiskey. Then he quickly poured himself another. Swallowing it in one mouthful, he took a deep breath and paused for a moment. Every new day brought with it longer, more intense pain, and it seemed minutes before his head cleared enough for him to continue.

Davis remained quiet. James knew the butler was smarter than to comment on his discomfort. He dutifully waited for James to compose himself, then said, "Mr. Pope is waiting in the lounge."

James felt his mood darken. He placed his glass on the desk and pulled at the cuff on his jumper. "Tell him I've already left."

Davis nodded and began to leave, but James called on him again. "Davis, get me my medication, and make it quick. My head feels as though it's about to explode."

CHAPTER THIRTEEN

Billy had zilch to go on.

No name. No address. No nothing.

Eliza's vague description of a tall man with a scar around the side of his mouth, wearing a baseball cap and Timberland boots, and whose name began with an *R* was just that – vague, and this led Billy to the conclusion that either Eliza was in fact experiencing temporary insanity, which was something that didn't sit well with him, or she was lying. And that really didn't sit well with him.

Several other officers had arrived at Eliza's house. Outside, nosey neighbours peered in through the open door from across the street. Their intrusion made Billy sick to his stomach. He walked to the door and stepped out onto the porch with every intention of telling everyone outside to piss off back to their own lives.

That's when Billy saw him.

A man, little over six feet tall, coat collars gripped together at the neck, his chin nuzzled to his chest. He glanced in Billy's direction, letting the streetlamp duck beneath the rim of his cap to light his face, and in particular the crescent scar around the corner of his mouth. He held that stare for a second or two, then stepped out from underneath the shelter of the oak and strode off down the lane – in his Timberland boots.

Billy remained still, his fingers gripped around his open notebook, and contemplated his next move. Was this the man Eliza had described? Did he actually exist? The man had all but reached the bottom of the lane when he stopped. He glanced up and down the street, then crossed the road to a small, silver sports car. Billy's knowledge of automobiles was about as expansive as his understanding of women's waxing, but even he knew an Aston Martin badge when he saw one.

The Aston's lights lit up and the car swerved away from the kerb, did a complete one-eighty without stopping, and accelerated down the road.

The guy was rich. Typical. As Billy glared after the glow of the back lights, the chance to give chase or follow slowly slipped away. He noted the number plate and hurried to his police car, needed a five-point turn before he faced the opposite direction, and took off after the Aston.

CHAPTER FOURTEEN

It took Roman just ten minutes to get back to his place.

He rushed into his tiny bedroom and, satisfied he was alone, shook his jacket free and dropped it to the floor. He glanced down at his bloodstained shirt, the sodden fabric already hardened. Several small holes ripped the cotton. This had been his favourite shirt...and the only clean item of clothing he currently possessed. He yanked it open, causing the buttons to pop in every direction, but it no longer mattered. The shirt was ruined.

His reflection in the mirror cheered him slightly when he saw his bruised and anaemic skin had once again returned to its normal bronzed gleam. He traced his fingers across his bicep. Smooth, silky skin showed no signs of where the earlier glass had stabbed him, and when he twisted, he noted his shoulder, too, was clear of any marks. His neck still ached, but then it always did after he'd broken it. Dying sure was a pain in the backside.

His jeans were still damp from the rain, but there wasn't any time to change them. Besides, he had nothing else to wear and was in a hurry. He needed to get to the hospital. He needed to get to Eliza. Yesterday's shirt remained by the side of the bed, this morning's dried noodles encrusted onto the cotton. He picked it up and scratched at them with bitten-down nails. The noodles flaked and crumbled until there was nothing left but a stain. A whiff of body odour wafted to his nostrils, and his nose crinkled in response. Sniffing under the arms, he gagged. *Shit*. It was this or the blood-soaked shirt that lay at his feet. Why the hell didn't he just go to the launderette once a week?

He ruffled his hair and shook the remaining noodles from the shirt. Oh, this was an all-time low, even for him. Still, he turned his head away from the stench and slipped it on. Catching a glimpse of himself in the mirror again, he paused. Staring back out at him, he glimpsed the man he'd once been, albeit briefly – a man who, when faced with a life-changing choice, had taken the easy way out. The repercussions of that decision had weighed heavy on his shoulders ever since. Could he really do it all again to Eliza and allow history to repeat itself?

Yes, he could. He would do anything to be with his Jane again – and nobody was going to stop him from achieving that.

He cleared his throat. God, he needed a smoke, and scooted through the bedside table drawer until he found another cigarette box. There was one cigarette left, perfect for a couple of drags. He lit it, sucked in the nicotine, and walked to the window. The cop had parked down the street, but Roman still saw him. It was the car parked right outside his house that concerned him. The black limousine hadn't been there when he'd arrived a couple of minutes ago, of that he was sure. His mobile buzzed, and he retrieved it from the jacket he'd thrown on the bed. *Unknown caller.* Roman answered anyway.

"Mr. Holbrook. I thought you were going to Paris?"

"Just packing now."

The old man's hesitation, although only for a second, proved he watched from the car outside. "Mr. Holbrook, what exactly are you up to?"

Roman dragged on his cigarette. He really hated this arsehole. "Like I said, right now I am packing."

Another hesitation, this one a second or two longer. Then Roman heard the *snap*. His little finger jerked outwards and cracked. Pain erupted through his hand, and the cry left his lips before he had the chance to suppress it. "You fucker. When I get my hands—"

"Hands?"

Roman's index finger snapped upwards. A clean break.

Roman bit down on his lip. "I will kill you."

The old man laughed. "And then you will never have the wood to open the Gateway."

The cigarette quickly found its way back between Roman's lips, and he sucked on it as if his life depended on it. He gripped his hand, readied himself, and cracked his fingers back into place. He stifled the frustrated yell that tried to punch through, and puffed harder on the cigarette.

"Don't mess with me, Mr. Holbrook. Stay away from the girl and just concentrate on getting the wood. Leave everything else to me and you'll get your entry into Heaven. I promise."

The line went dead.

Roman dropped the phone and clutched his hand close against his chest. He would kill the old man for this, and it would be slow and bloody painful. After the fourth puff, the pain dulled a little, and his fingers were already healing. He stubbed the cigarette out on the window seal, slipping what was left into his shirt pocket for later.

He was going to enjoy killing the old bastard, but first things first.

Ditch the cop.

CHAPTER FIFTEEN

Davis was wafer-thin, and his seventy-eight-year-old body weighed less than seven stone.

Yet, James always heard his approach.

However, James was no longer here. James was on his way to Switzerland.

Davis opened the library door and entered, a single sherry glass balanced expertly in the centre of a silver tray.

Edward Pope sat nestled comfortably in the tapestry-covered armchair. "Where the hell have you been? I've been sitting here for the best part of an hour."

"I'm here now."

Pope leaned forward as Davis neared, and swiped the offered glass. "My father would have my scalp if he could see me now."

"Just as well he's dead then, isn't it? Now, do you have good news for me?"

"Yes." Pope held out a tube of rolled paper bound only by an elastic band. "The location is on that."

The open fire roared, its flames licking the flu above. It provided the only light in the room. Davis put the tray down on the nearby desk and pulled the rubber band free. The paper sprang open to reveal a blueprint of his Eliza's house. "You're sure it's in this house?"

"I'm sure." Pope took a sip of sherry. "Why, do you know it?"

"Yes. Yes, I do."

"What about James' daughter?"

"Eliza will be brought here later tonight."

A look of anxiety clouded Pope's eyes. He downed the rest of the drink, leaving the sherry glass empty. "What about Paris?"

"What about it?"

"Have you acquired what's there?"

Davis thought of Roman, and smiled. "I have my best man on it."

He lifted a poker from its stand and prodded the coals. Flames soared higher into the air, lighting the sweat beading Pope's forehead. "Is this too hot for you?"

Pope felt his face. "No, not at all." He pulled a handkerchief from his top pocket and dabbed it across his brow.

Davis turned from the fire and raised the poker, the tip glowing red.

Pope eyed it for a second, a look of uncertainty in his eyes. "I don't think I can be a part of this anymore."

Davis licked his finger and brushed the end of the poker. An abrupt hiss finished as quickly as it started. The tip dulled and Davis stabbed the poker back into the flames. "Okay. You want out, you're out."

"Just like that?"

"Don't you trust me?"

"Of course."

Davis turned his back, letting the heat of the flames warm his face. "Have you mentioned any of this to anyone else? Your wife? Your mistress? That Soho prostitute you frequent on Sunday mornings?"

"Never." Pope loosened his tie.

"That's good. It would be a shame if that loose tongue of yours blabbered something it shouldn't."

Pope put the glass on the small, round side table and pushed himself up out of the chair, taking a while to steady his balance. "Good luck, Davis. After tonight, we probably won't see each other again."

"I was just thinking the same thing."

Pope unbuttoned the top of his shirt and loosened his tie further. He glanced at the near-empty glass of sherry, a sudden look of fear in his eyes. "What have you done?"

"Nothing. You did it yourself by thinking you could trust me."

Pope clutched his chest and staggered to the door.

Davis replaced the poker, and took hold of the silver tray again. "I'll see you to your car."

CHAPTER SIXTEEN

Billy shivered.

Since he'd turned off the engine, it hadn't taken long for the heat inside his car to disperse. He rubbed his hand over the windscreen, wiping away enough condensation to see the house he'd followed Eliza's mystery man back to. Twenty minutes earlier, the top right-hand room had lit up and Billy watched the man smoke part of a cigarette. A limousine had pulled up outside, stayed long enough for Billy to note the number plate, and then driven away again. Then, three and a half minutes ago, the room light had gone out. Now, Billy counted down his imaginary timer, waiting for the man to re-emerge from the front door.

He didn't.

Billy waited. If the man was still inside, whatever he was doing, he was doing it in the dark. Billy flipped open his phone and hit 1: his speed dial for the station. Immediately, the pre-recorded communication asked him to leave yet another message. As he'd already left five asking George to run a number-plate check on the Aston, he just hung up. He had a bad feeling about this whole night. Eliza's delusional state when he'd found her mumbling of vanishing men, and giving no reasonable explanation as to how her house had been wrecked other than she'd done it herself, had led him to believe she was nuts. He felt guilty as hell for that now.

Eliza's mystery man was real.

What did all this mean? Billy had no freaking idea. But too much time had now passed. He grabbed a torch from the back seat, opened the door, and got out of his car. An unusual veil of mist had replaced the rain, and the lack of moonlight meant visibility had become much more difficult. Lampposts lined the pavement, each one orbed by a golden glow, and the desolate street showed no sign of life. Dampness suffocated the evening air, and Billy wished he was anywhere but here. He took a deep breath and gripped the rubber handle of the torch tighter. Never in his entire lifetime had he seen Eliza 'lose it.' Doubting her had been an error on his part, and one he was determined to put right. He zipped up his jacket, and switched on the torch. The fog brightened under the beam and completely hampered what little vision he had left. Heck, he didn't need the torch out here anyway. He turned it off and, with one last check up and down the street, closed the car door and headed towards the house.

Every step echoed on the tarmac, and the garden path wasn't any better. Gravel crunched beneath his boots, and dew from the overgrown grass brushed against his trousers, soaking his skin. Mail bulged from the metal post box screwed to the front porch and Billy pulled some envelopes free to find a name. Every letter was addressed, 'To the occupant.' Having hit a brick wall and being no closer to uncovering who Eliza's mystery guy was, Billy shoved the letters back in the box and scanned the street one last time. A loose brick wobbled beneath the house step and tested his balance. The house was worse than a bloody minefield.

At this point, Billy knew he was going to enter the house. The question was, how? He had no warrant or probable cause. If he broke in and found the guy upstairs asleep, he was going to have a hard time proving any lie he told. He pressed the doorbell, but heard nothing. Judging by the state of the house, Billy assumed the bell hadn't worked in years, so instead he tapped his knuckles against the door. Softly at first, then a little louder, each strike magnified by the stillness in the air. Net curtains hung in the window and blocked his view inside, and no matter how hard he knocked, the house remained in darkness with little sign of life.

Billy checked his watch. It had just gone ten. If this guy had left the house already, then where in the hell had he gone? He glanced towards the Aston that remained parked in the driveway. The man had to still be inside the house, and Billy needed a decent excuse to go in.

He tried the door handle; to his amazement, it opened. Still, he hung back, the re-ignited torch beam separating the darkened hallway into two halves. Few items hid in the shadows: a side table, newspapers, pizza boxes, all barely visible even under the torchlight. Whoever he was, this man looked to be one hell of a slob. A baseball cap, a different colour from the one Billy had seen him wearing earlier, hung from one of the coat hooks near the door, a leather belt hanging from another. Everything appeared quiet and normal, just as Billy would expect when nobody was home.

He crossed the threshold, his hand close beside his Taser. "Police. Is anybody home?" he said, deciding to blame his intrusion on a suspected burglary. When there was no reply, he took another step forward. The grandfather clock at the end of the hall ticked away endlessly. The torchlight found it. Of course, in a house this messy, it seemed only right that the time was incorrect. Billy lifted his elbow towards the light switch, and pressed.

The room brightened, the bulb popped, and the hallway plunged back into darkness. Under the light of the torch, the lightshade swung back and forth, its once-clean floral material now mustard coloured from cigarette smoke. Inside, burned soot blackened the bulb. Billy tried the second switch – the porch light. Nothing. The blown bulb must have tripped the fuse.

"Great." He waited, unsure whether to continue.

The man wasn't here, of that Billy was certain, and he wanted to get back to Eliza at the hospital. But what would he say when she woke and asked if he'd found the man? 'By some miracle I ran into him outside your house and followed him home, but then I left'?

The small kitchen housed a large table and not much else. It took Billy less than twenty seconds to clear the area and move on, less to examine the two mismatched chairs, beanbag, and television in the sparse living room. Thirteen uncarpeted stairs led to the first-floor landing. Billy didn't bother with the lights. Adrenaline still rushed his veins from the blown bulb, and he didn't need or want any more surprises.

Four rooms completed the upstairs. Two bedrooms looked out over the front of the house. The bathroom and the toilet, split from one another by a thin wall, both viewed the rear of the property. From the top of the stairs, Billy saw the narrow toilet was empty, as was the toilet roll holder. He turned his attention towards the bathroom beside it. The endless *drip, drip, drip* against porcelain echoed in the otherwise silent space around him. The torch beam searched the room. Dried water stained the cabinet mirror, and toothpaste smeared the sink. Behind the door, clothes overflowed the wicker basket, and wet towels dirtied the floor. A grey shower curtain stretched the length of the bath, hiding the area behind it. Billy gripped the torch tighter and reached for the end of the fabric. If this had been a horror film, he'd have deemed what he was about to do as idiotic.

Taking a deep breath, he whipped the curtain back.

Water droplets fell in unison from the showerhead and splashed into the bath. Mouldy grout surrounded grey tiles, and a blackened loofah hung from the lime-scaled tap. Billy let go of the curtain and almost laughed aloud at his own idiocy. Two bedrooms to go, then he could return to the hospital knowing he'd searched all he could. In the morning, he'd up his investigation, and then think about bringing Eliza up to date.

He entered the bedroom, where the stale stench of cigarettes hung in the air. And what in the hell was that other smell? Chinese? Billy tried the light, but of course it didn't work. The torch shone across the crappy furniture until it found the back wall. The bedroom was as sparse as the rest of the house.

On the bedside table was an empty bottle of vodka. Lower, and just catching his eye, the beam touched beneath the unmade bed, the saggy mattress far too big for the shrunken sheet stretched across it. Billy knelt to get a better look. A foil carton crumpled beneath his knee, and he directed the light towards it. Dried noodles, now crushed into powder, and remnants of whatever the hell sauce that had once been, soiled his trousers.

Billy pushed the tray away and, gripping the torch beneath his chin, reached under the bed and pulled out a scrunched-up piece of paper. He unfolded it. Scrawled in black biro was an address. Billy paused, brow furrowed. His father's address. Why the hell did this guy have his father's address? Had he been watching Eliza? Billy peered further under the bed and saw the white shirt, torn and bloodstained.

Damn it. Eliza had been telling him the truth.

Outside, a car engine roared to life. Billy ran to the window and saw the Aston Martin reverse out of the driveway and speed off down the road.

Damn. He hurried to the stairs. His mobile phone started to vibrate against his leg and he reached into his pocket. The caller hung up just as Billy answered. Billy cursed and redialled.

George answered. "Where the hell are you? A Jag's crashed off Old Brewer's Road. Get your backside over here now."

Shit. "Okay, I'm on my way." Billy hung up. He glanced at the shirt. This was going with him.

CHAPTER SEVENTEEN

A familiar sound resonated in Eliza's thoughts: *Beep. Beep. Beep.*

Her tired eyes flickered but barely opened. In the darkness beside her, a green line repeatedly jumped the width of a small screen.

Beep. Beep. Beep.

Behind it, tilted blinds blocked out the majority of hallway light, and with her eyes now starting to ache, she closed them again. Dryness scratched the back of her throat, and she mustered what little saliva she could and swallowed. When she opened her eyes again, the blurred objects appeared a little clearer. The starched pillowcase pressed against her cheek, its stiffness in dire need of some fabric softener, and she rolled onto her back, igniting the dull ache in the base of her neck.

Outside, a car engine revved. Headlights penetrated the fabric blinds and danced across the far wall, laying bare a lamp hanging above her, a plastic bead that dangled from a static cord, and some paint, which had scratched away from the wall beside the door. She was in the same hospital room as the night before.

The car engine stopped, and the light inside the room went out. The lamp disappeared behind the gloom, and apart from the low bleep of the heart monitor, the room fell silent.

Something moved in the corner of the room. Eliza rushed to find the lamp's cord but pain cramped her stomach and restricted her from reaching it. She winced, and doubled over. Short, sharp breaths flowed through dry, parted lips, and the beep on the monitor quickened. When she pushed back the blanket and glanced down through the neck of her hospital gown, she saw a square piece of gauze taped just above her navel. The soreness slowly calmed, and this time when she reached for the cord, it was in a more gradual and controlled manner. Fingertips brushed the plastic bead, and the cord swayed backwards. The beep's momentum quickened and Eliza yanked the monitor's clip from her finger, at last having total silence. She shifted to sit up. The bead swung towards her and she grabbed it, immediately lighting up the room.

Apart from the uncomfortable armchair the hospital insisted every room should have, the area was as it should be.

Eliza lay back against the pillow, but she couldn't relax. Either she had just seen the Shadow, or she was losing her mind. Whichever, she wouldn't sleep again tonight. She pushed back the blankets and slid her legs out of bed. Someone passed in the hallway, their silhouette behind the closed blinds slow and undisciplined. They stopped inches from Eliza's door, and although Eliza expected it to be a nurse on her rounds, nobody came in. After a brief pause, the figure shuffled onwards, and the door to the adjoining room could be heard opening and then closing shut. The mattress squeaked, and Eliza changed her assumption to that of the old lady with the bad varicose veins returning from yet another toilet visit.

Eliza stood, her toes curling against the cold floor, and her hideous open-backed gown doing nothing to cover her modesty. She found her jeans and T-shirt folded across the back of the chair, but her trainers were nowhere to be seen, giving further victory to the cold floor when she started to dress.

Bruised skin and patched wounds hurt with the slightest movement, and if the wall clock was anything to go by, it took her a full seven minutes to get dressed and a further ten while she searched for her mobile phone, certain she must have left it behind the day before. She needed to get out of this room, and she needed to call Billy to come and get her, but no matter how hard she searched, her phone was nowhere to be found. Determined not to spend the rest of the night laid up like some invalid, she opened the door and headed to the nurse's station.

The endless trill of a telephone could be heard long before Eliza reached the vacant desk. Normally she would have obliged and answered it, but tonight she just wanted to call Billy to come and collect her.

Instead, she waited patiently for its eternal ringing to finish, and then started to dial Billy's number.

079... She paused. So reliant was she on her mobile's pre-stored numbers that she had no clue as to the rest of the digits. She replaced the phone and let out a defeated sigh. She didn't want to stay the night in hospital, but she also didn't want to make her own way home after it had ended so badly for her the night before.

Tiredness no longer consumed her, and only a light fuzziness behind her eyes reminded her of the drugs she must have been given. She wouldn't be able to sleep, but as she glanced up and down the empty corridor, it didn't look as though she would get any conversation either. Where the hell was everybody? Even with the latest hospital cutbacks, the night-shift skeleton staff usually still managed to spread themselves around enough to be seen.

A door opened down the corridor; the room next to hers, and Eliza expected to see the old lady with the varicose veins head out on yet another toilet run. The hospital had supplied her with a bedpan a week ago but she'd refused to use it, waving her cane at the newly appointed orderly and scaring him half to death. Eliza couldn't blame her, though. Women just didn't have the same point, aim, and shoot capacity that men had.

To Eliza's surprise, it was her motorbike crash patient, Jason Devlin, who tottered through the door. Although a fair distance separated them, Eliza saw enough of him to trigger her heartrate to quicken. The handsome if not slightly bruised face she'd witnessed the evening before had gone. Now, shaded areas hollowed out his cheeks, and darkened eyes emphasised just how ashen his skin tone had become.

He shouldn't be here. He should have been discharged today, and Eliza called out to him.

Jason stared aimlessly towards her, his gaze unmoving. His arms hung straight against his sides as though weighed down with bricks. His crinkled and creased hospital gown hung loose around his shoulders, and claret-coloured goo stained his mouth and chin. He turned from her, seemingly uninterested, and began to stagger towards the fire exit. The gown's tie was undone, and the bareness of his white bottom could have been mistaken as comical on any other night. The cast, which had earlier supported his broken leg, had disappeared, and a small piece of card attached to his toe dragged along the floor behind him with each unsteady step he took. He continued to trudge away from her. His legs shook under his weight and his knee popped from its socket. His leg folded outward, and he tumbled sideways.

Eliza gasped and reached for her own knee, rubbing away the discomfort she felt for the man before her. Jason wobbled back on his heel, and glanced down at the protruding bone. Slowly, he slapped the side of his leg. His knee cracked, and the shin jerked straight. Eliza swallowed the saliva stuck at the back of her throat, and glanced down to where her own knee hid protected beneath her trousers, perfectly unhurt, yet still aching. When she looked up, Jason was nowhere to be seen.

CHAPTER EIGHTEEN

Billy arrived just in time to see George, his sergeant, bite into a cheese and coleslaw bap.

George clocked him, and frowned. "It's about time. Where the hell have you been?"

"Flat tyre. What happened here?"

"Car accident. Looks like the driver took the bend too quick." A dollop of mayo slopped from the side of George's mouth and landed on his chin. As he spoke, it slowly slid towards his dimple. "Divers had to dig the bumper out of the mud."

George took another bite, and noticed Billy staring. "Wabs s'mabba?"

Tiny spots of mayonnaise hit Billy in the face. "On your chin..."

George felt under his lip, knocking the blob of mayo onto his shirt. "Shit." He flapped open his handkerchief and wiped his face.

The yellow tow truck at the side of the river shuddered, and the winch ground to a halt. Suspended two feet above the water hung a black Jaguar, a waterfall of murky river pouring through the door joins. The winch rotated further, and the car slowly swung across to the bank, spilling water onto the grass until emergency workers had it settled on the churned mud. A fireman tried the door, but it wouldn't open. He shouted something to a colleague and a second fireman appeared with a large metal-cutting device. *Boys and their toys*, Billy thought as the cutter roared to life, its thunderous sound resonating into a scream when the blade touched the metal shell and sliced into the top of the roof. Sparks exploded in every direction, and for a brief moment Billy thought back to his boarding school days, and the time he and a group of friends let off a Catherine Wheel in the gymnasium. He'd copped hell for that and had nearly been expelled – until his father stepped in, waving his cheque book about.

The blade worked across the roof, buckling the metal, the sharp edges ready to take anybody's hand off. Down the blade cut, ripping and chewing, until it reached the bottom and the severed metal fell away. Firemen shut off the cutter and stepped back, allowing three scenes-of-crime officers to move in on the vehicle. The body of a man sat in the front seat, slumped over the steering wheel. He looked older than Billy, his face ashen and his hair grey. One of the crime scene guys turned and handed something to George: a black leather wallet holding various credit cards, and at least a hundred pounds in ten-pound notes.

"His name's Edward Pope," George said. "Going by his business cards, he's a shrink from London."

"Any idea how he died?" Billy said, taking the wallet from George.

All three SOCO guys looked up. "Give us a chance," the nearest one said.

"I mean, does it look like an accident or foul play?"

George turned to Billy. "Why'd you think it'd be foul play?"

"I don't. Just being thorough." Billy turned back to SOCO. "Any chance the sat-nav in that thing can tell us where he's been, or where he was going?"

SOCO sighed. "I'll let you know as soon as we know."

"Good enough." Billy handed George the wallet. "Are you hanging around here for a while?"

"Yeah, why?"

"'Cause I need to go check on something back at the station."

"I got your message about the DMV check. Don't hold your breath finding it anytime soon. The computers have crashed."

Billy straightened his belt. "Guess I'll have to find out the old-fashioned way, then."

CHAPTER NINETEEN

It didn't take a genius to figure out that something wasn't right.

Eliza reached for the phone again, pressed zero, and waited for security to answer. They did on the third ring.

"This is Nurse Hamilton. Can someone come up to the first floor?"

Two men worked security on the ground floor. One was in his mid-thirties and married to the nurse who should have been manning the desk where Eliza stood now. When a grunt acknowledged that someone would be up shortly, Eliza realised it was the snotty school leaver who'd been hired from the local job centre that had answered.

Eliza hung up and pushed the urge to get the hell off this floor to the back of her mind. Her gut told her to sit tight. It was light here, and the man in her living room had said she'd be safe in the light. If she wasn't losing her mind — and at this point she seriously doubted her sanity – and if the Shadow did come for her again, this seemed as good a place as any to be.

The lift at the end of the corridor remained closed, and Eliza watched the row of numbers above the door, willing them to light and assure her security was on its way. They didn't, and with nothing more to do but wait the three or four minutes until the young kid arrived, she perched on the desk and rubbed her cold feet, wishing she'd been able to find her shoes, or even a pair of socks.

Like a house in the dead of night, the slightest noise echoed along the corridor – something Eliza had never noticed before, not even on the quietest of nightshifts. Creaks and groans and the uncertainty of their origin prompted her to move behind the desk, where she happily allowed the enclosed area to fool her into thinking she was safe. She pulled out the high-back chair, still watching for the elevator lights to illuminate, and sat down. Now she had a better view, and could see both ends of the corridor with just a slight tilt of her head.

Various papers and open books lay across the work surface, and she couldn't help but cast an eye over some of them. Bob had signed out for the night an hour earlier, along with four other members of staff, and going by the roster, medication for the old lady with the varicose veins was half an hour overdue. Eliza walked the chair closer to the desk, the cold linoleum floor suddenly feeling wet and slimy beneath her feet. She wheeled the chair back to let in a little light, its wheels marking out trails of red paint. Eliza froze. The first instinct of denial kicked in.

This is not blood. This is not blood.

But it sure as hell looked like blood.

The lift bell pinged, and the scrawny security kid stepped out on to the first floor. He saw Eliza immediately and walked towards her, the bunch of keys hanging from his belt jangling so loudly it was enough to wake the dead.

He reached Eliza, a bored look on his face, probably because he'd been summoned here, and put his hands on his hips. "Well, what's up?"

Eliza couldn't find the words to explain the relief she felt at no longer being alone. "There's blood," she said, wheeling the chair back further so the young lad could see.

The security guard didn't glance down, and his expression didn't change. He looked just as bored as ever. He stared at Eliza, a sure sign that he thought of himself as the one in charge and would only look down when he was good and ready. Five seconds later, he glanced down. A couple of seconds after that, his forehead creased as he too raced through the first stages of denial. "That's not blood."

Confirmation. The excuses of drugs and concussions, and even that she was going mad, vanished from Eliza's mind. The security guard could see the blood too. Eliza wasn't imagining it. This was real, and she didn't know if she felt relieved, or more worried than ever.

"Whose blood is it?" The security guard hovered at the front of the desk, not attempting to come around and check it out. "Is it yours?"

Eliza shook her head.

"Who does it belong to then?" He didn't give her a chance to reply. "How much is there?"

Eliza could clearly see the pool of blood beneath the desk. Not a huge amount, but enough for her to think that someone, like the nurse − and wife of the security guard still downstairs − could be in trouble. "Enough."

"Enough? What's that mean? Enough for a stubbed toe? Enough for a burst blood bag? Or enough for a human slaughter?" The security guard paused. Perspiration glistened across his forehead, and sweat marks darkened the shirt under his arms. "There isn't a dead body, is there?"

"No." Eliza stood and walked around, each footstep printing a crimson path to the front of the desk. The sight was enough to make her vomit. Nearly. "We have to call the police."

The security guard nodded, but Eliza doubted he'd heard what she said. His young face had paled, and his spiky blond hair looked drenched more from worry and shock than from the gel fingered through it. Eliza picked up the phone and punched in the first of the three nines.

The door to room 202 opened.

The security guard didn't notice, but Eliza had. The whole of her body stilled.

Jason Devlin trudged into the corridor, his shinbone jutting through the grey-white of his skin. Unlike before, when Eliza had called out and he'd turned away, he now lumbered clumsily towards them. Eliza stepped back until her legs pressed against the desk. Anything she'd been doing now became a distant thought.

The security guard must have seen the look of horror across her face, because he whipped around. His eyes widened when he saw the disfigured movement of Jason. "Is that normal?"

"That's the reason I phoned you."

"You mean it wasn't about the blood?"

"No. I found that after."

"But that guy is dead."

"What do you mean?"

The security guard started to back away from the desk, clearly readying himself to flee. "Look at the tag on his toe."

Jason neared, his cold eyes staring at both of them. Blood caked his mouth and soaked the front of his gown, much more than when Eliza had seen him minutes earlier. He looked as though he'd just survived a massacre – or started one. Maybe finished one. His arms lifted and he reached out, almost like he wanted a cuddle.

"This shit ain't right. That ain't human," the guard said and, as Eliza had expected, he turned and fled.

Eliza watched him go, yelling at the top of his voice for help. She couldn't blame him. She too wanted to run with him to safety, but her feet remained planted to the floor, her frightened joints rigid and unable to move. She tried to call out, beg the guard not to leave her, but the words stuck in her throat.

Jason shifted past, his hair lank and his skin dry and coarse; something she'd seen many times on bodies in the morgue. However, the bodies in the morgue had been dead, stiff as a board. That wasn't – couldn't be – Jason now. He was mobile, semi-responsive. Eliza held her breath, the urge to run now gone. Now she wanted to be still, unmoving, invisible.

To her relief, Jason didn't look at her. He seemed more intrigued by the guard escaping down the hallway, which also happened to be a dead end. The scrawny guard turned like a frightened cat, the earlier look of boredom now replaced by an unnerving show of panic and fear. He saw Jason's interest was with him and raced for the nearest door handle: a locked storeroom. He moved to the next door, this one open, and darted inside, slamming it shut behind him.

Jason followed, albeit at a slower pace. Eliza needed to do something. She had no clue what Jason would do, but it couldn't be good. None of this was good. She forced herself away from the desk and moved into the middle of the corridor. Her hands shook. Her throat was dry, but when she called out, her voice was louder than she expected. "Jason."

Jason paused.

Shit.

Slowly, he turned to face her, a look of death hanging over him.

Eliza didn't wait to see what he did. She turned. Not wasting time for the lift to arrive, she raced for the fire exit. The stairwell door crashed open and Eliza rushed though, leaving no time to determine whether danger lurked on the other side. She sprinted downstairs, ignoring the pain in her stomach or the pounding inside her head, and burst onto the ground floor.

"Hello? Security?" Her heart raced, thumping against her chest so hard she wondered if this was where the term 'dying of fright' stemmed from.

Two naked patients, an elderly man and woman, lingered in front of the security desk. Eliza tried to search past them, praying to find the older of the two guards sitting there, but his chair was vacant. She glanced towards the main entrance, her path blocked by the elderly couple. The gentleman groaned and they both turned in unison towards her, heads tilted to one side, saggy old skin covering their bones, their grey hair brushed back from their faces. Eliza recognised them instantly as the husband and wife who'd crashed their car into the old oak up on Cliff Edge Road several days earlier.

The problem Eliza now faced was this: they had arrived at the hospital as DOAs – Dead On Arrival.

The words punched Eliza over and over again. *Dead On Arrival. Dead On Arrival.* She was staring at two dead people, and yet here they were, alive, and staring directly towards her. Eliza edged back into the stairwell and let the door swing shut. What should she do? She had no idea. She'd practiced fire drills and evacuation drills, but never a zombie-invasion drill.

Zombie. The term made her want to laugh and release the hysterical madness that seemed to prove without doubt she was losing her mind.

But the guard upstairs had seen the blood. She hadn't imagined that.

She looked at the options in front of her. Zombies blocked the main entrance, so she was left with either going back up to the first floor where Jason was, or down into the basement – where the morgue was. Neither choice sung out to her. She cranked her neck and stared upwards. Although only one floor high, the stairwell seemed to tower above her like a vortex leading straight to Heaven. Below, then, was clearly Hell. The first floor was where she had to return. She couldn't go to the morgue, and one zombie was easier to deal with than two. Besides, the guard was up there.

A hand appeared on the bannister above her. *Jason?*

Eliza stiffened until her neck ached, waiting to see whether the person or thing it belonged to would go up to the roof or head down towards her. It stilled for a moment, maybe because the corpse it belonged to was doing the same as her – waiting and listening. Eliza re-examined her options. If the person came down the stairs, she'd have no choice but to head back out to the ground floor and tackle the old naked couple. Nothing on this earth would get her down to that morgue.

The person above her started to descend the stairs. Eliza stepped back towards the ground-floor door, and quietly opened it. A quick check confirmed the corridor on the other side was clear, and as silently as she could, she started to back through. A wrinkly arm yanked her back by the scuff of her T-shirt. Eliza screamed and grabbed the doorframe, pulling herself free until her T-shirt ripped, and she tumbled forward on to the stairwell. The old man stepped into the doorway, a piece of cotton fabric clenched between his fingers. Eliza screamed again, and jumped to her feet. She rushed for the door, catching the dead guy's arm as she slammed it shut. With no other option available, she fled to the basement.

The morgue was situated at the end of a long, cold corridor, and the stench of disinfectant and death hung heavy in the air. Light slivered out from underneath the doors, and Eliza raced towards them. The assistant, who looked after matters for the coroner, was not at his desk. This didn't surprise Eliza one little bit. He was a slimy son of a bitch who spent far too much time with the dead for Eliza's liking. However, at this point in time, she'd rather tackle slimy than zombie. She grabbed the phone off his desk and pressed zero for a line out. There was no dial tone whatsoever.

Shit. She threw the phone back down on the table, and pushed open the morgue doors. A large sterile room awash with stainless steel cabinets, trolleys, and two large sink and drain units greeted her. Randomly lit panels in the ceiling and an x-ray machine fixed to the far wall provided little extra blue light.

"Ted?" Goosebumps pricked Eliza's skin, and she rubbed them away. Like the two floors above her, the room was devoid of any staff or activity.

She shuffled forward, not too much, just enough to let the door swing shut behind her. The room seemed colder than usual. Four out of the five chamber doors hung open, but inside, they were as vacant as the room around her. Three trolleys commanded centre stage, two empty, with a white sheet draping the furthest one. The familiar outline of a body lay beneath it. Dryness hit the back of her throat, and a feeling of dread washed over her.

The sheet moved. Only slightly, but enough to turn Eliza's dread into full-blown terror.

It's just the air-con.

The cadaver bolted upright, and the sheet slipped from his body and floated across the floor like an ocean spray across a sandy shore. Eliza watched it, her eyes transfixed and fighting the urge not to look up. But she did glance up, and stared directly towards the trolley.

Adrenaline raced through her veins, and her whole body shuddered with uncontrollable fear. A tag hung from the deceased's toe, the printed barcode the only identity the corpse had left. Eliza rubbed the coldness from her hands, but her sight remained fixed on the tag. Back and forth it swung like a pendulum, and she stared until her eyes ached. She didn't want to look at the dead man. She wanted to run, to get to the stairs and race to the main entrance, not giving a damn who or what blocked her way. But her body refused to move. Her feet, so cold she could no longer feel them, ignored her brain's command to turn and run for her life.

Eliza felt the cold metal door against her back, and grasped the handle. The dead man flinched and his eyes opened, lifeless and too dark for Eliza to see what colour they had once been. She gripped the door handle, and froze. *Please don't look at me. Please don't look at me.*

The corpse turned, stone-like, and stared into her eyes.

Fear paralysed Eliza. Silent tears burned into her cheeks, but she didn't move. She stared at the man, and the man stared at her.

He was the first to move. His legs slid to the side of the trolley, the first leg plunging over the side like a car off a cliff, dangling in mid-air until the second one joined it. Then he slowly slithered from the trolley until both feet landed squarely on the tiled floor. He stood silent, unmoving. Dark eyes glowered and penetrated hers. His head twitched and he took a clumsy step towards her. The unbalanced movement had no coordination, and yet he remained standing. His trailing foot thrust forward and tangled in the sheet, preventing further progress. Confusion contorted his face, and his torso tilted forward until he saw the cause of the problem. A groan bellowed from the back of his throat, and he jerked his foot again, but the sheet only wrapped his ankle tighter. He returned the same cold glare towards Eliza, and lurched his foot forward. This time, the tangled sheet stretched and pulled the trolley with it, wheels squeaking with every step he plodded towards her.

Eliza's brain screamed for her to move, and she turned for the door. The squeaky wheel fastened behind her, and then something seized her by the hair.

The morgue door burst open, knocking Eliza off balance. She stumbled onto her backside, pulling the zombie down with her. Hysterically, she wrestled with the ice-cold hand that gripped her scalp, until she felt a rush of air sweep past her. She glanced up, and for the third time in twenty-four hours, she saw him: Roger? Raymond? Roman. That was it. The man from her house – his baseball cap pulled low over his face, and the ends of his jacket flapping in the air like the wings of a wild bird. *But he died.* Was he now a zombie too?

He moved swifter than the other zombies, and fought the dead man with ease. The corpse took a succession of punches until finally it tumbled back against the row of gurneys, their steel edges colliding and sending medical instruments crashing to the ground. One last punch from the man and the corpse fell to the floor, his face no longer recognisable, clotted tissue and bone exposed around his severed elbow.

Eliza's fingers flinched across the cold, stiff hand still tangled in her hair, and comprehension turned to dread. Without warning, her body started to jolt. Hysteria took over, and she yanked at the dismembered limb, trying to get it out of her hair.

Two hands gripped her shoulders, and she screamed again.

"Stop," she heard Roman shout. But she wasn't going to stop. She was going to keep going until this dead, mutilated carcass was away from her being.

"You're bleeding."

Eliza shook her head, her arms, her whole body. "Get it out. Get it out."

A slap hit her across the face. Not hard. Not enough to bruise or even leave a mark, but the shock instantly stilled her. The severed hand remained tangled in her hair, its skin rough and cold against her, but she didn't move.

"Hey? Look at me. You're bleeding."

Eliza glanced up and saw her saviour, his face still hidden beneath the shadow of his hat. "Are you one of them?"

"One of what?"

Eliza looked towards the corpse lying on the floor. "One of them."

"No."

"But you died. I saw you die."

Roman sighed, almost silent, but she heard it. The hardness in his eyes softened, and the urgency towards her bleeding withered.

"How can you be alive when I saw you die?"

His warm hands covered hers and lowered them to her lap. "Just hold still."

Eliza felt his fingers move quickly through her hair, and within seconds he held the severed hand in front of her. A twinkle sparkled in his eyes, a mischievous look she hadn't seen before, and he smiled. "Safe to say he won't be needing any more manicures."

Eliza vomited.

Roman casually threw the detached hand over his shoulder, where it landed in the sink. "Now we need to stop that bleeding." He pointed to her stomach, where a small circle of blood stained her T-shirt.

"You smashed his face in?" Eliza wiped her mouth.

"Mash the brain any way you can."

"But he was already dead."

"And now he's dead again."

"But he was walking."

"It happens." Roman wiped a splatter of blood from across her neckline. "Are you bleeding anywhere else?"

"How? How does it happen?"

"Now's probably not the time for a Q and A session."

"You were dead too, I saw you die." This man was supposed to be her proof that she wasn't losing her mind. Instead, he seemed to be like everything else – part of her crazy imagination. "Are you like him?"

"No."

"But you did die."

Roman stood. "For a bit." He turned for the door, bloodstained boot prints marking his retreat like hers had at the nurse's station.

"Where are you going? There are others like him upstairs."

"Shush." Roman paused in the doorway. His shoulders tensed, and he rubbed the back of his neck. "Wait here."

He didn't turn to face her, and instead walked to the door. "And check you're not bleeding anywhere else."

Then he was gone.

The corpse, who'd now died twice, lay only yards from Eliza. His left eye hung from its socket, his nose pushed somewhere to the back of his head. *Like hell I'm going to wait here,* Eliza thought, getting to her feet.

She was at the door when something thundered past inches from her face and smashed into the mortician assistant's desk. She jumped back, and when she refocused she saw Jason Devlin lying face down by her feet. His head twitched, as did his arms and legs. Then, slowly, he got to his feet. His head turned towards her, losing interest in whatever had pushed him back, and his demeanour changed. Dragging his broken leg behind him, he came for her.

"Jason? It's Eliza... Nurse Hamilton." She edged back into the morgue.

Jason followed.

Roman appeared in the doorway and watched, back in control. "You won't get much conversation out of him."

"Aren't you going to help me?"

Roman said nothing.

"Help me." Eliza's hand brushed against a toppled gurney. Fallen instruments lay around her feet. She grabbed one, a steel thermometer, and stabbed it forward, plunging it deep into Jason's navel.

Jason paused. His arms dropped to his sides, and he glanced at the metal rod protruding from his stomach.

"He's not dying. Why's he not dying?"

Jason stepped towards her.

"Do something," Eliza yelled at Roman.

Roman unfolded his arms, and casual as could be, grabbed Jason by the shoulder and spun him around. Jason raised his arms in the same slow, awkward manner the cadaver had shown moments before. In the blink of an eye, Roman slammed his palms against Jason's temples and twisted. Jason's head rotated with a sickening crack until all he saw when he glanced down was his own bare arse. He looked back up and focused on Eliza. The stunned expression that clouded his face changed to one of bloodthirsty hunger. He still wanted her.

Eliza scrambled to put distance between them, but Roman stepped forward and punched Jason in the back of the head. His knuckles exploded out through Jason's forehead, and clotted blood and brain sprayed Eliza's face and splattered her clothes.

Roman's fist withdrew, and Jason dropped to the floor. "I told you to stay where you were." Roman reached for a paper towel and wiped the mess from his hand. He scrunched the towel into a ball and threw it across the room. It landed in the sink along with the severed hand.

"Here." He took another towel and passed it to Eliza. "Wipe yourself off. I need to be sure none of that blood on you is yours."

Eliza stared at him. No words came.

"What's wrong with you? Can't you move?"

Eliza didn't move.

Roman approached her. A flicker of warmth flashed across his otherwise emotionless eyes, and he sighed. "Shit. Look at the state of you."

He dabbed another towel gently across her forehead. Stopped, and sighed again. "C'mon. Let's get you back upstairs."

"I'm not going anywhere with you."

"Yes, you are." Roman reached into his pocket and pulled out a white handkerchief.

"What's that?" Eliza said.

"Just something to make you sleep."

Eliza backed away. "I don't want to sleep."

"I'm afraid you don't have a choice."

Eliza turned to run, but the toppled gurney blocked her escape. The cloth covered her nose and mouth, and hard as she lashed out in retaliation, an arm wrapped her chest and pulled her into a vice-like hold. Gradually, Eliza's hearing faded. Her legs trembled beneath her and gave way, but she didn't hit the floor as expected. The cloth left her face, and Roman scooped her into his arms. Eliza's head lolled against his chest, and thoughts of Shadows and zombies whirled through her dazed state. Maybe she would wake to find it had all been a nightmare...or maybe she wouldn't wake at all.

The subtle smell of body odour wafted beneath a stronger one of aftershave. She had just watched this man butcher two dead people, and all that came to mind was how nice he smelled. Exhaustion, both physical and mental, drained her to her very core. Her eyelids drooped until she could no longer see, and the last thing she remembered hearing as Roman carried her up the stairs was a comment about her stinking of puke.

CHAPTER TWENTY

Roman kicked the emergency bar, and the stairwell door to the ground floor flew open.

Moments earlier, he'd felt Eliza's hand slip from his shoulder, and now it dangled somewhere around the base of his spine. He stepped into the corridor, letting the door bang shut behind him. There were no signs of life, or the walking dead. When he passed the open-doored rooms, he didn't look in. There was no need. The sleeping patients inside had been ripped apart by the old naked couple. The same went for the security guard stationed by the entrance. His bloodied remains splattered the inside of the staff toilet. But behind other closed doors, some lucky patients survived, still sleeping and totally unaware of just how close death had been.

Roman glanced down towards Eliza. Ceiling light, artificial and unflattering, lit her sleeping face. Her eyes raced from side to side beneath their lids. Her lips parted as though she was about to speak, then the frown dispersed, and her body relaxed. Once again, she looked at peace. Against his better judgement, he let his gaze linger, her soft porcelain skin masked by fragments of Jason Devlin's brain. On her neck, her pulse throbbed in perfect symphony with her beating heart, slow and rhythmic as his had once been.

God, she was beautiful.

The base of Roman's neck tightened, and he forced himself to look away from her.

Refocus. She's just your key to getting to Jane.

But he was struggling. The smell of her freshly washed hair almost masked the stench of vomit. At her house earlier, this girl had been given the chance to run, yet she'd stayed and fought...to help him. Nobody had ever helped him. The tightness in his neck started to ache. Compassion did not come easy to him, and in all the years he had walked this earth, he only felt guilty about one thing. To feel any kind of emotion towards this girl irritated the hell out of him, and his inability to control it only added anger into the mix. Eliza's wellbeing was not his concern, just as both his son's and Jane's deaths had not been his fault.

The entrance doors automatically slid apart, and he walked outside to his car. Carrying Eliza's body in his arms felt good, too good, and the lure to steal another glance...

He focused on his car, his one joy in life, and carefully put Eliza in the passenger seat. With the corner of his shirt, he began to wipe Jason Devlin's blood from her face. Then down across her neck, her shoulders, the soft ivory of her skin, inviting and alluring. Roman stopped, his fingers lingering on the neckline of her T-shirt. He closed his eyes for a second, clearing the lustful thoughts from his mind, then stood and closed the door before she could screw with his head anymore.

He didn't bother buckling her seatbelt.

CHAPTER TWENTY-ONE

It was just before sunrise when Billy reached the records office.

If he couldn't run a number-plate check, he sure as hell could find out who owned the house he'd followed Eliza's mystery guy back to. He parked in the empty car park, got out, and strolled along the brick-paved pathway to the front of the building. He wasn't at all surprised when he pulled the doors and they shuddered but remained closed.

Inside, the security guard looked up from his desk. He waved his hand dismissively, and returned his attention to the small television monitor.

Billy hammered his fist against the glass until he had the guard's attention again.

The guard shook his head with obvious irritation. He slapped his hands on the desk. "Do you know what freaking time it is? We're closed." He pushed his chair away from the desk, re-zipped his trousers, and waddled to the door.

"I thought my uniform'd give away the fact that I'm here on police business," Billy said. "I need to check some information on a property."

"At this hour?"

"This can't wait. Our computers are down."

The guard grumbled again and pulled a bunch of keys from his belt. He prodded a long silver one into the lock and pulled open the door.

Billy stepped into the foyer and, although low, immediately heard a woman's pleasurable groans over a dated porn composition. Billy turned to the small television set on the guard's desk. "I'm not keeping you from anything important, am I?"

The guard straightened. "What floor do you want? We're still repairing damage caused by the freak storms last week. The entire basement was flooded, y'know."

"I want land registry on seventh."

The guard eyed him for a moment, then relocked the door. "Follow me," he said, plodding back to his desk. He slumped into his chair, which groaned for mercy beneath his weight, switched off the TV monitor, and slid the visitor's register across the desk. "Sign this."

Billy scrawled an illegible name, and pushed the book back towards the guard. "Anyone else up there?"

"You're kidding, right? At this hour?"

"Are the computers working there?"

"No. Like I said, the place is closed due to water damage. Everything's off."

"Not the TV though, right?" Billy pocketed the guard's pen and turned for the lifts.

"You need a visitor's pass."

"What for?"

"In case you get stopped by security."

"But you are security."

A victorious smile curled the corners of the guard's lips. "Those are the rules, pal."

Billy shook his head and trudged back towards the desk. He snatched the laminated badge from the guard's hand, shoved it into his trouser pocket, and started to head back to the lift.

"It has to be visible."

Billy smiled and pressed the lift button. Patience had never been a strong point of his. He bit his tongue, fighting to hold back the build-up of profanities, and stabbed the pin through his cotton shirt. It pricked the skin just above his left pec and, in frustration, he whacked the lift button again.

"Lifts are turned off after midnight," the guard said, enjoyment oozing from his voice. He made an obvious effort to check his watch. "Missed them by some fourteen minutes. You'll have to use the stairs."

Billy glanced towards the stairwell. Seven flights? Sometimes, police life sucked.

By the time he reached the seventh floor, he was more out of breath than he liked to admit. He gave himself a minute or two for the ache in his legs to ease, and then pushed open a large set of doors. The room inside was dark, and the musty smell of old books and papers clung to the place like mist to an evening ocean. The stuffiness of the room and the lack of oxygen tickled the back of his throat, and he coughed. Unable to find a light switch that worked, he manoeuvred past various outlines of furniture and drew back a wooden shutter from the window. With no sunlight, it made little difference to aid his sight, so instead he pulled the torch from his belt and switched it on. Millions of dust particles hovered in the air. Beyond them row upon row of bookshelves, all crammed with records dating back centuries, to when Fowey was a little fishing village and smugglers inhabited the area. Billy removed his hat and ran a hand through his hair. Registry records for the village he wanted were kept upstairs. The balcony was where he needed to be.

The spiral staircase wobbled as he climbed the cast-iron steps. Ten short bookcases, which was five more than there was room for, squeezed alongside each other. This made the space cramped and claustrophobic, something Billy wasn't entirely happy with. He hung his hat on the top of the handrail, and walked to the eighth aisle. The torchlight flickered and died, its battery life expended no matter how hard he whacked it. He fished a lighter from his trouser pocket and struck the wheel.

Files and manuscripts packed the shelves in a disorganised mess, and even with the light of the flame Billy found it hard to read the worn and frayed book spines. He held the lighter closer, and finally found what he was looking for. The burgundy spine lit up, and the gilt lettering sparkled under the flickering flame: Fowey's housing records – before the days of computers, when people still used paper and pen. It was a long shot. Who was he kidding, it was a million-to-one shot that some anorak geek still kept these written files up to date. Regardless, he found the area he was after, honed in on the most up-to-date copy he could find, and pulled the thick, leather-bound book from the shelf. It was dated from 1800 to 1959. Disturbed dust clouded the air in front of him, and the inside of his nose tingled with an impending sneeze. He waited for it to arrive, which it did half a minute later, followed by a second, and then a third. He paused, nose poised, waiting for a fourth. When it didn't manifest, he crouched down, balanced the heavy book on his thighs, and began to fan through the handwritten inscriptions.

A list of illegible signatures scrawled the paper, the black ink of the older ones now grey and faded with decades of age. Pages turned and further dust wafted from the book, and the fourth sneeze arrived.

A page caught Billy's eye, and he stopped to read the name of the road he was after: Orchard Lane. Running the tip of his finger over the addresses, he paused midway at number twenty-four. His fingernail dug into the paper as he underlined the words: Purchased 30th April 1937: Mrs P A Gardener.

Who the hell is P A Gardener?

The lighter burned hot in Billy's hand and he flipped the lid shut, letting the dark surround him for a moment. Some old dear who'd be at least a hundred years old by now – if she wasn't six feet under – was definitely not the man he'd seen enter the house. *Grandson? Great grandson?* Or no relation at all. The house had probably been sold five times over since 1950 anyway.

Shit.

Nothing but a waste of time that could have been spent with Eliza at the hospital. And that's where he should be now.

CHAPTER TWENTY-TWO

FRIDAY
The Catacombs. Paris, France

Roman leapt the wall.

On the other side, loose gravel and rock crumbled beneath his boots and he slid rather than walked the bank, not stopping until he reached the disused rail tracks below. He was way out from the centre of town right on the edge of Paris, and when he glanced inside the underground tunnel, he found – as he had been informed – the French authorities hadn't yet sealed this illegal entrance into the Catacombs.

Eliza, bound and gagged, pushed her way into his mind, and although confident the drugs he'd sedated her with would hold her in slumber for a few more hours yet, he wondered if she'd still be where he'd hidden her by the time he returned. But he couldn't worry about that, or her, now. Not while he had a job to do. He pulled a laminated map from his backpack.

The tracks would lead him a mile into the tunnel, where he would find a hole in the ground to crawl through. He glanced up at the tunnel opening, old brick walls covered in moss and years of neglect. He'd been a thief for over two decades, and never once had he failed to obtain what he'd gone after. The Catacombs, with its labyrinth of ancient tunnels and passageways, would be no different. The third piece of wood was in there, over three hundred feet below street level and buried among the resting places of millions of corpses, all exhumed from Paris cemeteries and dumped into the Catacombs at the end of the eighteenth century.

But it was in there...and it was his for the taking.

Moonlight soon evaporated into darkness, and by the time he'd walked the first mile, only the light from his torch spot-lit the tunnel walls. He'd never known darkness like it, and nearly walked right past the tiny hole on the left-hand side of the floor – a perfectly formed circle just big enough for him to squeeze down through. He snapped a glow stick and dropped it, the amber light landing in a puddle of water six or seven feet below. This hampered the glow from reaching even a meter in distance, making it hard to detect whether anything lay in wait. Regardless, he slid off his backpack, the removal of weight from the extra battery supply he carried a welcome relief to his shoulders, and pushed it through the hole. It hit the watery floor and then, as planned, Roman lowered himself through feet first.

Over four hundred miles and at least seven levels of tunnels made up the Catacombs, and one wrong move on Roman's part meant he risked never finding daylight again. Every so often, as Hansel and Gretel had done with breadcrumbs, he cracked another glow stick and dropped it. As no light whatsoever reached these passageways, the amber glow could be spotted easily, and although his route was clearly marked on the map, having the added security of the sticks to guide him back to civilisation was more than a little comforting.

He walked on, every so often stumbling on loose rocks and human bones. The lower he went, the more water flooded the route. When it eventually reached knee height and began to spill over the top of his wellingtons, he considered abandoning the job altogether and getting the hell out of there. Air had become stuffy, and his chest tightened as he worked harder to breathe. Several times, while concentrating on the route ahead, he tripped and nearly tumbled into holes and crevasses so deep his torch light couldn't even touch the bottom.

Roman felt his little finger, still sore and taking an age to heal. Old Man Davis could break any bone he wanted, and that was one hell of an incentive for Roman to keep going.

So that's what he did, trudging on through the water until it became too much and he had to climb onto the small ledges and hunch, so as not to hit his head on the low ceiling. Three times he stopped to stretch and empty his boots of water, the stench almost enough to make him gag. Collapsed walls revealed hidden rooms, and when he shone his torch inside, skeletal remains at least three feet deep covered the ground.

The lower he went, the more bones he encountered, until the water disappeared and he had no choice but to walk across the graveyard of remains, bones snapping beneath his weight and sending chills down his spine.

It took him three long hours to reach his destination, some three hundred and twenty-two feet below street level. Many drawings and symbols, some centuries old, carved the walls along his route, but this one – the chalked figure of a man, arms and legs outstretched – was what he sought.

He turned to the small opening on his right, no more than three feet high, and sank to his knees. A shiver ran his spine, and he paused. Every ounce of his being screamed at him not to enter. Nausea stuck in his throat, and he very nearly turned and left. He sensed what was in the next room, and he didn't want any part of it. He took a deep breath and lay on the ground atop a bed of severed bones and skulls. When he exhaled, his breath trembled with fear. Was the cross that important to him that he'd put himself that close to evil? He took another deep breath, and pulled himself through the hole and into the room behind.

Inside, the five-foot-high ceiling stopped him from completely straightening. He shone the torch light around the small crypt, not really sure what he expected to see, and his blood ran cold. On the far wall, painted in something he didn't want to think about, were the Latin words: *semita ad immortalitatem.* The Pathway to Immortality.

He'd heard this phrase spoken only once before, back when he'd first started being a reaper, just before he'd entered Hell for the first and only time. And he'd never forgotten them. If he was smart, he'd choose now to turn and run. But he wasn't smart. He was greedy.

He looked for another door, or gateway, but only walls of bone surrounded him. He glanced at the sign again. Below, buried between rows of skulls and bones, was a timber plank, similar to the one he had taken from the Italian cathedral. He pulled a hammer and chisel from his bag and carefully started to chip away at the surrounding skulls. They splintered beneath each tap and crumbled from the wall until he was able to wiggle the wood free. That was the easy part. Now, he just had to find his way back to the surface and out of this hellhole.

The first sight of early sunlight looked as though Heaven itself beckoned him in. Rays broke through the tunnel entrance, turning an otherwise eerie place into one of beauty, and Roman trudged onwards, itching to feel the warmth of the morning sun upon his skin once again. He'd been underground for hours, and although very little ever unnerved him, he swore he'd never return to this place again.

A shadow broke the rays and a figure, smaller than he and much slighter in build, stepped forward. Roman raised his torch, the beam immediately finding the face of a young woman, extremely beautiful and, he estimated, a few years younger than himself. He paused, scanning for additional threats. When he was certain there were none, he stepped forward again.

When he reached the young lady, she wasted no time in getting to the point. "I need you to go back inside the Catacombs."

Roman laughed. Just his luck. A beautiful woman crosses his path and she's as nutty as a fruitcake.

"Please," the girl said, her French accent strong. "It's a matter of life and death."

Roman stopped. He took a deep breath and glanced over his shoulder at the spine-chilling darkness looming within the tunnel. His body ached from tiredness, and all he wanted was to eat, sleep, and get back to Eliza, although not necessarily in that order. "There ain't nothin' on this earth that could make me go back down into those caves."

"Not even five hundred thousand? Sterling?"

Roman glanced at the entrance where civilisation beckoned, and then back into the blackness of the tunnel. Half a million was a lot of money. But he couldn't be bought, at least not where the Catacombs were concerned.

He turned to leave, but the woman grabbed his arm. "My family is very wealthy."

Roman stopped again, and repositioned the wood on his shoulder. "Sorry, lady. I have business in England."

"I have just offered you half a million pounds. Are you not the least bit curious as to why?"

"Lady, I gave up on curiosity years ago. Takes too much energy."

The woman pulled a card from a dainty little bag that hung from her shoulder, and tucked it into the top pocket of Roman's shirt, letting her hand linger. Her index finger tapped against his chest, and she smiled. "Like I said, my family is extremely wealthy. Maybe one million pounds could persuade you, no?"

A million pounds could persuade him, if he didn't have to get back to Eliza. "Like I said. I have unfinished business in England."

"Well, maybe you'll call me afterwards?"

Roman glanced back inside the tunnel. "Lady, I won't be around afterwards."

CHAPTER TWENTY-THREE

Billy pulled the police car to a stop, and stared at the scene before him.

Members of the public congregated behind strips of blue and white police tape running the hospital's perimeter. A local news van pulled alongside Billy, and a young female reporter jumped out. He recognised her immediately from the six o'clock news on BBC One. Her hair was scuffed into a bun and there wasn't an ounce of makeup on her face; a far cry from the beauty he watched on the screen every evening. An older cameraman climbed out after her, overweight and struggling to keep up as she pushed her way through the wall of onlookers and disappeared into the crowd.

Billy tried to follow, nudging his car forward inch by inch, but the public, far too interested in what was going on inside the hospital, made no attempt to move out of his way. Some turned and shouted at him, another banged her fist on the bonnet of his car. Billy hit the lights. Neon pink and blue highlighted faces and the backs of others' heads. Slowly the crowd parted, and a quick burst of the siren made the ones who hadn't noticed him jump and follow suit.

Two policemen stood guard at the car park entrance, where Billy also found the news reporter, petite in frame, arguing with them like a crazed woman at being denied access. Billy wound down his window, heard her yell something about the freedom of the press, and motioned for the officers to let him through.

He drove into the car park and the reporter, clearly a risk taker, whacked his roof. "I have a right to report the news."

"And you can, right from where you are."

The reporter huffed, Billy's words only antagonising her further. She lowered to his eye level, clearly with more to say, but Billy pressed the window button up and pulled the car forward. In his rear-view mirror, he briefly glimpsed her trying to chase him before the two officers moved her back behind the barrier.

Now inside the car park, Billy could see the mass of destruction that held the crowd's attention. Emergency services swarmed the area: police, firefighters, doctors and nurses, some still wearing their uniforms while others, looking exhausted and dishevelled, were dressed in more casual clothes. Nobody stood still. One doctor helped an elderly woman into the back of an ambulance, and then climbed in alongside her. George's garbled message about Billy getting his arse over to the hospital ASAP had made little sense to him. Two police officers, suited up in black combats and protective vests, guns swinging from their shoulders, rushed another patient from the building.

The drizzle of rain that had started twenty minutes before had lifted, and an early-morning glow reflected across the hospital windows, warming the horizon behind him. Dew glistened across areas of lawn and trees, but the bright and glorious day that beckoned was marred by the sight of torment and pain. Nowhere could Billy see Eliza. He stopped the car and got out. Patients groaned and sobbed, and some hospital staff joined them. Billy saw Dr. Bob, dressed in a jumper and tracksuit bottoms, the cocky expression that always plastered his face now gone. In its place, a haunting picture of confusion and distress. He caught sight of Billy and stared at him, emotionless.

Billy looked away, searching the sea of faces in the hope of finding Eliza. But all he saw were strangers, their expressions plagued with torment and fear. He pulled out his mobile and dialled Eliza's number, but it went directly to her voicemail, just like the other twenty-five times. *Goddamn it, where are you?*

A series of gunshots blasted from inside the hospital. Patients and hospital staff screamed and fled to the safety of vehicles, where they ducked and hid from sight. Police officers contradicted those actions, some by running straight towards the building while others remained rooted to the floor, standing shoulder to shoulder with the firefighters as they watched the hospital's double doors, waiting to see what would emerge.

Billy grabbed a passing officer, a twenty-something chap he knew was stationed one village on from his. "What the hell's happened here? Is there a shooter inside?"

The officer stopped. "Nobody knows. Someone went nuts inside. Killed a whole bunch of people."

"Someone? You mean a doctor? A patient?"

The officer shrugged. "That's all I know." And he continued towards the hospital.

Billy headed after him. He had no idea what had happened, and no idea where Eliza was, but what he did know was that he couldn't stand around here waiting to find out.

"Billy, hold up." George grabbed his arm. He looked totally drained, not just from the obvious lack of sleep, but more likely from the stress of dealing with all the mayhem. His clip-on tie was gone, and the top three buttons of his shirt were undone to reveal the white stained vest he wore underneath. Usually Billy would have commented, but not today. Not now.

"George, what in the hell is going on here?"

"It looks as though some psycho's gone on a killing spree. It's a massacre in there, dead bodies everywhere. Even the corpses down in the morgue took a beating."

"What?"

George tutted. "What is the hospital world coming to? If the MRSA bug don't get you, some raving lunatic will."

"What about Eliza?"

George shook his head. "I haven't seen her yet. Firearms Unit are doing a final sweep of the building, but it looks as though the last patient has just been brought out."

"So then where the hell is she?"

"If she's still inside, Firearms'll find her."

"I can't wait that long." Billy turned for the hospital, but George stopped him and pushed him against the side of the ambulance. It was a show of force Billy had never seen from his sergeant before.

"Let Firearms handle it."

"She's my sister."

"I know, but there are people out here who need your help now."

"If everyone's out, what the hell are the guys inside shooting at?" Billy shrugged from George's grip only to be re-pinned against the van.

George swallowed, took a breath, and said, "There's some crazy talk making the rounds out here, none of which, may I add, I believe. If you want to help, help out here."

Billy glanced towards the entrance. Eliza could be inside, needing his help. How was he supposed to stay away?

Three officers emerged from the hospital entrance, all empty handed.

"Hey." George clicked his fingers, snapping Billy from his thoughts. He stepped back and removed his weight, allowing the heels of Billy's shoes to touch the floor. "I need your help."

Billy raised his hands in a show of surrender. He needed to get George off his back so he could slip inside the hospital unnoticed. "Okay, who do you want me to help first?"

"There's a young man over there, reckons he saw the maniac who did this..."

Billy listened, but his eye was on the entrance. As soon as George finished saying what he had to say and walked away, Billy was going in to find Eliza.

"...Some dude in a baseball cap and Timberlands. Now go take his statement."

Billy turned to George. "What did you say?"

"I said, go take his statement. He's scared half to death, and I want to know what he has to say before the bloody doctors tell us we can't question him."

Billy saw the young man sitting inside the back of an open police car, a beige blanket wrapped around his hospital gown, shoulders hunched, exposed hairy legs crossed at the ankles. Billy glanced back towards the hospital, but George blocked his view.

"Do I have to frog march you over there? I said go and ask him some questions."

Billy's body tensed. He took a deep breath and tried to relax.

"If you try to get in there for her, I'll lock you in the back." George raised an eye towards his police car.

"And then you won't be any good to anyone, least of all Eliza."

George was right. If Billy couldn't work, he was of no use to anyone. He ran his fingers through his hair until they interlocked behind his head. His shoulders tensed, and he stretched out the ache between his blades and slowly made his way towards the witness. Two minutes – one hundred and twenty long seconds. That's all this guy was getting from him.

The young man sat on the back seat of the car. He looked scared and in shock, and Billy knew getting any information out of him would require understanding and sympathy, both of which Billy didn't have the time to give right now. He had no idea where Eliza was, and her mystery man was still that – a total mystery.

The young man glanced up as Billy approached, eyes bloodshot, hardly any colour in his cheeks. "Did they get him?"

"Get who?" Billy leaned on the roof of the car.

"The guy inside. The one that..." The man looked down towards his lap. His fingers entwined around the blanket, scrunching the wool together until it bulged in his hand.

"Did you see what happened?"

The man nodded. "The guy...he just...he just ripped their heads off."

"What?" Billy crouched down beside him. "Whose heads?"

"The old couple."

"With his bare hands?"

The man nodded, almost trance-like. He pulled the sagging blanket back around his shoulders. "I expected more blood."

"What did this man look like?"

"Tall. I...I couldn't see his face. His hat was pulled down too low."

"What kind of hat was it?"

"Baseball cap. Navy, black, dark green. I'm not sure."

Billy's stomach tightened. "What else? What else was he wearing?"

The man thought for a moment. His head started to shake, as though his brain didn't want to remember any more.

"Think hard," Billy said.

The man closed his eyes. "A jacket, dark, I don't know what kind."

"Okay, that's good. What else?"

"Boots, maybe the Timberland kind. Again, I don't know. Everything happened so fast." The man opened his eyes. "He did curse about the amount of blood on them."

"Blood?"

A single tear rolled from the corner of the man's eye, its trail glistening across his cheek until it ran dry. "So much blood."

"I thought you said there wasn't a lot of blood."

The man glanced up. "Not from the old couple. But the security guard..."

"Security guard?"

"There was so much blood when they killed him."

"They? They who? You mean the man in the Timberlands, right?"

The witness shook his head. "The old couple. They were already dead, you know."

Billy waited a moment. Nothing this guy said made any sense, and he himself needed to get inside the hospital to search for Eliza. "What happened afterwards? Where did the man in the Timberlands go? Did he leave?"

The young man shook his head again. "He went to the fire exit. I saw him go down the stairs before the door slammed shut."

Billy stood and patted the guy on the shoulder. "You've done real good. I'm gonna get a medic over here for you, okay?" Now Billy needed to get inside the hospital more than ever. He saw George off to the right, preoccupied with a hysterical young woman who couldn't find her daughter.

"I saw him again," the witness said. "He left with a girl,"

Billy stopped in his tracks, and turned. "What girl?"

"A brunette."

"Nurse or a patient?"

The man shrugged. "She wasn't dressed like either. Wore jeans and a top."

Billy knelt beside him again. "Was she okay?"

The man shrugged. "I don't think she was awake. The guy carried her. She was covered in blood, too. No shoes on her feet."

"Where did he go with her?"

"Out the front door."

Billy waited for more information, but the man didn't volunteer any. "And?"

"I don't know. I just hid." A few more tears fell from the man's eyes. "I should have helped her."

Yes, you should have. "No, you did the right thing." Billy stood. Dr. Bob climbed out from the back of the ambulance, and Billy whistled and waved him over. He turned back to the man. "This doctor is going to help you now."

Billy's mobile vibrated. He still held it in his hand, and answered. "Yeah?"

"It's Linda from the lab. You wanted to know if the sat-nav from the car that crashed on Old Brewers Road had any information on it?"

"Yeah, but now's not a good time."

"Is there ever a good time? There was nothing on the sat-nav."

"You phoned to tell me you have nothing to tell me?"

"No."

"Then what?"

"The map app on his mobile. Movements for the last week, in fact."

"I'm only interested in just before the crash. Just email any info through to me. I'll deal with it later."

"I think you'll want to deal with it now. Seems your dead guy had just left Moneyready Road in Fowey. Your father's place, to be exact."

"What? Are you sure?"

"I'm always sure."

Billy paused. What the hell was his father up to? "Billy?"

"Yeah, Linda, I'm still here."

"I'll send the info through. Just thought you'd want a heads-up first." She hung up.

A hundred thoughts raced Billy's mind. His father was a slippery son of a bitch, but involved in murder? Then again, why not? Billy already suspected him of his mother's death. And Eliza? Could he be involved in his own daughter's kidnapping? *Shit.* This was his own father, for crying out loud. He redialled main division. "I have a missing person, last seen Looe Hospital."

Billy spilled out a description of Eliza. When he finished, he hung up and ran over to George. "The man who did this took Eliza."

George turned from the woman he was trying to console. The mother didn't stop her hysteria, and George took her arm, a show of reassurance that he was still listening. "Billy, what are you talking about?"

"Our witness over there saw a guy leave with Eliza."

"Leave? As in they were together?"

"No, I mean leave as in he carried her unconscious body out the front door. I've just called it in." Billy turned to leave.

George stopped him. "Where're you going?"

"Lab just phoned me. The dead guy from our car crash was last at my father's place."

"They said that?"

"Yep." Billy pointed to the witness. "And he just described seeing a man wearing Timberlands and a baseball cap, carrying Eliza from the hospital. Earlier, Eliza told me that a guy wearing Timberlands and a baseball cap was at her house. I then followed a guy wearing Timberlands and a bloody baseball cap to a house where I found my father's address written on a piece of paper."

George frowned. "And why the hell is this the first I'm hearing about it?"

"I needed to be sure. My dad's up to something, I know it." Billy waited for George to respond. When he didn't, Billy said, "I need to go and ask him some questions."

"No."

"Fine, then I need to let him know his daughter is missing."

George cracked his neck and rearranged his collar. "Okay."

Billy opened his car door and had one leg already inside when George stopped him.

"I haven't finished," George said. "You go see your dad, but only to inform him of Eliza's disappearance. You're too close to this, Billy. If I get him chewing my arse off later because you've overstepped the line, you'll be on desk duty for the next six months."

Billy started to protest, but George cut him off. "It isn't up for discussion. Missing daughter only."

CHAPTER TWENTY-FOUR

The smell of rotting food was the first thing Eliza sensed.

Then the barely audible chitchat of a radio.

She opened her eyes, her head drowsy and muddled, but she didn't move. Crouched several metres away, on the other side of the small cabin, was Roman. He didn't seem to notice her wake, his attention held by the patter of a rat as it took what was probably its daily route along the unpainted skirting board. Roman peered from under the brim of his cap, took aim, and fired the smooth and perfectly formed pebble he'd been toying with. It hit the rodent, who squealed and scurried to safety through a tiny gap beneath the broken fridge. Roman picked up another pebble, seemingly to wait for the rat to re-emerge. When it didn't, he scratched his chin and appeared to look for something else to keep him amused.

Through the moth-eaten curtain, which hung in tatters across the window, Eliza could see nothing but darkness outside. Rain pelted against the corrugated roof, making it hard to hear, and water trickled through rusted holes, soaking the dirty floor and periodically splashing her face. But still, Eliza didn't move. If this man was as bored as he looked, she sure as hell didn't want to give him something else to play with.

An overturned chair lay beside a decrepit, paint-chipped table. Roman stood the chair upright and straddled it. He glanced at his filthy Timberlands, muttered a string of obscenities Eliza couldn't quite make out, and grabbed a filthy old rag from the table. Shaking off dried leaves and debris, he began to wipe away what dirt he could. Mud smeared across the suede, and a look of annoyance creased his forehead. He threw the rag to the floor just as the rat reappeared by the fridge. Roman's fingers tightened around the pebble, and he slowly lifted his hand, ready to fire the next round. The furry rodent scurried out a foot or two then paused, as though aware of the impending danger. His whiskers twitched and, without warning, he darted back inside the hole. Roman's hand remained poised, and a determined scowl creased his brow. He looked like he really wanted to knock that rat's furry little nose right off his furry little head. Maybe that's what he had planned for Eliza.

At that thought, every bone in Eliza's body screamed for her to remain still, and as much as the nagging voice inside her head agreed, reason also told her she had to look for a way out. She slowly craned her neck just enough to view the rest of the cabin, but without drawing the attention of her captor. If she could just locate the door, maybe she could make a run for it.

Roman lowered his arm, and the corner of his mouth twitched into a half smile. "Nice to see you're finally awake."

Eliza paused. Goosebumps pricked her skin at the mere sound of his voice.

"You're not going to give me any problems, are you?"

Eliza shook her head just enough to send the message. "Where am I?"

"Bodmin Moor."

"Your place?"

Roman grinned and flicked the pebble across the room, now not seeming to aim at anything in particular. "Does this look like the kind of shit-hole I'd usually hang out in?"

"Are you going to kill me?"

Roman relaxed his arms around the chair and drummed his fingers on the back of it. "That's a strange question."

"Is it one you're going to answer?" A water droplet trickled down the side of Eliza's face and soaked into the neckline of a shirt she didn't recognise. When she tried to wipe it away, her stomach tightened with pain and she found she couldn't move her hands.

"I am not going to kill you."

Eliza didn't believe him. "But something is trying to, right?'

"Yes."

Eliza tried again to bring her hand around to her front, but realised they'd been tied behind her.

"It's just a precaution," Roman said, getting up from the chair. He crossed the room in four strides, and knelt beside her. "Are you aware that I have now saved you three times in two days?"

"And yet here I am tied up."

Another droplet splashed from the puddle beside her and hit her forehead, the bobble of water holding position for a second or two before trickling the same path as its predecessor. Roman watched it too, and just before it touched her jawline, he reached towards her face. Eliza turned her head and closed her eyes, flinching when she felt his thumb gently wipe the droplet away.

His fingers cradled her chin, and he tilted her head back to face him. "Would you like to get up off this floor?"

Eliza nodded, wincing when he hooked her under the arm and hauled her to her feet.

With her legs also bound, Eliza could move no faster than a snail's pace, and it soon became obvious that patience was not one of Roman's strong points. He searched around, kicked a chair out from under the table, and plonked her down.

"Who are you?" Eliza said, still struggling to free her hands.

Roman shook two JPS cigarettes from a pack, slipped them both between his lips, and lit them. He removed one and held it out towards her. When Eliza declined his offer, he shrugged and dropped it to the floor. "I've already told you."

"Why am I here?"

"Because if you were at the hospital, you'd be dead."

"*Why* have you been following me?"

"Because without you, I don't get what I want." Smoke curled from Roman's mouth, and he took a second drag.

"What is it you want?"

"You ask a lot of questions."

"You've given me good reason to." The ties around her wrists would not loosen, and Eliza relaxed her arms, allowing a moment for the soreness in her shoulders to dull. Over his shoulder, Eliza saw the door. If she could just get free.

"I watched you die."

Roman studied her. He rubbed the bristle around his chin and pushed his hat up off his face.

"I wasn't wrong about that, was I?"

Roman stiffened. He puffed on the cigarette and remained quiet until Eliza thought he would never answer. Finally, he said, "Here, drink some of this." He held a bottle of Evian to her lips.

"Will it kill me?"

He swigged down a mouthful himself, then put the bottle back to her mouth. "Satisfied?"

Hardly. But Eliza's throat was so dry she didn't see she had any other option. Cautiously, she parted her lips and slowly drank the liquid, a miniscule amount trickling down the side of her chin.

Roman watched, not once looking away. He held the neck of the bottle close for maybe ten more seconds, then re-screwed the lid and put it down beside the chair. "You're leverage."

"Leverage?"

Roman took a long drag on his cigarette and eyed her.

"So, what? You're ransoming me?"

"Call it what you want. Your father's butler—"

"Davis? He's like a hundred years old."

"He's a devious little bastard."

"And because of that, you kidnapped me?"

"Because of *that?*" Behind Roman, grime-covered plates littered the table. Cobwebs clung to blunt knives and dusty glassware, and bluebottle flies swarmed a maggot-infested squirrel. Roman pushed the dead animal away, and sat on the corner of the table. It creaked under his weight. "I guess so. Yes"

Panic took hold. Eliza twisted in her seat and pulled at her binds. Her stomach once again cramped with pain and she cried out.

"You cut your stomach. Remember?"

She glanced down. Noticed the unfamiliar shirt. "Why have you changed my T-shirt?"

"The last one had your blood all over it."

"What is so important about my blood? Why do I need saving? What's after me?"

When it was clear he wasn't going to answer, Eliza said, "How can you be alive?"

Roman dragged on his cigarette. The end brightened and smoke masked his face as he exhaled. "You talk way too much." He picked the old rag up off the floor. His glare hardened, maybe to try and frighten her, maybe not.

Eliza stared at the mud-covered cloth and sank back into her chair. "I'll be quiet. I promise."

Roman followed her gaze towards the rag, and for a second he seemed to contemplate her request. He dropped the rag and reclaimed his position against the table, crossing his arms and causing his biceps to bulge beneath the fabric of his shirt. He watched Eliza, unmoving and silent, and held the stare until Eliza broke it and turned away.

"How long do I have to stay here?"

Roman sighed. "That's not you being quiet."

"My father will pay you whatever you want, you know."

"Your father is a rich man who don't know shit about what's going on around him." A lone maggot wriggled beside him and he flicked it away, catapulting it into the air. It landed by Eliza's foot, and only when it started to crawl back towards his own boot did Roman step forward and squash it into the rotting floorboards. "My turn to ask a question. At your house, why didn't you run when you had the chance?"

"Is this a trick?"

"Is that you asking me another question?"

"But I don't understand what you're saying."

"Would it sound better if I asked it in French?"

"What? What kind of question is that? Who the hell are you?" Anger exploded, and Eliza pulled on her restraints. She felt them loosen slightly and thrashed harder. "Just let me the hell out of here."

Roman remained quiet, his arms still crossed, his glare never leaving her.

Eliza struggled until the energy drained from her body. The restraints didn't loosen any further, and her shoulders sagged. The rope around her wrists chafed her skin, her attempt at freeing herself having no impact whatsoever. She glanced up, not bothering to conceal her sense of defeat. "If I answer your question, will you answer mine and tell me how you can be alive, and what it is you reckon Davis is doing to you?"

"That's two questions."

The anger Eliza had thought gone resurfaced, and erupted like a volcano. "Then ask me two and we'll call it even," she yelled, tugging at the restraints more vigorously than before. The chair legs left the floor, and she crashed to the ground.

"Are you finished?"

Eliza lay on her side, tears overflowing, wrists and ankles still bound, her body totally exhausted. "Please let me go."

Roman took the cigarette from between his lips and stubbed it out on the table. "Why didn't you run from your house?"

"I don't know. Because I'm stupid."

Roman pushed himself away from the table. He bent down and took hold of the chair, lifting Eliza until she sat upright again. Strands of hair fell across her face and into her eyes, hampering her view when Roman knelt in front of her.

He stroked the stray hair away from her eyes, his fingertips lingering against her cheek. The slight stench of tobacco scented his warm breath when he spoke. "You've put me in an awkward position and it's causing me the biggest arse-ache ever."

"I didn't mean to."

Roman paused, seemed to realise he still stroked her face, and swiftly returned to the table. He took a mouthful of water and swallowed it. "The old man wants you dead."

"Davis? Don't be—"

"If I hand you over to him, you will die. If I don't, then I don't get what I want...And that ain't gonna happen."

"Davis loves me. I've known him since I was a child."

"He's going to sacrifice you."

Roman's gaze fixated on her, his blue eyes soft and filled with pain, and although Eliza wanted to look away, she couldn't.

"You're insane," she said, twisting her tied wrists to gain further movement. The knot unravelled and the rope slipped free, her fingers catching it before it fell to the floor. Roman swigged from the water bottle, oblivious to her imminent escape. Eliza glanced at the rope securing her ankles. It was much slacker and didn't look a problem to untie. Dried blood covered her cold feet, and dirt and other unknown crap wedged deep beneath her toenails. They looked how she'd imagine a shoeless soldier's to look after having walked a mile or two through the trenches.

Her heartbeat quickened and she scanned the room. There must be something she missed before, something that could cause a distraction and aid her in her escape. She wanted to feel her fingers tingle. She wanted the movie reel inside her head to begin playing. She wanted a way to—

"Don't waste your time trying to use your telekinesis. It doesn't work on me."

"You know what happened to me back at the house?"

Roman merely stared at her, a cocky smirk etched across his lips.

Oh, he knew alright. "Do you know how I did it? How I can do it?"

"Yes."

"I cut you back at the house, I saw the blood. That says I can hurt you."

"Did you kill me? Do you see any cuts on me now?" Roman lifted his shirt, his toned body showing no signs of injury of any kind. "I cannot die."

"What are you?"

Roman's brow creased and his eyes hardened, their wonderful blue darkening to near black. The softer side to him had dissolved. Now he looked pure evil again.

The two of them stared at each other, Eliza's mind racing through her options. Could she conjure up this telekinetic power of hers now, and knock him out? Even just stun him long enough to untie her legs and make it to the door? "Why can't I use my telekinesis against you? How can I even do it?"

"You really have no idea, do you?"

"I don't understand anything that is happening. You want to know why I came back to the house to help you? Because I thought you had the answers. Was I wrong?"

Roman eyed her. "You know, you are a very rare breed. I've only ever met one of your kind before."

"What? A woman?"

Roman smiled. "Jeez, at least the last one knew when to keep her cocky mouth shut."

Eliza didn't quieten. "Kidnap her as well, did you?"

"Let's just say an unforeseen stint in prison put paid to my plans."

"My heart bleeds for you."

Roman stood and walked to the window behind her. Eliza wanted to turn in order to keep an eye on him, but the pathway to the door was now clear. Yes, she wanted answers, but she also wanted her freedom. She dropped the rope and reached for her feet. Her stomach cramped under the movement, but it didn't slow her in yanking the bind from around her ankles.

Behind her, she heard Roman turn, but she didn't look back. She jumped up from the chair and bolted towards the entrance.

CHAPTER TWENTY-FIVE

The air hit Roman's face, the crisp, clean freshness like a shot of adrenaline.

The morning sun crawled into the sky at a lazy pace, and for as far as he could see, dew-covered terrain glistened under its golden glow. He'd always thought a sunrise to be a magnificent view no matter where he may be when he saw it. However, this morning it was the fleeing figure of Eliza that demanded his attention.

The rain had long since stopped, yet burst riverbanks still gushed down upon the valley below and the already sodden and drenched fields did little to soak up the excess water. Every stride Eliza slid across the mud saw the ground swallow her shoeless feet.

It was an amusing sight to Roman, and broke up the monotony of being cooped up in the cabin for the last hour. Every step tested Eliza's balance, her slender body jerking and reacting to each uneven rock and prickly weed she encountered.

"Eliza, there's nowhere to run," Roman called. He really didn't want to follow her, but to think she would stop upon his command and return without a fight was hoping for the impossible. He stepped from the cabin door. "Are you really going to make me chase you?"

Eliza didn't look back, continuing to clamber across the moors in her pointless bid for freedom.

Hell. She was going to make him go after her. If she tripped and started bleeding again, he'd kill her himself.

He began to walk, his leisurely pace soon turning into a slow jog. The wet ground also squelched around his boots, but they were sturdy footwear made for the outdoors, and the grip, although still unsteady, far outdid Eliza's. She turned and saw him, her eyes widening, and sped up, her feet slip-sliding across the mud like she was skating on ice. She showed spirit, he'd give her that. He liked that.

"Come on, Eliza. You know you're not going to outrun me."

Eliza glanced over her shoulder. Her foot whacked a rock and she sprawled to the ground, landing face-first in the mud.

Roman slowed to a casual plod. He didn't want to laugh – he was angry, after all, but as Eliza glanced up at him, mud caked across the right side of her face, clumps of hair wrapping her face and neck, Roman smiled. "You did notice the cabin wasn't equipped with a bathroom, right?"

CHAPTER TWENTY-SIX

Mr. McKenzie hung up the phone.

He knew his wife had been listening to his conversation, and she confirmed this by quickly popping her head around the kitchen door.

"Who was that?" she said, donning the innocent voice he'd heard her use countless times when conning the milkman out of an extra bottle of milk.

"I need to pop over to Eliza's house."

"What for?"

Mr. McKenzie glanced up. He walked towards his wife and gently held her by the shoulders. He was not a religious man. Not anymore, anyway. He never prayed, not even when his daughter lay dying of leukemia, and he never attended church. So it seemed reasonable to assume he wouldn't believe that ancient myths or folklores had any element of truth to them.

But, Mr. McKenzie was a believer.

Not in just any old tale. For instance, he didn't believe in fairies and leprechauns, nor that a pot of gold lay buried at the end of a rainbow. He believed in something bigger. Power. Not the kind found by being a politician or the CEO of a global company. This power was invisible. Supernatural. And it came from only one place: Heaven.

Thirty years ago this power had taken his darling daughter, and the years that followed tormented him further by snatching work colleagues and friends in any manner it saw fit: burnings, drownings, cancer. Some went quick like his Aunt Mable. An aneurysm dropped her to the floor like a sack of spuds, and she hadn't known what hit her. But the others... Their anguished screams drilled into his head and took months, sometimes years, to simmer and fade from his memory.

Like every child born today, the tale of the Crucifixion had played a big part at school. Mr. McKenzie made lollypop-stick crosses in Sunday School, and learned about an amazing man who rose from the dead, actually convinced that resurrection happened to everyone. The first he realised there was no life after death was three years later, when his mother and father died in a car accident. Mr. McKenzie attended their funeral, not crying like every other grieving relative. After all, he wasn't sad. His parents would resurrect in three days. He planted his much-loved crosses into their newly covered graves, went home with his aunt and uncle, and waited for his parents to rise and come find him.

It never happened, and it was left to his aunt to explain to a frantic eight-year-old boy how death really worked. To Mr. McKenzie, Heaven caused painful deaths worse than Hell itself could ever conjure up, and now it was payback time.

After the deaths of his parents, Mr. McKenzie looked further into the story of the Crucifixion, convinced he had missed something or done something wrong. For years he read, spending much of his spare time in the religious section of the local library, and when that didn't answer his questions, he begged his aunt to take him into the city so he could scour their larger reference libraries. All roads led him back to the same thing. Jesus only survived because he was the son of God. This angered Mr. McKenzie. All this time, he'd thought of God as a good man. But it was painfully obvious he was selfish and more evil than Lucifer himself.

So Mr. McKenzie hatched a new plan, a simple plan: to break into Heaven and rescue his parents.

By this time, his aunt and uncle had enlisted the help of a top London clinic. Every Saturday, Mr. McKenzie was driven two hundred and fifty miles – far from the Cornish village gossips – so he could sit with psychiatrist Edward Pope for sixty minutes and 'talk.' Although reluctant at first, Mr. McKenzie explained his dilemma. In return, Mr. Pope nodded and scribbled notes into a crisp new notepad. He became the only person Mr. McKenzie trusted. And it meant Mr. McKenzie spent most of his weekends in the English capital.

Edward Pope was the perfect listener, and fascinated with Mr. McKenzie's determination to break into Heaven. For six years, he quietly listened while Mr. McKenzie prattled on about his plans to destroy God's sacred home and rescue his parents. It wasn't until his seventh year of attending these sessions that Mr. Pope introduced him to another man, well-dressed, in pleated slacks and a woollen cardigan rolled to the elbows. The doctor went on to describe how this man wanted the same as Mr. McKenzie, and that he knew how to get into Heaven and obtain the power needed to destroy it.

That was the day Mr. McKenzie met Davis.

Mr. McKenzie looked into his wife's eyes. "Remember I told you that one day I may need your help with something?"

"Is this it?" She could hardly mask her excitement. "Is this why we've been keeping an eye on the grandmother and Eliza all these years?"

Mr. McKenzie smiled at his wife. His aunt and uncle had frowned on him when he'd returned from London one year and introduced her as his new bride. He'd neglected to tell them he'd met her at his doctor's office, just as he neglected to disclose that her short-lived stay in the mental ward when she was a child was because she'd been discovered inflicting torture on the neighbour's pets. Further investigation uncovered she had in fact suffered terrible sexual abuse at the hands of her dominant father – a figure, it turned out, she couldn't live without and a role Mr. McKenzie now filled. "Yes, darling, this is why."

Mrs. McKenzie clapped her hands, a little squeal escaping her lips. "What do you want me to do?"

He opened a small door, which led under the stairs, and brought out a rolled sheet of blueprints. "I have to go up into Eliza's attic, and I need you to keep an eye out. Do you think you can do that?"

"Oh yes. Can we go now?"

"Yes. We can go now."

Mr. McKenzie crossed the small lane, closely followed by his wife, and strolled up to the front door as if the only thing he had on his mind was a good cuppa and a cosy chat with the young neighbour he'd watched grow since she was born.

He didn't bother ringing the doorbell. No need. He had a key.

Inside, the hallway looked as though a tornado had torn through it, and upon further examination, he saw the living room and kitchen mirrored it. Makeshift boards he'd nailed to the window after Billy had asked him to secure the house let in just enough early-morning light to see the aftermath. It looked grim. Smashed furniture piled against the far wall, broken glass swept in to the corner but not completely out of sight, and what looked to be blood staining the Egyptian rug his wife had loved so much he'd had to go out and get her one for herself.

He turned from the destruction. His wife remained by the door, peering out at the street through the spy hole. She was, if nothing else, dutiful. "Wait here and alert me if anyone comes."

Mrs. McKenzie nodded, enjoying her task far too much, but it pleased Mr. McKenzie to see her like this. Firstly, because her eagerness and loyalty lowered his chances of getting caught, and secondly – and probably more important than the first – Mrs. McKenzie was a joy to live with when she was happy.

He left her spying through the door and bound up the stairs two at a time to the first floor. Two of the three bedroom doors were closed, and a tapestry rug ran the length of the corridor to the far end, where net curtains draped a large window. Framed paintings and photographs hung mismatched along the wall, the missing two closest to him replaced by an outline of dust. Mr. McKenzie peered past the open door, it suddenly dawning on him that he hadn't checked with Davis as to whether Eliza was expected to return home again.

It's in the attic, was all the butler had said, and from that statement, Mr. McKenzie had just assumed the house would be empty.

The four-poster bed was made, and on the dresser was a clutter of makeup, face creams, and perfumes. Packing boxes, some flattened, the rest half empty, had been discarded along the far wall. Mr. McKenzie tiptoed to the second room. The floorboards creaked beneath his weight, and he winced. If Eliza did return home, what excuse could he use to explain his creeping around her house? *I thought I saw someone inside? I thought you may need help?* No, they were lame, and if he couldn't convince himself, how the hell was he supposed to convince her?

Ah, he had it. The truth. *Your brother asked me to secure the house.* Perfect.

He grabbed the door handle, this time with complete confidence, and twisted. Like the floorboards before, the door groaned as it opened, but he didn't care. He had an excuse to be here now. The drawn curtains made it harder to see than the last room. More half-empty boxes, an easel, blank canvases, and, hanging on a hook behind the door, a blue pinafore he recognised as being Eliza's grandmother's.

After checking the third room and seeing it was exactly the same as the first, an empty bed and no sign of Eliza, Mr. McKenzie headed towards the second stairwell. It was narrow, probably no wider than two feet, with a heavily painted cream door at the top. The attic. A cold breeze escaped under the door, and he blinked away the dryness. With a sweaty palm, he gripped the doorknob and twisted.

The door wouldn't open.

Mr. McKenzie turned the handle again and nudged his shoulder against it, gently at first, then with an impatient shove. The door flung open and Mr. McKenzie tumbled forward and into the path of a pale, ghostlike face. Even though pushing sixty, Mr. McKenzie's reflexes were that of any twenty-year-old. He punched the palm of his hand against the hardness of a chest, and the threat in front of him tumbled to the floor. He searched for the light switch, saw it against the doorframe, and quickly lit the room.

Undisturbed dust lay across the floorboards like a covering of snow. In the middle of it was the naked body of a female, her solid arms pointed towards the ceiling, her face holding the same plastic leer that had greeted him when he'd first come through the door.

Mr. McKenzie stared at the mannequin, then back towards the stairs. He straightened his shirt. Thank God his wife hadn't witnessed that, and stepped forward, the soles of his shoes leaving a trail of footprints in his wake. It was sloppy evidence to leave behind, but by the time anyone saw it and put two and two together, he'd be long gone.

He reached the far wall and unrolled the blueprints. The real blueprints. Not the manufactured one that failed to show the additional room he now wanted. He ran his hands across the mortar. Loose bricks, probably untouched for hundreds of years, wobbled between the crumbling cement. Slipping a screwdriver from his back pocket, he scraped between the bricks, disintegrating the mortar to nothing more than particles of grit that sprinkled around his feet. In less than a minute, a brick fell clear from the wall. Mr. McKenzie dug around the edge of another brick until it, too, prised free.

He continued this for some twenty minutes, pulling bricks loose. When he was lucky, others tumbled away with it and crashed to the floor, sending clouds of brick dust into the air. Several times, Mr. McKenzie patted down his clothes and wafted the air clean so he could pull another brick free. Finally, darkness stood where the area of brick had once been. He grabbed the pencil torch he always kept handy for emergencies, and shone it into the secret room on the other side. Cobwebs and dust as thick as a woollen blanket covered unknown shapes and objects.

He stepped inside, immediately spotting the rectangular item he wanted.

CHAPTER TWENTY-SEVEN

Eliza was surprised how easily Roman picked her up and threw her over his shoulder.

His arm wrapped her legs, securing them tight against his chest, and although she wouldn't normally foresee her weight of eight-and-a-half stone as a problem for any man, especially one as defined as Roman, she did expect the added weight of her mud-soaked clothes to make some, if only a little, difference.

Roman made it back to the cabin in record time, as though he'd made the same trek many times before. The notion he had, and that Eliza may not be the first woman he'd held captive here, exacerbated her panicked state.

Roman kicked open the cabin door, and promptly dropped Eliza to the floor. He grabbed her arms, and no matter how hard Eliza squirmed, he re-secured the rope around her wrists within seconds.

"Do I have to attach these ties to something more solid?" He glanced towards the rusted stove just beyond the table.

Having her hands tied was bad enough, but shackled to the oven? Eliza would never be able to escape from that. She shook her head and averted eye contact, bracing herself for the cold threats of what would happen if she attempted to run again.

They didn't come.

Instead, Roman grabbed her legs. Expecting her ankles to be re-tied, Eliza screamed and kicked out.

"I'm checking for abrasions," Roman shouted. He wiped away what he could of the mud and dirt from the soles of her feet. Once he seemed satisfied they weren't bleeding, he reached for her waist and lifted her shirt enough to see the stitched wound on her stomach was still intact. He left her alone after that, picking up the old rag he'd earlier wiped his boots with. He threw it down on the floor beside her. "Wipe your face."

The rag landed by Eliza's foot, the material hard like a dry chamois leather. It absolutely stank, and she declined to touch it. When his expression didn't alter, she said, "Why are you obsessed with me bleeding?"

"Do you want the Shadow to find you again?"

Eliza shook her head.

"Then don't bleed."

"I've bled loads of times. That Shadow thing has never come for me before."

"Well, the True Cross hadn't started being assembled before, had it?"

Coldness numbed Eliza's feet. She drew her knees to her chest and wrapped her tied arms around them, trying to distribute what little body heat she had left. "How long do I have to stay here?"

"I wouldn't be so eager to move onto the next phase of this situation if I were you."

"Why? Because my father's butler wants to sacrifice me? Do you know how ludicrous that sounds?"

"Why do you do that?"

"Do what?"

An old potato sack lay under the table. Roman shook it, dirt and debris momentarily polluting the air, and threw it around Eliza's shoulders. "Talk in such a way that could cause me to snap your neck like a twig?" He straddled the chair and stared down at her, his eyes wandering across her body until he finally looked her in the eye. "Let me make this clear. I don't owe you anything, got it?"

Fidgety hands drummed impatient fingers against the back of the chair. He removed his cap, swept his hair back from his face, then pulled the hat back on. His eyes looked everywhere but at her. "How well do you know your history?"

"I don't understand."

"Religious history. I take it you know something about it, even the basics?"

"Well, I didn't leave school with any qualifications on the subject, if that's what you're asking."

"There goes that smart mouth of yours again."

Eliza cringed beneath his glare. She closed her eyes and took a deep breath. "If you mean God and Jesus and all that stuff, then I know a little."

"Are you a believer?"

Eliza shrugged. "I go to church for funerals, weddings, and christenings, so you tell me."

Roman grinned. "Do you know the tale of the Crucifixion?"

"You mean the reason we have chocolate eggs and the Easter Bunny?"

The grin dropped from his lips. "Don't push me, Eliza." Roman tilted his head and although the sensual blue colour remained in his eyes, his face hardened.

Eliza let out a long sigh, a cover to mask the fear that swirled in the pit of her stomach. "Yes. I know a little about the Crucifixion."

Roman stood up and walked to the window. Over his shoulder, Eliza saw the red glow of the sun had reached the front of the cabin. The day looked to be a glorious one.

"I'm going to tell you a story," Roman said, keeping his back to her. "And you need to listen, because I am only going to tell it once."

Eliza wriggled her wrists. She didn't care about stories; she cared about getting the hell out of there. The rope rubbed against her already pink skin until it darkened to purple. She pressed her lips together, biting through the pain, telling herself it was nothing compared to the horror this man could and probably would inflict upon her.

"When the Messiah was nailed to the Cross, his spilt blood did something that nobody realised; it opened the Gateway to Heaven. The apostles took the magnificent ray of light, which shone down through the clouds and descended upon Jesus' dead body, as nothing but mere sunlight, but one guard recognised it for what it was: the Gateway to Heaven. And he wanted it.

"However, during the Messiah's Crucifixion, there were several, shall we say, supernatural events that also occurred. The guards, frightened of the unknown, were ordered to cut down Jesus' body and destroy the Cross, which they did by dividing it into four pieces and hiding them away so no living being could ever reassemble it. And for centuries its whereabouts remained unknown." Roman turned from the window. "But secrets always have a way of resurfacing."

For a brief moment, sadness and guilt clouded his eyes. "Many have claimed to find pieces of the True Cross. None of them were legit. The first real piece was located in 1389. It took five years of planning to acquire it. A hundred years later, it was stolen and didn't resurface until nearly two hundred and sixty years after that. Other pieces have also been found over the years...and stolen...and re-hidden...and found again...and lost again."

"Why are you telling me all this? I've nothing to do with this Cross."

"Ah, but you do. Davis wants the power that is to be gained from entering Heaven."

"And that's me? You're crazy."

"Am I? Explain the walking dead at the hospital. Explain the lunar eclipse. Explain the severe changes in weather. That shit is only happening here in Cornwall. Here, around you."

Eliza didn't want to think about any of the events. She twisted her hands again, unconcerned whether Roman saw her trying to free herself or not.

"The dead are rising from their graves, just as the saints rose from theirs during the Crucifixion. Davis has managed to acquire several pieces of the Cross, and as the sections are assembled, more events, such as earthquakes and storms, will mirror those that occurred during the Crucifixion."

"Davis is a Cornish butler, for Christ's sake."

"The Messiah's blood flows through your veins, Eliza."

"Oh please, everyone knows Jesus didn't have kids. Hell, I don't think he even had sex."

"Oh? And how would you know that?"

"'Cause...I just do. Everyone does. It's just one of those things that people know."

"Your blood is the key Davis needs to open the Gateway. It's the reason he got you in the first place."

Eliza stopped squirming. A mixture of emotions overwhelmed her. She wanted to laugh at Roman's ludicrous claims. She wanted to cry at the situation she found herself in. She wanted to scream for help and hope a passing hiker heard her. "First of all, I wasn't 'got,' as you put it. I was born to my mother and father. Second of all, Davis is a butler, not a powerful murderer who's hell bent on getting into Heaven to do... what exactly? And third, why would anyone go through all this aggravation to go somewhere when all they've got to do is kill themselves to get there anyway?"

"Evil doesn't go to Heaven."

"Davis is not evil. He pushed me on my swing when I was a child. He made me jam sandwiches and played hide and seek when my parents weren't home. For crying out loud, he read to me on stormy nights when I couldn't sleep."

"He was keeping you close. Your parents had a daughter, yes. But it wasn't you. Davis knew what you were because he knew what your real mother was. He planted you inside this family."

Eliza stood. "I've heard enough. My parents are mine. I am not adopted, or stolen, or swapped, or whatever the hell it is you're implying."

Roman rolled up his jacket sleeve. An inch-long cross inked the side of his hand. "I was marked with this a long time ago. It's how Davis found me. It's through me that he now has several pieces of the Cross."

"You're delusional. So you have a tattoo of a cross on your hand. Big deal. So do thousands of other people. You're just like one of those idiots who gets their teeth filed and then believes they're a vampire. You're nuts."

Roman shrugged.

"And why would you do anything Davis asked, anyway?"

Roman pushed down his sleeve. "I told you, we're partners. Have been for decades."

"Then why kidnap me if you're working together?"

"I told you that, too: Davis is a devious bastard."

"And you're not? If he is such a devious bastard, as you so eloquently put it, why give him the pieces of the Cross in the first place?"

"I knew the whereabouts of three pieces. The fourth piece – and your identity, of course – was down to Davis." Roman perched against the windowsill. "Not my finest hour, handing over the pieces, I admit."

"Pretty damn stupid if you ask me."

Roman took a deep breath and Eliza hoped he wasn't thinking of shoving the rag back into her mouth.

"So, what's in this for you? Entrance to Heaven?"

"Yes."

"Because?"

Roman stood and turned his gaze back to the window. "To be with my family."

Eliza let out an abrupt laugh. "Then just kill yourself and be done with it."

Roman turned to face her. Defiance flared in her eyes. "Maybe I should kill that cop boyfriend of yours instead?"

"That cop is my brother, and he has nothing to do with this."

"The cop at your house was your brother?" Roman paused. His stare held hers, and for a moment his eyes softened and he seemed relieved.

"Yeah, and he's gonna be looking for me."

Silence fell upon the cabin. Arguing the toss with Roman was getting her nowhere. The guy had serious mental health problems. Eliza had to get him to trust her, to find his weak spot and totally manipulate the crap out of it. That would be her only chance at getting out of this situation alive, she was sure of it.

"What is the Shadow?" Eliza said, biding her time while she thought up a solid plan of escape.

"That's the end of the Q and A." Roman reached for the water bottle.

"Does the Shadow have something to do with the Crucifixion, too?"

"I still have the rag..."

"How can you not die?"

Roman swigged from the bottle. "Last chance..."

"Why does the Shadow want me dead?"

Roman spun to face her, the rag clenched between his fingers. "It's a servant of God." He glared at her, his chest rising with every rapid breath.

"So God wants me dead now? That makes even less sense than a butler wanting to sacrifice me."

"Heaven cannot afford to let any kind of evil in."

"Including you?"

"Especially me."

"And these Shadows can only find me if I bleed?"

"Blood is a powerful thing."

"So, if I die anywhere other than on the Cross, then Davis cannot use my blood to open up Heaven's Gateway?"

"You got it."

"Why can't you just kill Davis?"

"I can't. I don't know where the Cross is being constructed."

"So?"

"So, I need the Cross."

"Oh, but it's alright for me to die?"

"Yes."

"But—"

"That's enough talking. I've told you what'll happen if Davis gets hold of you. It's kill or be killed."

"Why have I got to kill?"

"Because if you don't, he will kill you. You have the power, Eliza. When your blood touches that Cross, the gate to Heaven will open and I'll be gone. I don't intend to do Heaven any harm, but Davis? Davis plans to drop one hell of a shit-storm on this earth." Roman scrunched the rag into a ball. He walked over to Eliza, held her head steady, and pushed the soiled material into her mouth. "Believe me or don't, I no longer care. My conscience is clear. I've given you a heads-up about Davis. Only you will be able to stop him from entering Heaven."

Eliza pulled the rag back out but Roman forced it back in, holding his hand across her mouth. "Do you want your hands tied behind your back again?"

Eliza shook her head.

He removed his hand. "Are you going to behave?"

Eliza spat the rag from her mouth and glared at him.

Roman rubbed his chin, eyeing her for a second, then grabbed the rope from the table. Eliza seized her second chance and bolted for the door, but Roman's lightning reflexes were quicker, and he easily caught her. Eliza kicked and thrashed against his hold, but her struggle had little effect. Roman was strong. She was weak. Physically, she just couldn't beat him.

He carried her past the chair and dumped her in front of the stove where, immediately, she scrambled back onto her knees.

Roman stopped her. "I tried to be nice, to help you, but you've left me no choice." He grabbed her wrists and threaded one end of the rope between them. Within seconds he had her secured to the stove. He stuffed the rag back into her mouth, and a familiar tingling sensation returned to her fingertips, magnifying and burning its way across her palms and up her arms towards her shoulders. Random images started to flicker inside her head: the damp stone wall opposite, the chipped dinner plate lying in the corner of the room, smashed pieces of ceramic flying in her direction.

"I know what you're thinking, and I said you can't hurt me."

Eliza spat out the rag and glanced up towards him, the foul taste of grit stuck to the roof of her mouth. She swallowed to clear her throat. "No, but I can hurt myself."

Roman's grip tightened around the rag until the whites of his knuckles glowed. "What do you m—"

The ceramic plate lifted from the floor as if on invisible wires. It whacked against the brick wall and smashed into several pieces, the larger of which flew directly towards Eliza. Roman whipped his hand in front of Eliza's body, showing even more speed than before, and blocked the splintered ceramic from reaching her skin. But he wasn't ready for the second piece, or the third. A flash of white flicked across the room, nicking Roman's earlobe, and severing the rope that bound her to the oven. Another piece quickly followed, hurtling through the air and slicing Eliza's shoulder.

Roman stared at her, his face a picture of total bewilderment. "Why?"

"This time when the Shadow comes and you tell me to run, I will."

"What makes you think I'll stay around for the next time?"

"You said it yourself. I'm no use to you if I'm dead."

Roman glanced down at the broken piece of plate embedded in his palm and pulled it free, a spurge of blood oozing out with it. "You're a stupid girl." He wiped his hand down his trousers, the denim material quickly blotting red. When he next examined his hand, Eliza saw no trace of it ever having been cut.

"What in the hell are you?" She felt her own arm, smearing the wet blood around her recently injured skin. She'd never seen anything like this. "It's impossible for a human to heal that quickly."

Nothing made any sense. Shadows, zombies, Roman's resurrection. She'd almost talked herself into imagining how the last two days had gone down. Heck, maybe, at a push, she could be manipulated into believing Roman's death hadn't happened or it had in fact been a trick of the light. And maybe it wasn't a supernatural Shadow who'd attacked her at the train station or inside her house, but a mugger or intruder. Even at the hospital, she was prepared to accept that it was the hallucinate effect of the drugs given to her that made her see zombies. After all, the dead just did not come back to life, just as Jason Devlin's head couldn't have possibly twisted the full one hundred and eighty degrees she'd been convinced she'd seen. Thinking about it, she'd been so drugged, it wouldn't have surprised her if she'd witnessed Michael Jackson himself moonwalking down the corridor. But, there was no trick of the light in this cabin, no hallucinations from any drugs, no muggers or intruders. She was of a totally sane mind...and yet here she sat, witnessing Roman's hand heal faster than a person was capable of. "Are you even human?"

Roman turned from her. He walked to the chair and sat down, burying his head in his hands.

Eliza got up from the floor. To her surprise, Roman didn't try to sit her back down. "I have a right to know."

Roman remained quiet for several minutes, and Eliza began to doubt whether she really did want to hear an answer. She was a nurse for crying out loud, who enjoyed going to the theatre and eating out. She wasn't adventurous. She didn't dice with death by rock climbing or deep-sea diving with sharks. And as for the paranormal? It was laughable – nothing but a collection of myths and ghost stories. "Are you an alien?"

Roman scoffed, whether in distaste or in humour, Eliza couldn't tell.

"Does that mean you are?" She slowly inched back towards the door.

"Try and run if you want. You won't get far. You have no shoes on your feet, and you're miles from the nearest village."

"You have a car outside."

Roman raised his hand. A ring holding several keys dangled from his index finger.

Eliza glanced at her bare feet. "So I'll run. At least I'll be alive."

"You really haven't thought this through, have you?" Roman stood. "Let's forget for a moment that I won't let you leave. Where would you run to? If I'm not mistaken, your father's in Switzerland right now.

Or maybe you're thinking the cop could come save you?"

"Leave my brother out of this."

"Or there's the over-the-hill butler; the very man I said wants you dead?"

"When the Shadow comes looking for me, it will kill you."

"When the Shadow comes looking for you, it will attack you, not me."

Eliza hated to admit it, but Roman had a point. Back at her house, the Shadow had attacked her. It only turned on Roman after he intervened and tried to help. "I killed one Shadow. I can kill another."

Roman smiled and stepped towards her. He stopped just inches away, took her hands in his, and ran his fingers along the rope that bound her wrists. "And how successful do you think you'll be while you're tied up?"

The tips of his fingers brushed against the back of her hand, his warmth coming off him in waves. Roman's smile widened. He leaned in closer to her, his aftershave once again surrounding her as it had when he'd carried her from the morgue. Eliza froze, her eyes fixed on his while two thoughts battled in her mind: knee to his groin, or head-butt to his nose? Maybe she could do both.

Roman's hands slithered around her waist. The firmness of his chest pressed against hers, the fabric of his shirt still a little damp from the rain. Immediately, Eliza tried to move, but Roman held her tight. His hot breath moistened the inside of her ear, his gravelled tones shivering down her spine like sparks of electricity. "Do I scare you?"

He did scare her, yes, but that fear seemed to feed a morbid attraction towards him that she'd otherwise been oblivious to. He leaned back so she could see him, the tip of his nose almost touching hers, his eyes so near they were a blur to her without her glasses.

Was this her chance of escape? Seduction?

Eliza blinked. Often told her long eyelashes were her best feature, she knew that when she opened her dark-brown eyes, they would reappear with an extra shimmer. She lifted her chin very slightly so he wouldn't notice, but enough to reveal a little more of her slender neck.

Roman's breathing grew heavy, and a look of urgency filled his eyes. His lips parted slightly as though he wanted to tell her something. She felt his hand, at once gentle and yet somehow strong, masculine, cradle one side of her face.

He pulled her close, his lips lightly brushing hers. "I really do feel bad about the situation you're in."

Eliza remained still, wanting to push him away but faking her desire to feel his mouth against hers. She leaned into his hand and felt his fingers caress her cheek, her jawline, her neck, all the way down to her waist. His arms wrapped around her. The softness of his lips delicately met hers...

And then, she heard the distinct sound of the door being locked behind her.

Roman pulled back. He held the cabin key in his left hand. "And of course, for any successful escape, you need to be able to actually leave."

Speechless, Eliza stood rooted to the floor. This was not what she had expected, and anger quickly replaced her embarrassment. Her seduction ploy had failed. Worse, it had been used successfully *against* her. Roman had been one step ahead of her this whole time, and now Eliza was fresh out of ideas. She had no clue how to move things with her mind, and try as she might, both the old cigar box on the mantle and the empty beer bottles collecting dust on the table refused to acknowledge her telepathic wish to whack this man in the back of the head. The scent of his aftershave still engulfed her, and for a split second she allowed herself to recall the comfort of his warm body against hers. Why did these irritable feelings consume her? She held nothing but contempt and loathing for this fruitcake of a man.

"Tell me what in the hell you are."

Roman pushed up the brim of his cap and let what little light the cabin held brighten his eyes.

"Are you even human?"

Roman slid the key into his back trouser pocket, and returned to the chair. He removed his hat, ruffled some more life into his flattened mop, and said, "I was, once."

"Once? What does that even mean?"

Roman nodded towards Eliza's injured arm. His voice was even and emotionless. "I'd try and stop that bleeding if I were you – before it gets dark."

"Don't change the subject. What does 'once' mean?"

Roman glanced at her, a sudden sadness darkening his eyes. "I cannot die."

"But I saw you. I checked you. You were dead."

"Yes. And I do die. Have done many times. Stay dead for five minutes, sometimes hours, nearly two whole days once – although, to be fair, I'd knocked back a skinful and fell asleep in a cornfield. A combine harvester came along...well, it wasn't pretty."

Eliza starred in disbelief.

"I'm a Reaper." He watched her intensely, maybe waiting for his words to sink in, or maybe expecting some kind of shock to appear on her face.

Instead, Eliza said, "What in the hell's a Reaper?"

Roman cocked his head to one side, marred by a look of utter disbelief. "You don't know what a Grim Reaper is?"

"Of course I know what a Grim Reaper is. But you just said Reaper. You could have been a bloody farmer for all I knew."

Roman seemed stunned by her response.

"And, isn't a Grim Reaper's job to kill people?"

"No. We have the power to give life just as much as take it."

"So why not take Davis's?"

"Let me tell you a little about the rules of my universe. Firstly, I was told what souls to take, and what ones to save. If I strayed from that?" He pointed towards the air above him. "They'd know, and I'd have been up shit-creek without a paddle. Secondly, I am a Reaper, a servant of God. Protected. That means I already died once. I cannot die again; not by you, or that combine harvester...nothing. Thirdly—"

"Know what? I'm not even interested anymore. You talk a load of crap, and people will be out there looking for me by now."

"You mean the cop?"

"Yes. I mean my brother, Billy. He would have been to the hospital by now. He will know you've taken me, and he won't stop until he finds me and makes you pay."

Roman glared at her, wrinkles lining his slightly squinting eyes, tiny creases etching his pursed lips. "Clean up your arm."

This time, Eliza didn't hesitate to pick up the old rag. As hard as it was with her hands tied together, she began to dab at her wound.

"Wiping it isn't good enough. You need to seal it."

Eliza ignored him and continued to wipe, but the cloth was way too old to soak up any of the blood, and eventually she gave up and threw the rag to the floor.

Roman stood, pulled a lighter from his pocket, and lit one of the candles on the mantle.

"Oh no. You ain't burning that thing over me." Eliza backed away until she felt the hardness of the door against her again.

"It's just a little wax."

"I said no." She turned and pulled on the handle.

"It's this or die." Roman grabbed her hands and trapped them under his arm.

"I'd rather die." Eliza struggled, but Roman twisted to his side, leaving Eliza no option but to twist off balance with him.

He lifted the candle above her shoulder, and a blob of wax dripped onto the laceration, scalding her skin. Eliza cried out, struggling until her shoulder felt it would pop from its socket.

Another drop of wax splashed onto her skin, and tears sprang to her eyes. "Please stop," she begged.

"I'm doing this to save your life."

Did he know how ironic that sounded? Knowing he was going to deliver her up to Davis – supposedly to be sacrificed? She bit down on her lip while wax dripped onto her arm. The blurry image of Roman flying back across the room began to materialise inside her head. Wax hardened over her wound, and Eliza's pitiful sobs died in the back of her throat. Then, to her relief, Roman set the candle down on the table, and the picture reel inside her mind faded.

"This will be over soon."

"How did you become such a deranged psychopath?"

Roman stepped back from her. He looked hurt by her accusation. "I am not a psychopath, Eliza. I just want to get back to my family."

"Just let me go, then." Eliza went to rub her arm, but stopped. If the wax flaked away, would he put her through all that again?

He pulled Eliza's shirt over her head and tore it free from her wrists, leaving her to try and cover her bra-clad body. "I can't."

"How did you get to be like this?"

He paused, his eyes lingering on her bareness for a moment. "I was chosen."

"By who?"

"God." He looked up, the blue in his eyes brighter than ever before. "I didn't want the job."

"Then why take it?"

"I didn't get the chance to turn it down."

"When did you die?"

Roman poured what little water was left over the fabric, and began wiping the blood clean from her arm. "A while ago."

"How did you die?"

He paused, but didn't release his gentle hold on her. "Plague." He didn't look up.

Eliza wanted to laugh. He talked utter nonsense and she detested him for what he was putting her through. Yet, suddenly, she didn't feel like making fun of him or arguing with him. He needed a doctor or a shrink along with a comfy bed in the nearest nut home.

Maybe compassion and a little reasoning would get her out of this mess? "You're wearing well for your age."

He raised his head and she held his gaze. "So, let me see if I have this right. You need to find the Cross, deliver me to Davis, and sacrifice me. Only then will you be able to return to Heaven to be with your family, while I'm left to kill the butler I have known all my life, right?"

Roman's face hardened, and Eliza wondered if her question had sounded too patronising.

He threw the rag on to the table. Their short-lived truce was over.

"I do have one question that may throw a spanner in the works. How can I kill Davis if I've already been sacrificed and am dead?"

"I don't intend on letting Davis kill you."

"Then I'm confused. You just said I had to kill him."

"I told you worst-case scenario. Bottom line, all Davis needs is your blood on the Cross. A pinprick amount will do."

"A pinprick? So I'm not going to die?"

"You will if Davis gets hold of you."

"Then, here." Eliza held out her arm. "Take your pinprick and let me go."

"That mouth of yours is driving me up the wall."

She re-offered her arm. "Then take it."

"Oh, Eliza, I wish it were that simple. For my own sanity, I want rid of you."

"Then what's the problem?"

"It needs to be fresh, like minutes fresh. I need to get it immediately before I meet Davis at the Cross. I'm afraid we're stuck with each other until then."

"So, even after all this, you're still going to take me to Davis?"

"Not directly to him. But you will be nearby. Once I take your blood, you're free to go. He won't get you."

Exhaustion began to take hold. She felt like they were going round in circles. "Why can't he just take the pinprick?"

"Because he's a—"

"Devious bastard, I know, I know."

"He killed your so-called mother."

Eliza tensed. How dare he bring her mother into this? She felt anger burn in the pit of her stomach. "My mother's death was an accident. She fell down the stairs."

"Engineered by Davis."

"You're lying. I found her."

"She began to suspect you were not hers. That made her dangerous to have around. You were a pawn in Davis' plan. Who wouldn't believe the innocent devastation of a six-year-old witness?" Roman grabbed the cloth again and set back to wiping the blood from Eliza's arm.

Eliza shrugged from his hold. "How could you possibly know what happened?"

"Because I was there."

"That's impossible. You would've only been a boy yourself."

Roman stopped wiping. "I told you, I'm a little older than I look."

"Ah, yes. The plague, right?"

"I've been nothing but honest with you, Eliza."

"Did you kill her?"

"I am not a murderer."

"But you stood by and watched it happen?"

Roman started to wipe her arm again.

"You let my mother die?" Eliza shook her head. Billy had been right. Their mother had been murdered, only not by their father. "Why didn't you go to the police?"

"That was not an option." He glanced up. "I am not the bad guy here."

"You're just an insane one. You're toying with my mind and trying to turn me against my family. What's it called? Stockholm Syndrome? Some crap like that? Is that what you're trying to do? Because it's not going to work."

Roman threw the shirt to the floor. "Stockholm Syndrome? Seriously? After everything I've told you, that's the conclusion you're settling with?"

"Yes."

Roman laughed. He retrieved his flimsy jacket from the back of the chair. It was still damp from the previous evening's rain, but he wrapped it around

Eliza's shoulders regardless. He twisted Eliza in the direction of the door, and unlocked it.

"Where are we going?" Eliza said. Going outside now felt like a bad idea.

"Away from here. This cabin reeks of your blood."

"I'm not going anywhere with you."

"Eliza, you are. Now, whether you spend the journey sitting in the passenger seat or crammed in the boot, is entirely up to you."

CHAPTER TWENTY-EIGHT

Davis clapped his hands together.

Today was going to be a good day. Mr. McKenzie's van pulled off Moneyready Road, and Davis waited while the iron gates at the bottom of the driveway closed behind him. Giant oaks, still holding their greenness, shaded the winding brick-paved driveway, and cold-hardy mums and pansies like the ones Eliza used to pick for her mother bloomed in the flowerbeds. These flowerbeds lined the drive all the way to James Hamilton's house, a French-designed building with a slightly pink, stone exterior. It was the perfect backdrop for the front courtyard, where sculpted hedgerows ringed a fountain, and a continuous burst of water erupted high into the air. Four ·garages stood to the side, each housing an expensive vehicle, including the one his employer had purchased anonymously at auction last year. It had cost him just under four million pounds, and to this day he'd never driven it.

Rounding the final bend, Mr. McKenzie slowed to a stop a couple of metres from the first garage. The engine died and Davis waited for his visitor to emerge.

"Did you get it?" Davis said, accompanying Mr. McKenzie around to the back of the van.

Mr. McKenzie smiled and opened the doors. Inside, partially wrapped with a white sheet, was the third piece of the True Cross.

Davis stood back, and the beginning of a victorious smile twitched the corners of his mouth. For decades, he had searched for all four pieces of the Cross, and not only had he at last accomplished the task, which at times he'd thought impossible, but he'd also managed to locate the Messiah's bloodline. He took a moment to savour his achievement.

"Davis," Mr. McKenzie said. "The police are here."

Davis turned to see the iron gates swinging open as a clearly marked police car pulled onto the driveway. "It's Billy. Take your van round to the servant quarters and unload there. Then wait for me." Davis cracked his neck and tried to fight the tiredness that burned behind his eyes. He needed sleep, especially before tonight arrived and James Hamilton returned home. But instead, he straightened down his suit jacket, forced one of his warmest smiles, and waited for the police car to reach him.

Of all the careers the boy could have chosen, why did it have to be the police?

CHAPTER TWENTY-NINE

Billy hadn't worked out what he was going to say.

Even with the extra fifty minutes, courtesy of the rush-hour traffic, he still hadn't decided how to break the news of Eliza's disappearance. Nor was he sure how to possibly throw in a question about his father's involvement with the man who'd taken her. George had told him not to mention it. Actually, George had ordered him not to accuse his father of anything – that the consequences of being wrong were too great. Billy, on the other hand, didn't care. His father was up to his neck in whatever was going on, and all Billy needed to see was a flicker of recognition on the old man's face to betray his involvement.

Billy rounded the driveway to find Davis waiting for him. He pulled to a stop, grabbed his hat from the passenger seat, and got out of the car. The majority of tourists down by the cove had vanished with the summer sun months ago, and apart from the last-minute few who'd returned in the last couple of days to enjoy the freakishly warm weather, it was overall a quieter place again. Seagulls circled high above the Cornish coastline, which was adjacent to the family's estate, looking to scavenge the odd chip or discarded ice cream cone before the bin men arrived and swept the streets.

Billy pulled on his cap and straightened his tie, not wanting to give his father the opportunity to ball him out over his grubby uniform for a second time, and proceeded towards the butler. "Is my father home?'

Davis looked startled to see Billy standing before him. Not surprising, since Billy hadn't been there in years. "My boy. How nice to see you again. You look well."

"Thank you, Davis. Is my father home?"

"He is in Switzerland on business. He won't be back until later tonight."

"Switzerland? When did he go?"

"Yesterday. Is there a problem?"

"I need to speak to him about Eliza."

Davis stiffened. He glanced over his shoulder – at what, Billy couldn't see. "Is everything alright?"

Even though it wasn't the warmest of mornings, perspiration dampened Billy's underarms. "There's been an incident at the hospital," he said, unsure where to take the conversation from here. "I really need to speak to my father."

"I can try and contact him."

"Yes, please."

"It may take some time. Can I pass on a message perhaps?"

Billy stalled to answer. His father hadn't even been in the country when his crash victim visited.

Davis took his hand, his eyes pleading. "I've known Eliza all my life. I love her like she's my own daughter. Please, Billy, if something is wrong, tell me."

It was against every rule in the book, but Billy said, "She's missing."

"Missing? Missing where?"

If I knew that, I wouldn't be here. "It appears she left with a man."

"A man? What kind of man?"

"Well, we know it wasn't a doctor."

Davis seemed panicked, and Billy prayed the revelation wouldn't kill him. "Did she leave willingly?"

"Our witness confirms that she did not."

"How long ago was this?"

"Just before midnight."

"And you're only just bringing notification? Fourteen hours later?"

"Emergency services had to confirm patient numbers. I came as soon as I knew."

"I see." Davis turned his back and walked to the first garage where, through the open door, Billy saw the unmistakable badge of his father's 1912 Silver Ghost. It was the same car in which, numerous times as a boy, he had found his young sister hiding from their angry father.

Davis walked the width of its bonnet, his fingers trailing across the gleaming paintwork, his previous hysteria now calmed. "What else did your witness say?"

Billy held off answering. Something about Davis' actions didn't sit right with him. Why wasn't the old man running for the phone to notify his father? Billy decided to play along. "He gave us a description of the man."

"Oh? And?"

"Cap, Timberlands, dark jacket."

No emotion. No concern. No running for that damn phone. Billy found himself standing on a cliff's edge, the voice of reason telling him to step back and not ask any questions as his sergeant had ordered. *Don't accuse Dad. Only notify him of Eliza's disappearance.* But Billy wasn't accusing his father. His father wasn't here. Davis was here. And Billy's sergeant hadn't said anything about questioning Davis. "The man was spotted several hours ago."

"Was he apprehended?"

"No." *Here goes nothing.* "He entered a property in Orchard Lane but was gone by the time officers arrived. We're running checks on his car now."

Davis looked Billy straight in the eye, his calm expression clearly forced. "I'll inform your father as soon as I can. I assume you will keep me updated on the situation?"

"Absolutely." Billy turned back to his car. He'd been wrong all along. His father wasn't the guy he was after... It was his butler.

CHAPTER THIRTY

Goddamn it. Billy knew.

"McKenzie!" Davis stormed the three stone steps that led to the impressive arched mahogany front door. Fury bubbled inside him. He needed to punch something, his first option being to whack the door open with enough force that it would release the frustration that burned like acid inside him.

However, the weighty door only moved at one speed. Slow.

"McKenzie!" Davis entered the hall.

His second option, two original suits of armour, was much lighter. The one on the right held a two-handed sword, and Davis charged it. The stand toppled, and pieces of armour broke free and crashed across the marble floor. Davis waited for the echoing calamity to cease, sucking in breath after deep breath in a bid to calm himself.

McKenzie appeared from the library. "I heard a commotion. Is everything alright?"

He glanced at the armour, then back at Davis. "You need another minute?"

"No, I don't need another minute." Davis reached for the bannister and propped himself against it.

"Has Billy gone?"

"Yes," Davis said, his temper lessening slightly. "But he's close to linking Holbrook to me."

"He said that?"

"No. But it was written all over his face. Make sure he doesn't get the chance."

"You want me to make this a permanent situation?"

"I don't care. Just get him out of the way."

"And what about Holbrook?"

Davis knelt and began to gather up the suit of armour. "He's with Eliza."

"I thought he was going to Paris?"

"So did I." Davis stood with effort, the armour heavier than he'd anticipated. "Second thoughts, forget the cop. Go find Holbrook, and bring the girl here yourself."

McKenzie nodded. "And where will you be?"

"Checking on the Cross."

CHAPTER THIRTY-ONE

Roman didn't drive all the way to James' house.

Instead, he opted for a quiet wooded clearing half a mile out, and cut the car engine. He sat for a while and let his mind drift, wondering if when the time came and things went tits-up, he'd actually go through and hand Eliza over to Davis knowing what was in store for her. Of course, he didn't really see that he had another option. He needed into Heaven. He needed to see Jane and his son, and if giving up Eliza got him that, then it was a small price to pay. He'd walked away from Jane once before and he'd paid dearly for it ever since. Could he do it again to Eliza?

He got out of the car and stretched the ache from his legs. Sunlight filtered in through the trees, the rays struggling to reach the forest floor. He shook a cigarette from its packet, lit it, and leaned against the roof of his car. The heat of the metal burned hot through his shirt, but it didn't bother him. If truth be known, he actually liked the sensation. He dragged on the cigarette and watched the smoke dirty the air. Being holed up in the cabin with Eliza had caused a knot between his shoulders, and a migraine above his right brow. The girl was impossible. That she actually cut herself, risking the Shadow finding her simply as a means to escape, beggared belief. But she had balls, he'd give her that. Unfortunately, her stupidity outshone them.

Roman rubbed his chin, the new growth itching like mad, the bristles like tiny pins upon his skin. If only he could somehow slow the speed his stubble grew, it'd be one less daily hassle. He dragged on the cigarette until the majority of tobacco had burned away and only the stub of a butt remained, and walked around to the back of the car. The Aston didn't have a roomy boot, almost non-existent. If he had to be totally honest, he wondered whether cramming Eliza inside had been a good idea after all. The latch clicking shut had certainly astonished him. He ground the cigarette into the dirt and popped open the boot.

Immediately, Eliza squealed like a nervous pig, the rag that stuffed her mouth surprisingly still in place.

"I'll remove the gag, but I don't want you to shout, got it?"

Eliza obviously didn't get it because she squealed louder, her body thrashing around as though she had itching powder in her knickers.

Roman slammed the boot shut.

He heard Eliza bash against the inside of it. As he'd already called it: she was a nutcase. A minute passed, but Eliza's ranting from inside the car continued. *Doesn't she ever quit?*

Roman opened the boot again. "How the hell are you finding the room in there to move around so much?'

Eliza stopped squealing and stared up at him, her eyes glazed, her chest heaving with every breath she panted.

"Ready to try again?"

Roman waited for Eliza's compliant nod, then slowly slipped the gag from her mouth. No sooner had the cloth left her lips than she screamed for help at the top of her voice. Roman thrust the cloth back towards her mouth, but Eliza whipped her head from side to side, making it impossible for him to hit his target.

"Hold still." Roman grabbed her head and held it tight, forcing both his fingers and the cloth into her mouth.

Eliza bit down, and Roman saw his blood redden her lips. He tried to yank his fingers clear, but Eliza bit harder, holding on like a dog refusing to release a bone.

"You crazy woman. Let go." Roman pulled his fingers free and examined the damage, but the laceration was already healing.

Quick as a flash, Eliza swivelled onto her hip and kicked him backwards. She was out of the boot and jumping her escape through the forest within seconds.

Roman licked the blood from his finger and watched the last of the skin reseal. The woman was absolutely insane – and my God did he find that a turn-on.

"Jesus Christ, you're like a fucking squirrel. Where are you going now?"

Eliza continued to jump, her legs tied at the ankles, her bare feet almost stepping on each other. Just how far did she really think she would get? A couple of metres? Maybe nine or ten if she was really lucky? Roman let her jump what he reckoned was about twelve metres before he grabbed her around the waist. Immediately, Eliza kicked and screamed, leaving Roman with no other choice. He reached into his pocket for the white handkerchief and bottle of chloroform.

CHAPTER THIRTY-TWO

Davis wasn't as young as he used to be.

Along with his aging body came his intolerance for the cold, damp passageways his employer's house had hidden away. He entered the library, taking a moment to enjoy the warmth the room held, then tilted the hardback copy of *Henry V* back upright on the shelf.

The bookcase slowly swung shut and secured with a barely audible *click*. Now he felt calmer, and when he was calm, he thought more clearly. He reached for the brandy glass, but stopped when he saw Roman slouched in the armchair beside the fire; the same chair the deceased Edward Pope had occupied only hours earlier.

"How the hell did you get in here?"

"I walked through the front door. How else?"

Behind Roman, papers and various Cross-related documents covered the mahogany desk. Just how much had Roman seen? Davis forced a smile, and the calm he'd found quickly evaporated. "You should have been back here hours ago. Where have you been?"

Roman smiled. "Paris, like you asked."

Many thoughts swirled inside Davis' head, not least that Roman had seen how to open the secret bookcase. "Did you get the wood?"

"Yes."

"And? Where is it?"

Roman checked his coat pockets. "I had it when I left the house..."

"Don't mess with me, Roman."

Roman straightened down his jacket and settled back into the chair. "You'll get it tonight. When I know where the other pieces are."

"That wasn't the deal."

"Neither was you holding out on the girl."

An ache inside Davis' head started to pulse and he rubbed his temples, forgetting for a moment that Roman watched him. "Mr. Holbrook, where is Eliza?"

"Tucked away, safe and sound."

"And your reason for taking her is...?"

"Just covering all my bases."

Davis reached for another glass and poured Roman a whiskey. "The deal was that you would deliver the wood from Paris. The blood was my responsibility."

"Hmm, well I felt that deal was a little one-sided." Roman uncrossed his legs and leaned forward. "See, the thing is, I know what you're planning to do."

"Oh?"

"And killing her when you don't have to doesn't sit well with me."

Davis handed over the drink. "Mr. Holbrook, I am at a loss as to what you mean. The girl will not be harmed in any way."

Roman stared at him. "And how can I trust you'll keep your word?"

"My word is my bond, Mr. Holbrook." Davis walked to the fireplace. He grabbed the poker and prodded the coals. "That, and if you don't tell me where she is, I will kill you and find her myself."

Davis placed the poker back in its holder and turned towards Roman. He leaned over him and smiled. "I could break your bones in the blink of an eye. Where would that leave you then?"

"And I will re-heal. You cannot kill me."

"Oh, I know. Just like I know that the bigger the injury, the longer you take to heal. I can put you out of action for a while, Mr. Holbrook... Maybe just long enough to find Eliza and the wood myself?"

Roman remained quiet.

"I thought so." Davis stood upright. "Now, about our trust issues."

Roman sighed. "There's a cabin up on Bodmin Moor. The wood is there."

"And Eliza?"

"I'll bring her with me tonight."

"Then, Mr. Holbrook, you have a deal."

Roman swirled the whiskey around the glass, and it took all of Davis' willpower to keep from snatching it and forcing the drink down the man's throat. He walked back to the fireplace, once again picking up the poker.

"I'll tell you what." Davis unfastened a button on his shirt. He loved the open fire, but sometimes this room felt warmer than a funeral home furnace. "Drink your drink, go get Eliza, and tonight we will both be sleeping in Heaven."

"You almost sound sincere."

"I am."

Roman smiled. "You'd better be." He knocked back the drink in one gulp and placed the empty glass on the desk.

"One other thing." Roman got up from the chair. "I know why I want in to Heaven. Why do you?"

"Because I don't want to go to Hell, Mr. Holbrook." Davis stabbed the coals harder. Watching Holbrook swallow the poison was one of those rare and twisted moments in which he found pure happiness, and he didn't attempt to hide the pleasure. He had the wood's location, and he knew of Eliza's whereabouts. Roman had outlived his usefulness. "I'll call you later with tonight's location."

Roman smiled a cocky smile and turned for the door. Without uttering another word, he left.

Davis stabbed the poker into the coals, absorbing the heat the enraged flames tossed out. Holbrook annoyed the crap out of him, but in twenty minutes it would all be over, and the man would be out of his hair long enough not to be a nuisance anymore. He called out for Mr. McKenzie, who arrived within seconds. "Follow Holbrook. The girl is with him. Then get over to Bodmin Moor. The wood's there."

Collecting the whiskey glass, Davis left the room.

CHAPTER THIRTY-THREE

Roman opened the car boot.

Sunlight filtered down through the trees and lit Eliza's sleeping face. Whether a trick of the light or just a yearning desire, Roman found himself utterly besotted by her beauty. Her lips looked so subtle and soft, and he remembered what they'd felt like when he'd kissed her. Now he wanted to kiss her again, to press his mouth against hers properly, to feel her arms wrap his neck and let the strawberry scent of her hair engulf him. It had been an age since those desires had come to him, desires he'd worked so hard to bury. Damn Eliza Hamilton for screwing with his emotions.

Roman removed his hat and swept his hair back from his face. Only one woman had ever messed with his head as much as Eliza messed with him now: his Jane. A woman who'd stood in the house of God and rightly declared her love for his brother; a woman he couldn't live without and set out to seduce, only to then abandon while she carried his illegitimate child. But

Eliza and Jane were nothing alike. They looked different. They acted different. Jane had been compliant and gentle, whereas Eliza was a pain in his arse. Roman had wanted Jane more than anything in the world, whereas he couldn't wait to get shot of Eliza. Still, could he really live with handing her over to be sacrificed? The voice in his right ear cheered a 'hell yes,' because it wanted to see Jane more than anything. But his heart and his conscience knew different.

Eliza's image softened and blurred and he rubbed his eyes, the sting of sweat causing them to glaze over. He patted his shirtsleeve across his forehead and felt his face, his clammy skin hotter than the fires of Hell itself. What in God's name was wrong with him? Second by second, his body temperature rose. Ripples shuddered through his arms, leaving his hands and fingers almost immobilised. His knees weakened, his legs hardly able to hold him up. The forest around him swirled, with shades of green and autumn brown encasing him inside a murky blur of colour.

Roman closed the boot and struggled around to the front of the car. He fumbled with the door handle, pulling it open and flopping into the driver's seat. Breathing became a struggle, and he knew Davis must be at the root of this. He pulled his car keys from his trouser pocket, seeing only distorted shapes of silver. He was sure he hadn't been followed, but he had to get away from this place in case he was wrong. He had to find somewhere safer to hide.

He rubbed his eyes again. The first key scratched across the ignition, as did the second and the third. The key ring dropped to the floor. He cursed, reached for it, and started the process again. The first key didn't fit but the second did, sliding into the hole and sparking the engine to life when he turned it.

Roman wound down the window and ripped open the top two buttons on his shirt. Although the temperature was cooler beneath the trees, it couldn't chill the burning sensation creeping across his skin. He tore the rest of the shirt from his body, dropping it on the seat beside him. His semi-nakedness did little to cool him. He stepped on the accelerator, letting the air blow across his face. The car sped forward, bumping over the forest floor until Roman reached the clearing and pulled out onto the smooth tarmac of the A3082.

The road was quiet, the rush-hour traffic having already been and gone. Roman shook his head clear, and pressed his foot down harder on the accelerator. Ahead, just over the hill, he saw a vehicle heading towards him. It looked big, maybe a lorry, but with his vision impaired he couldn't be sure. It travelled downhill and disappeared behind the incline, and once again he was on his own.

Fields and trees whizzed past as he raced up the hill. Where he was going, he had no idea. He just had to get as far away from Davis as he possibly could. He had to protect Eliza. His eyelids grew heavy, and his head slumped towards the steering wheel. A car horn screamed and Roman bolted upright, oncoming headlights flashing before him. He twisted the steering wheel and veered the car back to the left-hand side of the road. Tyres squealed, unable to grip the road, and Roman slammed his foot on the brake. The car swerved, the steering pulled left, and the back end of the Aston Martin spun a complete circle before skidding to a halt in the middle of a T-junction. The engine stalled. Roman didn't try to restart it.

Jesus. He checked the rear-view mirror.

The lorry continued down the hill behind him, its two out-of-focus brake lights eventually fading. Roman rested his head against the steering wheel. Deep breaths wheezed from his throat. Pain pierced his chest, and he clutched beneath his breastbone. Another vehicle hooted, and Roman heard a string of obscenities about his car blocking the road.

Roman lifted his head and raised his middle finger.

Then he inhaled and held his breath.

A slow and controlled wheeze left his lips. He turned the ignition key. The engine moaned. Rage simmered in the pit of his stomach. It wouldn't take much coaxing for it to boil over. He turned the key again. Another noise groaned from beneath the hood.

"Bollocks." He smacked the steering wheel, and turned the key again. Life revved into the engine, and he sped off.

Another shot of pain tore across his shoulders and pierced into his chest, spasms paralysing his whole body. His fists clenched around the wheel and the car veered towards the roadside, scraping the side of a giant oak and crashing through the makeshift barbed wire fence used to keep cattle in. The vehicle nose-dived into a ditch and the engine shut off. When the back wheels finally stopped rotating, only the sound of the shallow stream that trickled beneath his car could be heard.

Roman reached for the key, but another spasm ripped into his heart. He had no choice but to clutch his chest and ready himself for the inevitable.

Death.

CHAPTER THIRTY-FOUR

Eliza couldn't hear anything.

A sliver of daylight pierced a tiny hole in the corner of the back brake light and she wriggled closer, craning her neck just enough so she could look out. A canvass of cloudless blue painted the sky, and only when she raised her head could she see trees on either side. Without a landmark, the view resembled seventy percent of Cornwall, and she was none the wiser as to where Roman had driven her.

She rolled onto her back and thumped the balls of her feet on the underside of the boot.

She kicked again and her hands, although still tied, pounded along with them. Nothing could be heard above the succession of hammering, and between the lack of air and the rapid rise in warmth, exhaustion crippled her in less than a minute.

She waited, expecting Roman to open the boot, but he didn't. She tilted her head and glanced through the hole again. A light breeze whistled through, drying her eyes and causing her to blink several times while she tried to figure out where the hell she was. An engine purred in the distance, and Eliza quietened. The purring grew louder, growing into a hoarse growl, and a white van hurtled past. Eliza kicked and banged the boot again, screaming to be heard even though she knew the van would be long gone and out of earshot. She quietened again, listening for further traffic. It was pointless. A passing car would never hear her, and considering the speed at which the van raced past, they probably wouldn't see her either.

Eliza rolled onto her back and pushed the boot with every ounce of strength she could muster, until her arms collapsed back onto her chest. She lay there and let the ache dissolve. The boot certainly wasn't going to open through sheer strength or determination, that was for damned sure. She needed to find another means of escape. Maybe punching out the backlight, or finding a release latch on the inside of the boot. Wasn't that what people did on the silly television dramas she watched? But there was no latch, at least none she could find, and the backlight proved even more stubborn than the boot to move.

"Hey!" She shuffled back onto her side and peered through the hole again. "Is anybody out there?"

No answer.

"Shit." She turned her attention to the back seat, her strength all but gone. Legs drawn back, she drew a deep breath and kicked out. Her heart nearly skipped a beat when she felt the seat shift upon impact.

Eliza craned her neck to gain a better view, pressing the soles of her feet against the cold metal again. This time, instead of kicking, she just pushed. The top corner of the seat bent away from her, and a stream of daylight shone into the boot like a torch beam. She pressed harder, her legs shaking under the pressure. The gap between the seat widened, and further daylight brightened the inside of the boot. This was it. This was her way out.

How long she kicked and pushed she didn't know, just like she had no idea how much time remained before Roman might catch her.

The seat buckled under the force of her desperation, and finally it collapsed away from her. She shuffled over, pulling herself out of the boot and onto the back seat. Roman wasn't anywhere to be seen, and she wasn't going to wait around for him to show up. The first thing on her agenda was to get out of the car and up to the road. It didn't matter that she was tied. She just needed to flag down a passerby.

It wasn't until she dragged her legs clear of the boot and sat up that she spotted Roman, half-naked, slumped over the steering wheel, his face turned away and partly covered by his arm. What on earth had happened to him? Had he crashed and knocked himself out? Was he dead? Her first instinct was to reach over and check on him. To care for him. He looked vulnerable. His eyes were closed and any hostility he'd shown towards her over the last twenty-four hours was long gone. But common sense told her different.

Common sense told her to ignore him and get the hell out of there.

She reached for the door handle. *Shit*. The Aston didn't have a back door. Eliza peered over the driver's seat. Roman's body remained still, but that didn't mean he was dead. After all, according to him, he couldn't die. She honed in on the side of his neck and searched for a rhythmic pulse.

She couldn't see any.

Maybe Roman was dead, or maybe he wasn't. Eliza couldn't tell the difference between black and white anymore. She did know one thing, though. If Roman wasn't dead and he woke up before she got out of the car, she'd lose her chance to escape.

As quietly as she could, she climbed over the passenger seat and pulled on the door handle. It opened, allowing the autumn breeze to rush in. Without a second to waste, she clawed her way up the verge towards the road.

Not one car in sight. Only Roman's zigzag tyre marks blackened the tarmac. Eliza turned back towards Roman's car and saw for the first time the mangle of barbed wire and broken fence that tangled around the side of the vehicle. Whatever had caused the crash, she didn't care, she just wanted away from it. Unfortunately, her options for escape were limited. She either waited in the hope that a vehicle would pass by or, in her current bound state, she jumped her way to the nearest police station. Neither alternative appealed to her.

She studied the landscape around her, looking for a flicker of familiarity to help decipher where she was. In the far distance, and assuming she was still in Cornwall, the Atlantic Ocean met the horizon. Between the water and her current position, there were miles of fields and, in the middle of them, five wind turbines. Suddenly, Eliza knew exactly where she was: just a couple of miles from her father's estate.

She squatted and fell back onto her arse. Although her hands remained tied, her fingers easily worked loose the knotted rope around her ankles, and within minutes she was free and on her feet again. The rope around her wrists was harder to untie; in fact, it was impossible. Maybe something inside Roman's car would aid her to cut through it, but she wasn't going back in there. Tied hands would not stop her from running to her father's house.

Snippets of earlier conversation came to mind. Roman had not spoken well of Davis, nor of his intentions towards her. Of course, Eliza believed none of it, betting that as far as the residents of Cornwall went, sacrifices probably didn't rate high on their list of priorities. If Davis really did plan on sacrificing her, surely she would have sensed it. Nevertheless, as she ran along the roadside towards Fowey, she found herself wanting Billy and the safety of the police station rather than the pretty pink rendering of her childhood home.

Behind her, the warm breeze carried the hum of a car engine. She slowed her pace, her first instinct to dive behind a tree in case Roman had woken and somehow managed to get his car back on the road. Instead, she shielded her eyes from the sun and waited for the blur of the oncoming vehicle to sharpen.

It was a red post van. Eliza ran into the middle of the road and waved her bound hands until the van slowed and pulled alongside her.

A middle-aged man got out, shirtsleeves rolled to his elbows, his navy blue shorts not looking entirely Royal Mail uniform. "Are you okay?"

"I need you to take me to Looe police station."

"What happened to you?"

Eliza glanced down at her bare feet, dirt covered and desperately in need of a wash. "I need to get to the police station."

The man wavered, his sudden look of apprehension dissolving into a more concerned expression.

"Please," Eliza said. She stepped towards him and held out her hands. "I need to get this rope off and get to the police station."

"I have a phone—"

"That's great, call Looe police and ask for Officer Hamilton, but please don't leave me here."

The man eyed her for a second then let out a long sigh. "Get in the van."

CHAPTER THIRTY-FIVE

The Cornish fishing port of Looe had a population of just over five thousand.

Therefore, Eliza wasn't surprised when she raced into the police station and found it empty. The waiting area, which consisted of two chairs and a magazine rack, was separated from the main office by a security door and serving window. The office was a little bigger. This had the luxury of two filing cabinets, a water cooler, and three desks. In the far corner, a doorway led out back to a six-by-eight holding cell and a toilet cubicle. As nothing exciting ever happened in Looe, the station warranted no more than three officers to run it – two of them constables. Of those constables, Billy was the brains of the outfit, while Eddie Wilkins was an energetic kid fresh out of the training programme and a little too overenthusiastic to serve and protect his community. At present – according to the local paper – Eddie was on sick leave after a failed cat rescue left him with a broken leg. Then there was

Sergeant George Collins, who, in Billy's own words, was a grouchy old git who spent the majority of his time on desk duty.

Eliza banged her fists against the glass partitioning. She didn't care which officer was on duty, she just wanted to see the security of their pale blue shirt and dark slacks stride into the room. It was George who walked in from the cells and hung a bunch of keys on a nearby nail. Eliza whacked the glass again, startling him. For a split second, he did nothing but stare at her. Then he rushed to the door, pressed the release button, and let her in.

Eliza raced into his arms, allowing a moment to soak up the awkward pat on the back he consoled her with.

"What on earth's happened to you?" George held her at arm's length and looked her square in the eye. "Billy was frantic when you disappeared from the hospital."

"Is he here?"

George shook his head. "No doubt he's out looking for you." He led her towards Billy's desk, kicked out the chair, and sat her down.

"Can you contact him?"

"Yes." George wheeled his own chair beside her and pulled a handkerchief from his pocket. He sat down, his heavy bulk too wide for the seat cushion, and began dabbing the side of her head. "I can also phone your father?"

Again, Roman's comments about Davis' intentions came to mind, and as much as Eliza didn't believe anything Roman had told her, something held her back from letting George make that contact. "I just need Billy."

George seemed to contemplate her request. "Here, hold this. Your head is bleeding." He lifted her hand to replace his against the tissue, then walked to the front desk where a pen and a stack of unused post-its sat beside a small radio.

He lifted the receiver and held it to his mouth. When he clicked the side button, a crackle of interference buzzed from the speaker. "Billy, you there?" He released the button and waited for a response.

After a few seconds' silence, he pressed the button again. "Billy, this is George. Are you there?"

This time when he released the button, Billy's voice bellowed out. "I'm here, but I'm in the middle of something."

"Eliza's here."

Billy took a second to respond, and even then confusion marred his voice. "At the station? Is she alright?"

"She's..." George eyed Eliza from head to foot. "Dirty and tired, and looks as though she's been dragged through a hedge backwards. How far away are you?"

"Twenty minutes, thirty tops. Don't let her out of your sight until I get there."

"Roger that." George dropped the receiver on the counter and traipsed his bulk back to Eliza. "The way he drives, it'll be more like ten minutes."

Eliza nodded. She glanced at the tissue, now blotted red with her blood, and scrunched it in her hand. It would be dark in a couple of hours, and the Shadow would come looking for her. She lifted her feet onto the chair and wrapped her arms around her knees.

George watched her for a second, then headed to the coffee machine. He didn't ask if she wanted anything, and just placed a wafer-thin plastic cup on the desk in front of her. "Hot chocolate. It'll warm you up." He whipped his coat from the back of his chair and wrapped it around her shoulders. It swamped her tiny frame, but she was glad of its size. It was something she could snuggle into and hide. She reached for the cup, ignoring the heat that scorched through the sides, and wrapped both her hands around it.

"It's not the best-tasting chocolate," George said. "But it's better than the tea and coffee crap the machine serves up."

Eliza sipped the brown liquid. It burned her lips and she quickly withdrew. George was right. It tasted terrible.

"Can you tell me what happened?" George said, reclaiming the seat in front of her again.

"I don't know where to start."

"How about you start with what went down at the hospital. Where did you go?"

Eliza took another sip of her drink. It still tasted awful, but she needed time to think. She wanted to tell George everything, but what exactly would that entail? That she'd seen zombies? And even if she bypassed that detail and just admitted to witnessing the inhuman things she'd seen Roman do, wouldn't that in itself open up a whole new can of worms? Simple ones like, 'what did this guy look like?' were fine, but the easy questions would inevitably lead to harder ones about what Roman had told her, and how would she answer those? 'He said I am a descendant of the Messiah and that my father's butler wants to kill me.' George would think her nuts, and knowing how her mouth had a mind of its own, she'd continue trying to justify her sanity with, 'No, really, I know he's telling the truth because I really can move things with my mind.'

Instead, Eliza stuck with the safe bet, and said, "I don't know anything, I'm sorry."

"Didn't you see what happened?"

You mean the zombies? Eliza shook her head.

George shifted a little closer. "There was a man there. Did you see him?"

You mean the Grim Reaper who killed the zombies and then kidnapped me? Eliza shook her head again. "All I know is I didn't wake up in the hospital."

George studied her for a moment, then leaned back in his chair. "Where did you wake up?"

"Somewhere in Fowey."

"'Somewhere' is pretty vague. Were you in a house? A barn? Outside?"

"I was in the boot of a car."

"Was anyone else there?"

Eliza thought of Roman's body slumped over the steering wheel. Again, the truth would lead to awkward questions she only wanted to speak to Billy about. She shook her head. "I just ran."

"Can you remember what sort of car it was? Or where it was? Think hard."

"No, I just ran."

"All the way here? From Fowey?"

"A postman drove me."

"Where is he?"

"I don't know. Gone. Said he didn't want to get involved."

George rubbed his chin, and smiled. The corners of his mouth didn't even dent his chubby cheeks. His eyes remained unmoving and suspicious. "Okay. It's all okay. You've been through a lot." He stood and pulled the waist of his trousers up, where it would have stayed if the overhang of his stomach hadn't gotten in the way.

"Where are you going?"

"I need the john. I won't be long. You're safe. No one can get in here." George turned and disappeared through the door at the back of the office.

Eliza watched him leave, and once again tried to drink some of her hot chocolate. The taste hadn't improved, and she put it down on the desk. The station was quiet. No phones rang, and no members of the public came in to report stolen bikes or complain about their neighbours. Eliza began to wonder what the three police officers actually did all day.

Somewhere out by the back of the office, she thought she heard a voice. She waited, expecting George to appear, but he didn't. She leaned over in the chair and tried to see along the narrow hallway. Everything was empty and quiet... apart from the voice, muffled and low.

"George? Is that you?"

The voice stopped.

A second later, George reappeared at the doorway, pulled up his flies, and flattened down his comb-over.

"I thought I heard voices. Are we here alone?"

George scratched his rotund stomach, where dried egg yolk and a splash of decaf looked to be the shirt stain of the day. "No one here but you and me, love. Must be that overworked imagination of yours." An open tin of Quality Street sat beside his computer keyboard. He plucked out a sweet, unwrapped it, and popped it into his mouth. His eyes gleamed with satisfaction.

He glanced at the full cup of chocolate. "Told you it was bad," he said, picking chocolate from his teeth. "So are you feeling better, or do I need to call an ambulance?"

"I feel fine." But Eliza felt far from fine.

CHAPTER THIRTY-SIX

"Where is she?" Billy burst through the station doors, nearly falling arse over tit.

Eliza spun the office chair to face him. His clothes, rumpled and marred with sweat and grime, looked to be the same ones he'd worn to the hospital the morning before. Perspiration glistened across his forehead, most probably from his hasty return to the station, and he wiped it clean with the cuff of his shirt, adding yet more grot to the already grubby material.

George buzzed him through, and mumbled something about needing to take a whiz again.

Billy pushed open the door, still an urgency to his movements. "Where the hell have you been? Are you alright?"

Eliza nodded. "You look cross."

Billy's shoulders slumped and loosened a little. He parked his behind in the seat previously occupied by George. "Cross? No. Worried? Yes. I went to the hospital. That man... He took you, didn't he? "

Eliza nodded.

Billy shifted in the chair the same way George had, only minus the excess bulk. He took her hands in his. "And are you okay? Did he hurt you? Did he—"

"Billy, I'm fine. He didn't do anything to me."

"He kidnapped you, Lizzy."

Eliza hushed him again. She glanced towards the cell doorway. George was nowhere to be seen.

Billy followed her gaze. "What are you looking at?"

"I lied to George before."

"About what?"

"About everything."

"Such as?"

Eliza pressed her finger to her lips, and glanced over her shoulder. Still no George.

"Hey?" Billy cupped her chin and turned her face to him. "Do you need a hospital, or a doctor?"

"No." Eliza lowered Billy's hand away.

"Then tell me what the hell happened."

"You're going to think I'm mad when I tell you what I saw."

"I'm leaning that way already." Billy sat back in the chair. He didn't speak for several seconds. Finally, he said, "Try me."

Eliza took a deep breath and tried to stop the trembling in her fingertips. She clasped her hands and rubbed them together, the newfound warmth failing to add colour to her pale skin. "That man took me from the hospital..."

"Yes, I already know that."

She glanced towards the back of the office. George still hadn't made an appearance and there was no noise to suggest he lingered out of sight, eavesdropping. "A dead man attacked me. I know it sounds like I'm nuts, but Roman saved me."

"Roman? Who the hell is Roman?"

Eliza hushed him again. Her eyes darted back towards the door, and only when she was sure George still wasn't listening did she continue. "He's the man who took me from the hospital."

Billy leaned forward again, only this time when he spoke, his voice was low and intended for her ears only. "A witness saw what happened. Your so-called hero is a killer."

"And a kidnapper." Eliza looked down at her bare feet curled on the seat in front of her. "And I hope he's nuts, too, because he said things I can't possibly let myself believe are true."

"Like what? Do they involve our father?"

Eliza looked up. Billy's question shocked her. "Dad? Why would you ask that?"

Billy dismissed her question. "Do you know where this Roman is now?"

Eliza nodded.

"Then I need to go get him." Billy stood, but Eliza grabbed his hand.

"I want to come with you."

"The only place you're going is to the hospital."

"I'm coming with you."

"No."

"I don't feel safe here."

"I said no."

Eliza stood. Immediately, she wanted to lift her feet off the cold floor and sit back on the chair. "If you want to find him, then the only way is for me to show you where he is."

"Absolutely not."

"I'm not staying here on my own."

"You're not on your own. George is here."

"I feel safer with you."

"Eliza, don't start with me. Not now." His lips tightened. "You don't even have any shoes on."

"I'll be in the car. I'll be fine."

"But you're hurt."

Eliza felt the dried blood. In a couple of hours the Shadow would come for her and that put Billy at risk. But what alternative did she have? To stay trapped in here with George? "I won't stay here, Billy."

Billy ran his fingers through his hair. A defeated sigh escaped his lips, and he grabbed a second set of keys from his drawer. "Jesus Christ. I can't believe I'm agreeing to this."

CHAPTER THIRTY-SEVEN

Davis no longer needed sleep.

He swallowed back the brandy he'd graciously poured himself, relaxed back into the armchair, and massaged his temples. From this distance, the fireplace provided a gentle heat, the flames erratic in their dance above the coals, that heat helping to soothe the headache this stressful day had caused.

The ache had almost diminished when the telephone beside him rang. Davis answered it, unhappy that he couldn't even have this single minute to himself, and listened intently as McKenzie informed him that Eliza had been found.

"Are you sure? You lost her once already." Davis sat forward, his headache a distant memory.

"I'm sure."

"You have her now?"

"No."

"Then where is she?"

"She's at the police station."

"The police station? What's she doing there?"

"I don't know. That's the message I received."

"And where is Holbrook?"

"He appears to be off the grid. As expected, he never made it back to the cabin. One can only suppose the poison killed him in a remote and as-yet-undetected area."

Davis drummed his fingers on the arm of the leather chair. Although pleased to have Holbrook out of the picture for the immediate future, Eliza being at the police station potentially caused a whole heap of new problems. "Where are you now?"

"On my way to the station."

"Good." Davis stood up. "I don't want any more slip-ups. If Billy becomes a problem, deal with him. Just bring the girl back here."

Davis hung up. He sat back down in the chair, and started to massage his temples once again.

CHAPTER THIRTY-EIGHT

The right knee of Roman's jeans had a hole in it.

He stared at it for several moments while his eyes adjusted, the white fraying torn and severed. It made no sense to him. Just as wanting to lift his head off the steering wheel now but being unable to also didn't make any sense. He closed his eyes again, and forced every unwanted thought from his mind.

Concentrate.

What had happened? What was he missing?

Roman opened his eyes, the hole in his jeans visible once again, and remembered. Bloody Davis and his goddamn poison. He didn't know who he held more anger towards: the old man for having the nerve to pull such a stunt, or himself for falling for it.

Two keys swung from the silver loop of his key ring, the third still in the ignition. He fumbled for a grip, his hands shaking and his fingers uncoordinated, and turned it. The engine groaned, its growl coming and going before it died altogether. Roman pumped the accelerator, and again twisted the key. Nothing. He lifted his head, this time without any hesitation, and shook away the grogginess. A chill shook his body. He glanced down at his bare body and a frown creased his brow. His shirt lay crumpled in the passenger foot well, and he reached for it. It was way too ripped and torn to wear, and he flung it back to the floor.

The door flung open with a swift kick, and he swung his legs out and stood. Outside, rays of sunlight shone upon acres of grassy fields. Nearby, cattle grazed, seemingly unbothered by his presence. Roman inhaled a fresh lungful of the countryside, and turned to examine the car he loved – his pride and joy. Broken fence dented the bonnet, and paint had been stripped from its sides, destroying its former beauty forever. He would kill Davis for what he'd done to the vehicle, let alone—

Roman stopped, and glanced towards the rear of the car. He remembered more. He remembered putting a chloroformed Eliza in the boot. The three strides it took to reach the back of the car mimicked more of a rushed jog than a walk. He patted his jeans for his keys, remembered he'd left them in the ignition, and fetched them. His fingers shook with fear, a rare emotion for him. He didn't like feeling it. What he expected to find inside he wasn't sure, but regardless, he slotted the metal into the lock dnd turned it until he heard the bonnet latch release. Slowly, he opened the boot.

Empty.

At first, not seeing Eliza inside, hurt or even dead, came as a welcome relief. Then frustration prevailed to beg the question, where in the hell had she gone? He noted the broken seat and spun to face the fields. The grassy meadows stretched for miles, but no matter how much he squinted, he could see no fleeing Eliza in the distance.

He slammed the boot shut and whacked the surface. It left a dent, and he cursed further at his own stupidity. Trees and bushes lined the roadside, the tarmac beyond only visible through the broken bushes made by his car. Ignoring everything else, he headed up the bank. It wasn't too steep, but still would have been tricky for Eliza to climb with her hands and feet tied. A familiar and discarded length of rope caught his eye and he knelt, cursing yet again. He clenched the rope in his hand, and gave in to the dismay of having to accept the cold hard truth: he'd given up the piece of wood's whereabouts, and now Eliza had finally succeeded in escaping him. He'd lost his only leverage against Davis and now stood no chance of finding the True Cross' location. He'd never see Jane or his son again. Not only that, but if the old man got to Eliza before Roman, then she would die for sure.

He dropped the rope and headed up to the road. Black tyre marks swerved across the tarmac, ending where he now stood. Given the severity of the skid, he was almost impressed Eliza had been lucid enough to make it out of the boot at all, let alone travel any further. He glanced right, then left. No sign of traffic, not even the hum of an engine in the distance. A bird chirped somewhere above him – a blackbird, if he wasn't mistaken – but his feathered friend was of little help in finding a solution to the predicament he now faced.

Pacing back and forth didn't help much, either. He wore no watch, so had little idea how much of a head start Eliza had on him. Even if he had known, where would he begin looking for her? North? South? Back at her father's? A police station?

He remembered the paperwork on Davis' desk, in particular the whereabouts of the last piece of the Cross. Finding Eliza was important to him, but getting possession of that last piece of wood was his final chance to reach Jane, and save Eliza – that was, if Davis hadn't taken it already.

Way down the road, the glimmer of sun reflected off a windscreen like the sparkle from a highly polished diamond. Roman listened. Sure enough, the low rumble of an engine followed. He took several paces into the middle of the road, and waited. The chug of the vehicle neared. Eventually, an orange Mini Cooper appeared over the top of the hill. When it was close enough for him to read the number plate, Roman held up his hands and flagged the driver to pull over.

A young kid got out, twenty years old if he was a day. He eyed Roman for a second, his eyes seeming to linger on the hole in his jeans, and Roman fought the urge to point out the dangers of stopping for strangers along the roadside.

"Are you okay?" the kid asked, looking hesitant to step out from behind the security of his open door.

Roman pointed to his car. "Deer ran out. I swerved to miss it but..."

"A deer? Really? Here?" The young boy glanced at the broken foliage. From his point of view, Roman guessed he could just about see the tail end of the Aston. As expected, curiosity got the better of the driver, and the boy stepped out from behind his door and walked closer to the accident site. "Whoa, that's a neat ride."

"It was a neat ride."

"You want me to call a tow truck or something?"

Roman shook his head. "What I really need is your car."

"My car?"

It was obvious to Roman that his intentions didn't sink in with the boy straight away. In fact, it felt like a full minute before the boy started to slowly withdraw from him and make a dash back towards the open door of his Mini. Roman rushed after him. He had to give this lad his dues, he was a fast little bugger when he got going. He made it back to his car before Roman could reach him, a defeat Roman chalked up to the fact that he'd just died – again – and pulled the door shut, hitting the locks and quickly starting the vehicle. The engine revved far higher than the Mini allowed for, and the kid glanced towards Roman one last time, a look of confidence breaking through the fear that he was indeed going to make a clean getaway.

Roman smiled. He wasn't without a trick or two up his sleeve, and punched his fist through the side window. He grabbed the boy by the scruff of the neck and smashed his head against the steering wheel. Not too hard. Roman didn't want to kill the guy, just daze him enough so he wouldn't be any more trouble. The lad's foot slipped from the clutch, and the engine stalled. When Roman pulled his head back, a purple lump already bruised the bridge of the kid's nose. He tried to speak, but Roman opened the door and let the lad half fall, half stagger, onto the road.

Roman turned for the car and stopped. The young lad was smaller in build, but even a tight jumper would less inconspicuous than none at all. "Give me your sweater."

The lad frowned.

Roman took a step towards him and the boy quickly pulled his jumper over his head and threw it towards Roman.

Roman caught it, and got into the car, his legs too long for the pedals even after he adjusted the seat. He glanced at the lad. "A guy your age really should think about getting one of those boy racer cars."

CHAPTER THIRTY-NINE

"It's just over that hill," Eliza said, not entirely sure Roman's car was in fact where she thought it might be.

From the corner of her eye, she saw Billy glance in her direction. He said nothing. In fact, he hadn't said anything since she'd told him of her abduction and the conversations it had spawned with Roman back in the cabin. So, following his lead, she'd remained quiet for the duration of the journey, and only spoke when she needed to direct him left or right.

The police car climbed the hill until trees, fields, and the open road beyond became visible. Eliza searched ahead, now certain she was at the right place, and that Roman's car was somewhere buried among the bushes along the left-hand side.

"There're skid marks across the road," Billy said, slowing the car. "Looks like you weren't lying."

"Why would you think I was?" Eliza waited for the car to come to a complete stop and turned towards him. "Do you think I made the whole thing up?"

"As hard as it was to hear what you had to say, I actually believe some of it."

"Some? What bit don't you believe?"

Billy didn't answer. He glanced out through the windscreen and pointed to the skid marks again. "Looks like the car skidded off into the trees over there."

Eliza didn't accept his change of subject. "Billy, what part don't you believe? That this guy is involved with Davis, or that apparently Davis wants me dead?"

"I already had a feeling this family of ours wasn't all it was cracked up to be."

"So what part then?"

Billy took a deep breath. As he exhaled, he spoke in an even, controlled tone. "I'm not sold on the whole sacrifice thing, or that you can move crap with your mind. I think someone is up to something. Whether it's Davis or our father is anyone's guess, but this Roman guy knows and is somehow involved."

"It's not Dad, it's Davis."

"Whatever. I think Roman's spun you a whole yarn of lies to mess with your head."

"Why would he do that? What possible reason is there?"

"He's nuts. Do people like that need a reason?"

Eliza knew she had no explanation for the things she'd done in the past few days. She opened the door to get out, but Billy reached across her and pulled it back shut.

"Where do you think you're going?"

"Roman's car is just through there."

"And I can find it on my own."

"You're making me stay here?"

"Yes."

"But—"

"It's non-negotiable, Eliza. You wait here or I'll cuff you to the steering wheel. Got it?"

Eliza raised a brow, but Billy's mind was made up; that narrowing of his eyes told her he wasn't about to budge on his decision. He opened the driver's door, the twittering of birds suddenly audible, climbed out, and slammed the door shut behind him. Eliza sat back against the seat and folded her arms. Her father constantly treated her like a child and she hated it. Now Billy was doing the same? She watched him near the point of impact. He kicked a broken fence panel to one side, glanced back towards her – probably to check she hadn't followed him – and stepped into the undergrowth.

Eliza waited until he was out of sight before quietly opening the door. She had no intention of staying put. In the last forty-eight hours she'd battled everything from the advances of Doctor Dick to the mysterious and violent unknown. To be treated a victim now was almost laughable.

She tiptoed the few metres between Billy's police car and the crash site, and peered through the bushes. Billy was already beside Roman's car, hunched and leaning in through the open passenger door. Eliza rounded the bush, needing to see if Roman was dead or alive, no matter how insane with rage Billy would be when he saw she'd ignored his order to stay away. She reached the top of the ditch. A twig snapped beneath her bare foot, and Billy whipped his head up to face her. She expected a look of surprise, but instead he gave a disapproving tut and turned back to the car.

"Is he dead?"

"No."

"He's alive?"

"No."

Eliza took a single step forward and tried to peer into the car. Billy's body blocked any view of the driver's side. "Billy? Is he dead or isn't he?"

Billy backed out of the car. He straightened and stood to one side, waving a hand towards the driver's seat like a magician revealing a vacant box.

Eliza took another step forward and saw the car was empty. Loose dirt crumbled beneath her weight, and she slid a little way down the bank before regaining her balance. "Where is he?"

Billy shrugged and walked to the other side of the car.

"But he was right there, slumped over the steering wheel."

Autumn leaves and debris crunched underfoot somewhere behind the bushes to their left. Billy pressed his finger to his lips. More slowly than Eliza had ever seen him move before, he made his way to the front of the Aston.

Branches rustled. A twig snapped. Eliza backed up towards the road. If Roman emerged through those bushes, she wanted to be in easy reach of the police radio. A hand pulled back part of a branch until the twig snapped in two. Billy said nothing. He just waited, his hand poised near his belt and the Taser clipped to the side of it.

"Help me," came a young voice.

Billy still didn't move, his eyes fixated on the trees in front of him. "I am a police officer," he stated, his voice holding the same authority she'd heard moments earlier in the car.

A young lad, naked from the waist up, stepped out from the bushes. Bruising swelled the bridge of his nose, and his voice was nasally when he spoke again. "Thank God, the police."

"What's your name, boy?"

"Stephen."

"Stephen what?"

"Banks. Some dude stole my clothes and my car."

Billy glared at Eliza, a knowing look spread across his face. Without looking at the lad, he asked, "And what did this dude look like?"

"Tall, dark hair. I didn't really take much notice. Said a deer ran out in front of him."

"You always stop for strangers?"

"No."

Billy's hand lowered from his belt and he stepped forward, helping the young lad to the passenger seat of the Aston. "You got a broken nose there, Stephen."

"He whacked my head against the steering wheel."

"What car'd you say he stole?"

"A Mini."

"Number plate?"

"OLM..." A frown creased the boy's forehead. "383L"

"An old one, eh? Done up, or a rust bucket?"

"Mint condition until he smashed the window."

"What colour?"

"Orange."

Billy patted the boy's shoulder and waved Eliza down to join them. "Stay with him," he said, pausing for a second to push Eliza's hair back from her face. He wet his thumb and wiped what she presumed to be dried blood from her face, once again reminding her that the Shadow would come for her if she didn't clean herself up.

"Where are you going?"

"To call it in. The guy needs an ambulance."

Eliza watched him climb the bank. He disappeared from sight, and suddenly she wished she'd stayed in the car when first ordered to.

"Are you a police officer?" the lad asked.

Eliza glanced down at him. Although only five or six years seemed to separate their ages, he looked like a young son needing comfort from a mother. She knelt. "No."

"Why don't you have any shoes on your feet?"

Eliza studied her feet, skin hardened and covered in dirt and mud. She'd forgotten all about her lack of footwear. "It's been a long day."

"As crazy as mine?"

Well, let's see. I've been drugged, kidnapped, fought zombies, and told I have to kill my father's murderous butler using only the power of my mind before he sacrifices me to open the Gateway to Heaven. "No, it's been nothing like your day."

Billy appeared at the top of the mound. The dirt crumbled like a mini avalanche beneath his feet, and he slid the last couple of feet down the bank. "George and an ambulance are on their way. The ambulance will take you both to the hospital in Liskeard."

"I'm not going back to any hospital, never mind Liskeard. Not after the last time."

"Eliza, don't argue with me."

"I'm not going to any hospital, Billy."

Billy cursed under his breath. "Fine. Then George will take you back to the station."

"I need to go home. Get a change of clothes and clean myself up."

"Do I look as though I'm in the mood for an argument? Go with George to the station. I'll meet you there once I know this chap is on his way to hospital."

"Then why can't I wait with you?"

"Because you have no shoes on your feet, you're a victim yourself, and it's safer back at the station with George."

"But—"

"It's not up for negotiation. George will take you back, you will give him a full statement, and you will wait for me there."

Billy turned his back on her, and Eliza heard him ask the young man if there was any family he wanted to call. The young man shook his head. Eliza waited for Billy to face her again so she could further argue her case to stay with him, but he didn't.

CHAPTER FORTY

Roman didn't bother hiding the car this time when he arrived at Eliza's house.

His head ached enough to irritate the hell out of him, and he didn't plan on being around long enough for anyone to catch him. He entered through the front door, bold as brass, and headed upstairs towards the attic. The notes he'd seen on James' desk in the library showed the attic as the resting place for the fourth and final piece of the True Cross. Careless for such important papers to be left out for all and sundry to see, and ironic that it had been under Eliza's nose the whole time, but it had saved Roman immense time and aggravation having to search for them. Getting to this last piece before Davis was his only hope of ever seeing Jane again.

Considering the day he'd had, the climb wasn't an easy one. Yet, Roman still managed to reach the attic in record time. Daylight filtered through the open doorway and lit the top of the landing. Inside, footprints disturbed dust-covered floorboards, and broken cobwebs left an uneasy feeling in the pit of his stomach. He walked to the far side of the room, where daylight barely touched the walls, and saw the broken bricks prised from their lime surroundings and smashed on the floor. He kicked a path clear and peered in through the hole. Visibility was almost non-existent, but he could still see there was nothing in the small cubbyhole on the other side.

Roman punched the wall. A lone brick fell and missed his foot by inches. Without that last piece of wood, Roman had nothing to bargain with. He'd lost Eliza, he'd lost the wood, and he'd lost his last chance to find Jane and apologise for everything he'd done to her. He just could not see what his next move should be.

He turned from the hole and left the room, annoyed that he'd arrived too late, and doubly annoyed that Davis had outsmarted him. Two options now faced him: give in and let the old man win, or kill him. Whichever he chose, the outcome was the same. He'd never get to Heaven. This scenario did not sit well with him.

The stairs down to the hall seemed longer now that he had no interest in rushing. Everything had gone to shit, just as it had after he'd walked away from Jane and his unborn child. It had taken days leading up to that abandonment to convince himself it was for her own good; that her husband – his brother – was best suited to care for them both. And he'd spent every day since trying to wash their blood from his hands. Jane had been everything he desired, but he'd left her, and she'd ultimately died.

Is that what was happening now? Was history repeating itself?

Eliza certainly awoke a yearning inside him, but whether it was one of genuine emotion or just plain lust, he didn't know. Whichever, he intended on leaving her for Jane, and would probably never know if she died at the hands of Davis. Could he honestly live with another's blood on his hands because of his own selfishness?

The front door remained open just as he'd left it, and he stepped out onto the porch, casting an eye at the few houses scattered in the hills around him. At the top end of the lane a neighbour fussed with the flowers that bordered his lawn and, two houses down, a harassed blonde packed her four kids into a grey 4x4, moaning that they were late for karate.

Roman stood and watched her, bemused that she'd allow her simple life to cause so much aggravation. What he wouldn't give to have her kind of worries. He turned to close the door and an open packing box caught his eye – or, more accurately, the contents that lay on top of it. He stepped back inside the hall. Various trinkets and photo frames crammed the box, half wrapped in paper and bubble wrap. One picture in particular held his attention. He picked it up and grinned with conceited satisfaction. In front of him he held the answer. In the picture, a smiling Eliza stood beside a handsome dark-haired man in a smart-looking police uniform. Of course. Davis didn't have Eliza... The cop did.

The game was back on. Roman could still get Eliza back, although what he did with her now, he wasn't sure. With a newfound spring in his step, he turned for the door.

Mrs. McKenzie stood in the entrance, a flash of something across her face he took to be concern at seeing him inside. "Can I help you?"

"I was just leaving." Roman sidestepped her, but Mrs. McKenzie leaned against the doorframe and blocked his exit, seemingly unbothered that her low-cut blouse revealed way more than he wanted to see.

He stepped back and surveyed the woman. He would have expected more anxiety from a woman finding a strange man in her neighbour's house. She didn't even seem intimidated, considering her dumpy frame barely reached his breast bone.

Mrs. McKenzie pushed herself from the doorframe, patted her over-styled hair, and walked into the hall. Her hips swayed, a display of sensuality obviously emphasised for Roman's benefit. It didn't work. "What you came for has gone."

Roman glanced towards the stairs. Did she mean the Cross or Eliza? He decided to go with the Cross. "You took it?"

"No." Mrs. McKenzie laughed, and kicked the door shut behind her. With the sunlight blocked, the room took on the same cold and dismal feel it had the other evening when the Shadow had come for Eliza.

"But you know who did?"

Mrs. McKenzie smiled, and it was obvious she wasn't going to dignify his question with an answer.

"So, if there's nothing of any importance left in this house, why are you here?"

"Maybe I'm just looking out for my neighbour."

"Then you would have called the police."

Mrs. McKenzie laughed again, clearly enjoying herself. "There sure ain't any flies on you, is there, sugar?"

Roman drummed his hand against the side of his thigh. He didn't have time for idle chitchat. "Question is, do you know anything that my torturing you would unveil?"

The corners of Mrs. McKenzie's mouth turned, and the look of fear he sought replaced her overconfident demeanour. She glanced to the left. "I don't know anything. I was told to keep an eye on this place and that's what I'm doing."

Her transition from survivor to victim was good. Almost believable, in fact. But Roman had been around enough liars in his time to know when someone was playing him. "You looked to the left."

"I'm sorry?"

"When you spoke, you glanced to your left. You're lying to me."

"I'm not." Mrs. McKenzie opened the door. "Look, just go. I won't tell them you were here."

"Tell who? Davis?"

Now her eyes rapidly searched off to the left.

"Don't say a word unless you are going to speak the truth." Roman reached past her and pushed the door shut again. "Now. Do you know where Eliza is?"

Mrs. McKenzie stared at him, eyes wide like a cornered wild animal.

Maybe she was nothing but a pawn in a dangerous game, but she knew alright. Still, it was a game Roman didn't have time to play. His hand still drummed against his leg, and he leaned in closer towards her. "Do you hear that?"

"What?"

"My hand tapping against my leg."

"Yes."

"That's a sign I'm growing impatient. Now, you have exactly thirty seconds to tell me where Eliza is."

"Then what?"

"Do you really want to know?"

Mrs. McKenzie swallowed, and fished through her jeans pockets. She brought out a folded piece of paper and handed it to him. "Please don't kill me. I have it here, written down. I'm supposed to meet—"

Roman snatched the information and opened it. Handwritten in a scrawl he thought only doctors used, was a list. He read the first four items: washing powder, bleach, fruit cake, beef. "What the hell is this? A shopping list?"

He glanced up, but Mrs. McKenzie already had the knife in her hand. She plunged it deep into Roman's stomach, and before he had time to react, she withdrew and stabbed him a second time. "You should never underestimate a woman," she said, knifing him a third time.

Roman stumbled back towards the kitchen. Lunge after lunge, Mrs. McKenzie came for him. All around, light reflected off the blade: above, to the left, to the right. Roman blocked every frenzied attack the tiny woman made to finish him off. Renegade jabs carved his arms and chest. His clothes sliced apart, and blood soon soaked them. He felt his legs weaken and knew he couldn't hold her off much longer. The knife came at him again and he raised his hand to block it. The blade speared clear through the back of his hand, the point exiting his palm and stopping inches from his heart.

Mrs. McKenzie didn't pull it free. Instead, she laughed and pushed harder. Roman held her off, his arm shaking with pain. He had little strength left. He was losing.

"Why don't you just die?" Mrs. McKenzie said.

"I already did that today." Roman grabbed her hair at the roots, and kneed her in the stomach.

Mrs. McKenzie's hand released the knife. She doubled over but Roman yanked her head back up and slammed the knife into the side of her neck. The steel penetrated her jugular and embedded deep in her throat. Only then did he pull it free. Blood followed, spurting out like the Bellagio fountains in Vegas.

Roman shook her. "Where's Eliza?"

Life had all but drained from Mrs. McKenzie's eyes. Her arms fell to her sides and she stared vacantly at Roman.

"Tell me."

Mrs. McKenzie dropped to the floor and Roman collapsed beside her. "Tell me where Eliza is." He grabbed her head and banged it against the floor.

For a second, Mrs. McKenzie eyes widened and focused on him.

"Is Eliza at the police station?"

A slight smile from the woman revealed bloodstained teeth, and then her eyes rolled to the back of her head.

Roman collapsed back, his breathing growing heavier by the minute, and examined his arms. The wounds were already healing, and given he was still alive, he assumed the stab wounds to his abdomen had miraculously missed every vital organ. Lucky bastard. He didn't have time to die again. He grabbed a tea towel and pressed it against his side. The blood would soon stop flowing, and he just prayed it was before he passed out. To lose more time now while his body healed was something he couldn't afford. He climbed to his feet, his body begging for a longer rest, and staggered to the door. Outside, the woman with the kids had already left, and the man tending his garden now mowed the lawn.

Yards from where Roman stood, the Mini Cooper sat in the driveway...with two slashed tyres.

CHAPTER FORTY-ONE

George pulled the police car to a stop and switched off the engine.

He unclicked his seatbelt and opened the driver's door. It whacked against the wheelchair ramp, leaving himself little more than a couple of feet to squeeze out through.

Eliza made no attempt to move.

George noticed, and said, "You're safer here, you know that?"

"Since when do you take orders from Billy?"

"I happen to agree with him."

By Eliza's reckoning, George spent a full three minutes trying to exit the car. He twisted this way and that, removed the torch and Asp from his belt, wiggled, sucked in as much of his stomach as he could, and when he finally stood, his shirt was untucked, his tie skew-whiff, and he was missing his hat. Was this really the best protection the police could offer until Billy returned?

George waddled around to Eliza's side of the car and tapped on the window. "Come on, I'll make you a really bad cup of tea."

Eliza watched him disappear inside the police station. How easy it would be to run in the opposite direction. To head to Scotland, or Wales, or America...or anywhere that wasn't here, and start a new life away from all this horror. Probably not as easy as she thought. She didn't have a penny on her, her clothes were ripped and bloodstained, and the soles of her filthy feet were sore and in no shape to flee anywhere. Begrudgingly, she slid off her seatbelt and opened the car door.

George reappeared at the door and held it open, encouraging her to hurry inside. Eliza trudged past him, opting not to look at him until she'd entered the office.

She glanced at the same chair she'd occupied less than a few hours before, and said, "I really need to clean up."

"Sure, the toilet's through there." He pointed to the back room, then grabbed a shirt off the coat stand. "Here, Billy's spare."

Eliza took it and hurried to the toilet at the end of the corridor. Inside, she filled the small basin with water and removed Roman's jacket. The wax had flaked away from her arm and although dried blood covered her skin, the wound no longer bled. She soaked some paper towels, cleaned herself before washing as much of the blood from her top as she could, and flushed them away. Slipping on Billy's shirt, she prayed to God she'd done enough to stop the Shadow finding her.

By the time Eliza returned to the office, George had kept his promise and made her an awful cup of tea.

He sat at his desk and took some papers from his drawer. "Why didn't you tell me you knew where the car was?"

"Billy just drove around the area until something looked familiar, and then we found the car," she lied.

"Uh huh." George didn't believe her, she could see that. He scribbled some notes, noticed the pencil was blunt, and sharpened it.

Eliza remained quiet, feeling guilty she'd kept things from George in the first place.

He must have read her mind because he said, "You could have saved us a lot of time if you'd told me what had happened straight away. We may have even caught the guy who took you."

"I wasn't sure—"

George held up a hand. "Let's just fill out this paperwork, shall we? That's if you're going to tell me the truth this time."

Eliza was back at square one. The truth couldn't possibly be written down, especially on official paperwork that would be filed. She sat in the spare chair. George knew she was holding back. She had to give him something.

"Okay, name?"

"What?"

"Your name." George pointed to the form.

"Eliza Hamilton."

"Address."

"George, you know my address."

George glanced up. "I also know your date of birth and that you're a female, but I'm still going to ask seeing as you're not telling me much else."

Eliza reached for the drink, changed her mind, and looked George straight in the eye. "Okay, I'll tell you everything I know."

"Good. Now, let's start with what happened at the hospital."

Eliza shifted position. "I woke up and went looking for a phone."

"Who were you going to call?"

"Billy, but I couldn't remember his number. He's changed it since..."

"And did you find one?"

Eliza shook her head. "I even checked the morgue, but I must've passed out or something because the next thing I knew, I woke up in the boot of a car."

George finished writing, noticed her silence, and said, "And?"

"And what? You know the rest after that. I got out of the boot and ran. A postman brought me here."

George seemed to consider her for a moment. "Did you see who took you from the hospital?"

Answering 'no' wasn't going to cut it. Eliza had to give George something else. "It was a man."

"How'd you know that?"

"I came to at the hospital, after I fainted. He was carrying me up some stairs, but I didn't get a good look at him."

"Black? White?"

"White."

"Dark-haired? Fair? Ginger?"

"Brown. I think. It could have been darker."

"Any distinguishing marks…?"

Eliza thought about the scar that curved the side of Roman's mouth, but shook her head. George looked up when he didn't hear her answer, saw her movement, and jotted the motion down on the paper. "Did he speak to you?"

Again, Eliza shook her head, causing George to glance up again. He seemed annoyed she wasn't using her voice, and placed his pencil down on the desk, interlocking his fingers. "It's been more than a few hours since you went missing from the hospital. What was he doing all that time? Just driving around?"

Eliza shrugged. "All I know is that I woke up in the boot. When I got out, I flagged down the postman and came here."

A tap on the security window startled her.

"Ah, finally." George got up and pressed the door release. "Where have you been?"

Eliza twisted in her seat. Her throat tightened when she saw Mr. McKenzie enter the office.

"Halfway to Bodmin Moor," he said, scanning the room. "Where's the brother?"

"At the accident site, although I don't know for how much longer."

Mr. McKenzie grunted and brushed past George. He strode up to Eliza, clasped her chin, and tilted her face from left to right. "Didn't you give her the sedative?"

"Of course I did, in her tea, but she needs to drink the thing for it to work."

"Whose blood is that?" Mr. McKenzie glanced at the bloodied tissue used earlier to wipe Eliza's head.

"The girl's. Why?"

"Burn it."

Eliza pulled from Mr. McKenzie's grip. "What's going on?"

Mr. McKenzie smiled. "I'm taking you home."

Eliza stood, and backed away. "I'm waiting here for Billy."

Mr. McKenzie grabbed her arm, his callused fingers digging into her skin. She turned to George for help but he just glanced at the station doorway, as though scared Billy would walk in and catch them.

"Let go of me."

Mr. McKenzie laughed, his head tilting back to reveal a mouthful of fillings. Gone was the warm and friendly neighbour Eliza had grown up around. He turned to George. "Get the door."

"George, don't let him take me. They're going to kill me."

George walked to the station door and opened it. "I'm sorry, Eliza."

"You're in on this?" But the sergeant turned his head away. "George, please."

Mr. McKenzie pushed Eliza towards the door, and she stopped struggling. She turned, complying with her neighbour's command.

"Good girl." Mr. McKenzie loosened his hold. "We'll have you home in no time."

Eliza stepped forward, then pivoted suddenly. Without warning, she raised her knee and planted it firmly in McKenzie's groin.

Mr. McKenzie released her and doubled over. "My fucking balls."

Eliza fled to the back room and pulled the door shut behind her. The old lock didn't look as if it would hold up under attack, but she bolted it regardless. From the office, she heard Mr. McKenzie scream for George to get her, and then footsteps hurried to the door. She had to get out of here.

The narrow hall gave access to one cell and the toilet. As the cell was nothing but a small space surrounded by three thick walls and a row of bars, she opted for the toilet, and the tiny, cobweb-covered window.

Eliza climbed up onto the toilet seat and yanked at the latch, but years of over-painting had long since sealed it shut. She heard the locked door smash open, and heavy boots thud towards her.

"Eliza, get down," George said.

Eliza let go of the latch and faced him. George had a Taser pointed towards her.

"Don't make me use this."

"George, what is going on?"

"I said get down!"

Eliza jumped down, and George stepped back into the hallway, keeping a healthy distance. "Now, I want you to walk back into the office. If you try anything, I will Taser you."

Eliza stared at the gun. Would George seriously use it? She stepped out of the toilet, George backing up into the corner of the hallway to let her pass.

"Put your hands on your head, Eliza."

Eliza did as he asked. "George—"

"Don't talk." He motioned her towards the office.

Mr. McKenzie waited, bent over and massaging his groin. "You little bitch," he said when she entered, then to George, "Why didn't you Taser her?"

"She came willingly."

"Fuck willingly." Mr. McKenzie snatched the gun from George's hands and pointed it towards Eliza. He leered at her for a second, and fired.

A small dart punctured just below Eliza's breast. Fifty thousand volts of electricity zapped her insides, and her body involuntarily tightened. She dropped to the floor, spasms her only movement until the sensation stopped and her muscles relaxed, leaving her unable to move.

CHAPTER FORTY-TWO

Billy watched the ambulance disappear over the hill and out of sight.

He slammed the Aston's car door shut, having found nothing to help him track that bastard Roman down, and waved to the breakdown recovery driver that he was finished.

"You sure? I'm paid by the hour, so can wait as long as you need."

"I'm sure."

The driver looked put out. He folded his newspaper and threw it on the dash. "Suit yourself." The truck roared to life. Without another word he pulled away, towing Roman's car behind.

Billy didn't watch it leave. Instead, he hurried back to his own car, grabbed the radio, and called George. When his sergeant failed to answer, Billy dropped the radio on the seat and started the engine, tyres spitting gravel as he screeched away.

He'd travelled no more than a mile when darkness suddenly descended. He switched on the lights, the beams cutting through the dense surroundings, and eased his foot off the accelerator. Outside, high in the sky, the sun was eclipsed. At least Billy assumed the circle of green light, like a lone Olympic ring, was an eclipse. He'd seen this before – the night Eliza had been attacked at the train station, and nothing good had happened that night. He accelerated again, even more desperate to get back to the station. Outside, trees swayed in the growing gale, and fallen leaves swept across the lit tarmac, swirling and fighting each other as if unsure of which direction to go. Billy sped up. Although he believed very little of what Eliza had earlier told him, he knew one thing for sure: something strange had been happening in Cornwall these last forty-eight hours, and if he were a betting man, he would bet his apartment that something bad was brewing now.

The steering wheel gyrated in his hands. At first Billy thought he had a flat tyre, but beneath him, the ground rumbled again. The car rocked one way, then the other. Fight as he might, he struggled to keep the vehicle on the road. Ahead of him, the tarmac cracked apart like an eggshell. Fences tilted, some sections severing apart for the gales to thrust into Billy's path. Branches snapped from trees and fell to the ground while others hit the car roof with deafening thuds.

Shit. It's a fucking earthquake.

Billy swerved the car, first to miss the gaps in the road and then to miss the falling debris that showered his vehicle. But the winds picked up, ferociously hammering the side of the car. Soon, his control over the steering was lost. Blow by blow, the storm nudged the car across the road, but Billy didn't ease off the accelerator. The speedometer hit sixty. Broken tarmac rose from the ground like speed bumps, and several times the tyres hit them and sent the car through the air. Wind battered the vehicle. The back end swerved out, and Billy wrestled to keep the steering straight. Lightning cut through the dark, lighting the debris-littered, tree-lined road ahead of him. Thunder grumbled somewhere over the hills, and rogue raindrops began to splash upon the windscreen.

A second bolt of lightning splintered across the sky, and somewhere in the distance Billy saw an explosion of fire. Rain turned to hail, and lightning stabbed down from above once more, its target a tree some fifty metres ahead. An orb of light burst from within like a fireball. Branches fizzed like gunpowder and the trunk divided in two, the severed parts splitting before they crashed across the road.

Billy slammed his foot on the brake. The tyres locked, and the car skidded across the wet surface. He panicked, everything taught to him at police driving school forgotten. He turned the steering wheel, but the erratic action sent the car into an uncontrollable spin. It hit the tree now blocking the road, and the bonnet crumpled around it. A branch pierced the windscreen, broken glass showering the dash and the occupant.

The last thing Billy felt was the seatbelt cut into his chest as he was catapulted forward.

CHAPTER FORTY-THREE

Bang... Bang... Bang...

The noise pounded through Billy's head, wind rushing across his face. Opening his eyes, dull light blurred somewhere off to the side. Where in the hell was he?

Slowly, familiar objects became clear: the gearstick, the radio, the empty seat beside him. The passenger door swung open and whacked against a broken fence.

Bang... Bang... Bang...

Billy lifted his head from the steering wheel. Pain surged through his spine and exploded behind his eyes, and for a moment his vision blurred again. *I'm inside the car?* What was he doing inside the car? Something warm trickled down the side of his face and, without looking, he knew it was blood. He fumbled with the button on his seatbelt, and agitation turned to desperation when it didn't release. He gripped and tugged the strap, but it only tightened across his chest and further restricted his breathing. Adrenaline flooded his veins, and his heart raced. Outside, a tree burned, its leaves shrivelled, the bark charred. Inches from Billy's head, its branch clipped the headrest and pierced the back seat.

Pausing, Billy took a deep breath but calm eluded him. His eyelids drooped, and his head lolled back against the headrest. Once again he reached for the seatbelt clip. A composed push on the button, and the belt sprang across him. Within seconds, he'd opened the car door and fallen out.

The wind hadn't let up, and attacked him from all angles. Wearily, he got up and stumbled unsteadily to the front of the car. Hail stung his arms and face, and the wind howled louder than he'd ever known. He raised his arm to block what he could, and examined the vehicle. The bonnet curled around the tree trunk like a blanket wrapping a new-born baby. The front wheel buckled outwards, clearly no longer attached to the axle. This car wasn't going anywhere.

"Shit." Billy football-kicked the tyre. It wobbled free, and found peace on the muddy verge. Blood trickled into his eye. He wiped it away, and pulled his mobile from his pocket. No signal.

"Shit." He threw the phone down on the passenger seat.

For a split second, lightning lit the night, and through the torrent of rain he thought he saw movement on the road ahead. He shielded his eyes, trying to see through the day's premature darkness. It was impossible. A second burst of lightning brightened the sky again, illuminating several people some fifty yards away. Billy's shoulders relaxed. Thank God. Help had arrived.

He ran into the middle of the road and waved his arms. "Hello. I need some help here."

The flash of light disappeared as quickly as it had arrived, and Billy lost the group to the darkness once more. He waited for a response. None came.

The tree's burning embers gave off very little light, and his car's smashed headlights were worse. He spotted the police siren on the roof and hurried back to the vehicle. Flicking a button on the dash, red and blue lights started to rotate wildly, causing every object around him to shimmer under the purple glow.

Billy scurried back to the centre of the road and waited. It seemed an age before he heard the first groan. Hairs spiked on the back of his aching neck, warning him of danger. He stepped backwards. The wet tarmac glistened in the siren's light, but he still couldn't see anything beyond the fallen tree.

"Hello?"

Another bolt of lightning blazed across the skyline. Fifteen or so people, all mesmerised by the florescent lights, staggered towards him. Billy reached for his holster, but his Taser wasn't there. "Shit," he said again, stepping back towards his car. He had a shotgun in the boot, and patted down his shirt pocket. *Shit*. The key hung on the fob. The fob hung from the ignition...which was inside the car.

An older gentleman dressed in a grubby black suit and tie reached the car. He held out a bruised and bloody hand. Only two fingers and a thumb remained, each nail blackened with dirt. Decaying skin hung in tattered shreds, and when he curled his finger and motioned for Billy to approach, whitened bone jutted out just above his elbow.

Billy flicked his Asp towards the floor and it sprang free, extending a good three feet. The action momentarily stunned the man. Rot had eaten away half his face, and his eyes bulged from sunken sockets. A young woman moved alongside him, the same gaunt look on her face, the ragged hem of her dirty cream dress trailing the ground behind her. Thin, matted hair barely covered her scalp, remnants of eyeliner smudged beneath her eyes, and cheekbones pushed through barely deceased skin. Billy knew this woman. He'd attended her funeral weeks earlier.

Something touched Billy's arm and he screamed, whirling the Asp behind him like an uncoordinated athlete. A little boy, one arm hugged tight around the neck of a brown teddy bear, stared up. He tilted his head, his one remaining blue eye watching the stick in amazement.

Billy turned on his heel and ran for the fields.

CHAPTER FORTY-FOUR

The lights in Looe Harbour dotted the darkness like flicked paint across a canvass.

Without the aid of moonlight, the uneven fields made it almost impossible to navigate. Tree trunks lay fallen on their sides, and several times their deracinated roots caught Billy's clothes and face. Finally, the grainy tarmac touched the soles of his shoes, and he quickened his pace across the stony arch of Looe Bridge.

The police station doors burst open and Billy barged inside, gripping the Asp and ready to swing at anything he encountered. The small waiting room was empty. Fast, shallow breaths had little time to slow, and rainwater dripped from his soaked clothes and puddled around his muddy boots. He slammed shut the main doors and, wiping the sweat from his eyes, stole a cautious glance through the window. Outside, the car park appeared vacant, and in the distance all that could be heard was a mixture of sirens, house alarms, and people screaming.

What in the hell was going on?

On the other side of the partitioning, telephones rang while their message lights randomly flashed. Billy rushed to the security door and punched in the code. The digital screen flashed red, not green, and the door remained locked.

"Shit." Billy banged on the partition glass. "Eliza? George?"

Then, for the second time in as many minutes, the station doors burst open, and Billy came face to face with the dead.

CHAPTER FORTY-FIVE

James Hamilton stepped from his private jet.

Like a loyal dog, Davis stood by the open door of his limo. No doubt, inside a poured whiskey would be waiting in one of the four crystal-cut tumblers. James greeted him with a nod, waited for his coat to be removed from his shoulders, and then climbed into the car. The anticipation that soon he'd be home felt good after his long flight, and instead of opening his briefcase to continue unfinished work, he allowed himself a moment to close his eyes and relax.

"Did you have a good trip, sir?"

James opened his eyes. Davis looked back from the passenger seat, and as much as James needed to talk to him, it could wait the ten minutes to home. He closed his eyes again. "Yes, Davis. Everything went well." And raised the blackout screen between them.

CHAPTER FORTY-SIX

Eliza cowered where she sat.

Her wrists were tied in front of her, and thick cloth covered her head and face, letting in little air and no light. She struggled to shake the hood free, but some kind of tape wrapped her neck and held the fabric tight against her throat. She drew her knees to her chest, the clatter of chains scraping the hard floor, its clamps cold and heavy around her ankles. Maybe five minutes ago she'd heard voices. Not in this room, wherever this room was, but somewhere outside. She tried again to shake the cloth from her face so she could inhale anything other than her own breath. Nausea whirled in the pit of her stomach and drowsiness clouded her mind, and although the hood created complete darkness, she felt as though the room on the other side was spinning.

A door opened, and heavy footsteps walked across the floor.

Eliza held her breath. If she stayed quiet, maybe she'd go unnoticed. Strong hands gripped her shoulders, and she jerked away. The chain around her ankles tensed, and her attempt to gain some distance failed. The pair of hands held her tighter, and Eliza writhed and lashed out.

"Eliza, calm down."

"Daddy?" Eliza stopped moving. She felt her father's fingers tug at the restraint that tied her neck. "Daddy, we have to get out of here before Mr. McKenzie comes back."

"We will, but first you have to hold still."

Eliza felt the cold steel of a blade press against her throat, and she flinched. Never had she longed to see her father and feel his arms around her as much as she did this very moment. The blade sliced through the tape around her neck, and the restriction wrapping her throat loosened. He pulled the hood from her head, her clammy face welcoming the coolness of the room, and hugged her tight.

"My dear child, I should never have let you leave me."

Eliza sank against his chest, her cheeks welcoming the comfort of his soft, expensive shirt. "How did you know where to find me?"

"I have my ways." He pulled away from her, his palm cupping her chin, and held a bottle of water to her lips. "Drink this."

"No, we have to get out of here."

"We will, but first you need to drink."

Water trickled across her lips, and Eliza drank. The refreshing taste felt good. She'd swallowed half the bottle before her father finally took it away and placed it down beside him. He still held the knife, but made no attempt to cut her hands free. Instead, he cupped her chin and tilted her head from side to side, as though examining her.

Stone walls glowed under the flicker of candle flame, and hardened wax hung like disfigured stalactites around the base of their wrought-iron holders. A large wooden table dominated the centre of the room. On the floor around it, straw overflowed from open crates. The room looked medieval. "Daddy, where am I?"

The door opened and Mr. McKenzie walked in, his beige corduroys and tan leather loafers stained with what looked to be dried blood. He looked from Eliza to James, and smiled. "Well, look what we have here."

"Daddy, quickly, cut me free."

But instead, James turned from her and stood, the blade still in his hand. "What the hell is going on here?"

Mr. McKenzie stepped forward. "I don't know what you mean."

Eliza pulled at the chains around her ankles. "Daddy, don't trust him. He's the one who brought me here."

James stole a glance back towards her, then refocused on Mr. McKenzie. "You didn't sedate her."

"I wasn't instructed to."

Eliza's head started to swim, and she struggled to focus. Her hands dropped to her knees. "What's happening?"

James placed the knife on the table. A robe hung on the back of the door and he unhooked it and slipped it on, lifting its hood over his head. His face disappeared under a shadow of darkness, leaving only his jaw visible. "You're dangerous, child. I have to protect myself."

Eliza fumbled against her restraints, bruises ringing her ankles. The room swirled around her, and her vision blurred. The candlelight faded, and she slumped against the table leg. She glanced at the bottle of water beside her. "What's wrong with me? What have you done?"

"It's just a precaution... A little something to dull your senses." Her father knelt before her. "You've caused me many problems disappearing the way that you did."

"McKenzie's working for you?"

James flashed a grin.

Eliza's head lolled forward. "It's you who wants to kill me?"

"No, no, no. I don't want to kill you." James lifted her head. A smile that just wouldn't die beamed from ear to ear. "I want to crucify you, in the most glorious way."

Tears streamed Eliza's cheeks. As weak as she was, she still pulled at her restraints. "You're insane."

James stood. "My wife said the same thing, moments before she fell to her death."

Eliza glanced up and tried to focus. Had her father just admitted to killing her mother?

He reached for a whip. Several leather braids hung from a wooden handle, each embedded with acorn-sized lead, sharp glass, and nails. James admired it. "Glorious, isn't it?"

It wasn't glorious. It looked horrific.

"Your mother was one of a kind. Without her, I could never have created you."

"And yet you killed her."

Her father laughed. "My wife wasn't your mother. She was just a convenience. I created you with another, solely for this one purpose."

"I don't understand."

"My family has searched for one of your kind for centuries."

"My kind?"

"You're a Mind Mover, my child, as was your mother." James stood. "I made you, and I took you."

"Why?"

"Because my wife didn't possess the power."

"So Billy isn't my brother?"

"Only half of him is."

"I don't understand..."

"Heaven is a powerful place. Unfortunately, the Hamilton name isn't welcome up there. Your male ancestors, myself included? All destined for..." James tapped his foot on the floor. "I don't want to go down there."

He stepped towards her. "You're a descendant from Christ himself. Your blood will open the Gateway to Heaven. Up there I can summon my family, and rule...well, just about everything."

"Where is my real mother?"

"Someplace where she can no longer be a bother to me."

James caressed the leather whip. Seemingly no longer interested in their conversation, he turned his back on her. "Do you know what this is, my dear?"

Eliza tried to focus, but the objects around her danced in front of her eyes. She felt James' hand cup her chin and suddenly he was in front of her again. "Some call this a Roman flagrum; others, a cat o' nine tails. It was used on Jesus Christ himself moments before his Crucifixion."

Eliza's eyes widened.

Her father saw, and grinned. "Not with this exact whip, you silly girl. Even I can only obtain so much. No, this is a reproduction. A one of a kind."

He let the whip dangle in front of her, his eyes sparkling with delight as he watched her cower from it. Finally, he dropped it on the table. He glanced at Mr. McKenzie. "Strip her and get her up to the tower."

Mr. McKenzie waited for James to leave, then cracked his knuckles. He glared down towards Eliza with eager eyes. "Alone again," he said, grabbing the waistband of her trousers.

Eliza kicked out, twisting her tortured body in an attempt to free from his grip.

Mr. McKenzie laughed. His strength far outweighed hers, and he pinned her back, ripping apart her trouser zipper and yanking the denim to her ankles. "Nice panties."

"Get the hell off me."

He reached for the neck of her shirt and tore open the first two buttons. His fingers lingered an inch from her skin. "You sure have grown into a fine looking woman."

Eliza squirmed away from his touch, but she was weak and exhausted, no longer able to fight. "Please, don't..." She pulled against her restraints, but they only sliced deeper into her wrists.

"Relax. I don't want you for that. Not when I have a fine wife at home." He lifted his weight, and reached for the robe. Eliza seized her opportunity. She raised her knees, praying the chain had enough slack in it, and smashed Mr. McKenzie in his groin – for the second time.

Mr. McKenzie's eyes bulged, and he doubled over. "You whore," he said, hitting her across the face.

Eliza's head snapped to the side. Bells rang inside her ears, and when someone shouted, it sounded a million miles away. The sweet taste of blood filled her mouth. She had no doubt that the Shadow would now come for her.

A firm hand grabbed her by the hair and hauled her to her feet. She tried to focus, but every item in the room separated and became two. Mr. McKenzie glared down at her, the glint of the blade he held in his hand blurred but still painfully clear.

Eliza twisted away, but Mr. McKenzie gripped her arm and held her still. "If you try anything like that again, I will kill you where you stand. Do you understand?"

Eliza spat the blood from her mouth. It hit McKenzie's shoe.

He glanced at it briefly, but made no attempt to wipe it clean. When he looked up again, pure evil filled his eyes. A small smile found his lips and he reached for the whip. He struck Eliza across the legs. "Do you understand?"

"Yes, yes," Eliza cried out. Her legs weakened, and she buckled over.

McKenzie released her. "Now, put this on." He threw the robe at her.

Eliza saw the door only metres from her. Mr. McKenzie no longer held her arm, and although struggling to see straight, she raced towards the opening.

Mr. McKenzie was quicker. He caught her by the throat and squeezed his bitten-down nails deep into her skin. Eliza coughed and spluttered, her arms pushing against his until her body weakened and she had no choice but to submit.

"Now, let's try again." Mr. McKenzie released her, and reached for the knife.

CHAPTER FORTY-SEVEN

The works of Shakespeare had never interested James Hamilton.

His father, on the other hand, had sworn by them, often throwing a quote into a conversation whenever the occasion arose. James much preferred Dickens, or the poetic words of Keats. And yet, from the thousands of books lining the shelves of his magnificent library, it was Shakespeare's *Henry V* he most revisited. Gilt lettering shone on the dark green leather spine, and a pleasurable tingle made the hairs on the back of his neck stand. This book excited him more than he cared to admit.

He gulped back the last of his whiskey and placed the crystal tumbler on the nearby desk. A quick tug on the cuffs of his robe, and he reached for the book. Careful not to scuff the top of the spine, he pulled the novel towards him. A click resonated behind the shelf, and he released the book, allowing a section of the case to swing inwards.

Inside, stone steps led down into a dark passageway. Oil lamps burned from the ceiling, lighting the tunnel until they hit a pit of darkness at the very end that wouldn't have been out of place in a Lon Chaney movie. Decades earlier, when James' father had first made this secret part of the house known to him, he'd been apprehensive to enter. Today, he could hardly contain his eagerness.

A stream of cold sea air pushed past him. Several tunnels led off in various directions, all leading down to the caves below. For centuries, smugglers and pirates had used the tunnels to unload tobacco, ale, and whatever else the ocean brought their way. Nowadays, any sightseers or tourists who thought about venturing into the caves from the beach were greeted with darkness and claustrophobic angles; their fear eventually outweighed their inquisitive minds, discouraging them from exploring any further than thirty feet.

James reached for the wood, and grinned. The final piece of the Cross. He held it in his hands. Now nothing could stop him from gaining the entry to Heaven his family had sought for over eleven centuries. He entered the cold passageway and descended the uneven path. Fungus clung to damp rock, and water dripped from the arched ceiling. Beyond the darkness, a wood-panelled door sat at the far end of the corridor, behind which his daughter awaited her fate.

Ocean air raced the tunnels, and the passage he finally chose bore the wildest gusts. The length of wood was far too long to fit the narrow hallway, so James sidestepped and pressed against the wall, his back scraping every jutted stone behind him. Away from the main tunnel, darkness beckoned. Each step led further into shadow, until the glow of light totally vanished. Now, without vision, James had no choice but to rely on memory and footwork alone. Although familiar with this route, the wet and uneven floor always proved a challenge, even with the sturdy grip of his boots. Several times he slipped, his balance only saved by the tapered and damp passageway wall. When he collided into an iron gate, it brought him to an abrupt halt.

Years before James' birth, his father had installed the gate as a security measure to block unwanted access to the house, the passageway once being the sole entrance for his great grandfather's import-export business, which consisted of drugs, guns, tobacco, alcohol, and even people on occasion. However, since his father's death over three decades ago, it had gone unused.

James propped the timber sign against the wall and shook the ache from his shoulders. The sound of the ocean rolled through the cave. There wasn't much further to go now and he knelt, fumbling for the loose rock somewhere near the bottom of the gate. He found it and wriggled it free. Tucked deep inside the hole, James found a small bundle of dry cloth. He unwrapped it, feeling the smoothness of a newly cut key that slipped inside the brand-new lock with ease.

Lifting the wood back under his arm, he continued to edge forward until he squeezed out from the cave entrance to soak up the sight above him. Only a sliver of moonlight could be seen, the green halo of the eclipse almost fully covering it. Little had been mentioned of last night's three-hour lunar eclipse, and although the green halo had experts from various news channels baffled, it had received no more than a minute or two of air time.

James continued across the beach. Sand flicked across the toes of his shoes and into his socks, the tiny slice of moonlight leaving him little time to complete what he had to do. Worn steps hidden by foliage led up to the top of the cliff, and every steep tread challenged James' calves until he finally reached the top. He stopped to catch his breath. On a sunny day, the ocean could be seen all the way to the horizon. Not tonight, though. Waves crashed against each other, each spray catapulting high into the air. Late gulls, confused by the early darkness and still searching for food, hovered for many minutes before swooping down and disappearing into the water. James tugged on the cuffs of his robe again, and re-corrected his twisted collar. Leaving the sea behind him, he headed for a dirt path tucked inside a mass of trees and foliage.

It took only minutes for the path to lead towards the crumpled ruins of St Catherine's Tower. Legend had it that centuries earlier the tower had adjoined a prominent and respected church whose sworn duty had been to protect the Cornish coastline from evil and demons. Young girls were slain in unlawful sacrifices until, in the early seventeenth century, the charred remains of its priest had been found decapitated and tied to a tree far out in the woods. Whispers soon swept the neighbouring towns that the devil himself had been at work, and townsfolk, frightened for their lives, stayed away. But years of neglect, adverse weather, and many, many wars had taken their toll. Stone by stone the church had collapsed, and what hadn't tumbled into the sea had been taken by the ground and buried.

Ivy swarmed one side of the ruin. James edged along the narrow path surrounding the tower's circumference. His arms ached, as did his legs, and the ocean view no longer held his attention. The sky grew darker by the second, shadows nearly eclipsing the moon. In less than twenty minutes, he knew there would be no moon left to see. Only one entrance, a stone arch, accessed the inside of the tower. Undergrowth and weeds grew from cracks in the deteriorated frame, and tree roots pushed up through the earth and ran in bas-relief patterns on the forest floor. The uneven ground made it hard to navigate, and several times James stubbed his toe and tripped. Yet, he clung to the lump of old wood.

Inside, the tower roof had long since gone and, as outside, wildflowers and moss grew from stone walls. The previous night's rainfall still muddied the ground and, lying in the centre of the area, three wooden beams created what was soon to be the most perfect Cross history had ever known: the True Cross.

James stepped forward, his boots sinking in the sludge of previously left footprints. Excitement fluttered inside his stomach, and he smiled. The surge of exhilaration he felt was better than any sex he'd ever known, and he eagerly lowered the wood towards the top-end of the post. As it had with the wooden beams he'd assembled before it, the nearer the two items came together, the stronger an invisible force fought to keep them apart. James took a deep breath and pressed down harder, fighting to feel timber against timber. Mud seeped across his sinking boots, and he pulled them free to gain a better grip. He tightened his hold around the wood, grit his teeth, and let out a yell of frustration.

Only centimetres separated the wood, and James waited for the invisible force to switch movement and wrench the sign from his grip. As with the timber before it, it did just that, and a rapid flash of white light filled the small tower, the intense brightness blinding. James turned away and shielded his eyes. Tears rolled down his cheeks and he quickly wiped them away. When he finally opened his eyes again, the glare had died and his vision had blurred. For several seconds, the purest darkness known to man surrounded him. He blinked repeatedly until his spotted vision faded and gradually, stone by stone, familiarity surrounded him again. He wiped the last of the tears away. Scratches covered his palms, splinters embedded deep in his skin. He ignored all of it, his attention back on the wooden monument lying on the ground. The True Cross in its entirety, as it had been centuries ago.

Wind whistled in through a small hole in the wall, which had once served as a window, and James paused as the air cooled his clammy body. He was so close to achieving what his ancestors before him had failed to do.

He exited the tower. The eclipsed moon offered hardly any light, and he was barely able to make out the pathway back towards the steps. When he did, their treacherousness inspired little confidence that he would actually reach the bottom in one piece. The ocean rolled onto the sand below, the waves lapping over the last few rocks and washing away all traces of sand and mud from his boots. The higher tide soaked his trousers and splashed onto his robe, but he waded through until his feet found dry sand again. Within minutes he was back inside the cave, feeling his way through the dark until he saw the glow of flames flickering warm shadows in the passageway. With every piece now attached, the power of the True Cross would be at its strongest, with all seven supernatural acts mentioned in the Bible attacking together.

Only Eliza had her part left to play.

CHAPTER FORTY-EIGHT

Billy stared at the man standing in the doorway.

The man stared back: average build, average height...and completely naked with a postmortem 'Y' stitched into his chest. When he finally moved, it was slow and uncoordinated. Billy charged towards him and hammered a kick into his abdomen. The dead man stumbled backwards and fell onto the concrete path outside. Behind him, more bodies crowded the car park. They turned towards Billy and stumbled drunkenly forward. The dead man rose from the floor to join the gathering group, and Billy slammed the door and reached for the lock.

Zombies swarmed the station's entrance, banging against the doors with heavy fists. The glass rattled and vibrated under the attack and the door jerked inwards, causing the bolt to miss its latch. Billy pushed back, his shoulder wedged against the frame, and forced the door shut again. His shoes slipped across the linoleum, and he struggled to regain a grip as the weight of several bodies proved more than he could handle.

Finally, the door closed and he bolted the top lock. Hands thumped the glass, and the higher of the door's two windows cracked. Billy stepped back and swiped the Asp from the counter, reaffixing a sweaty grip around its handle. A decomposing hand punched through the already weakened window. Broken glass severed the corpse's right index finger, and it fell to the floor inches from Billy's shoes. Billy jumped back, the mere sight of it making him want to hurl, and kicked it against the skirting boards. Further glass shattered and broke free from the main entrance. Billy covered his face and turned towards the security window, pounding the Asp against the reinforced glass like a man possessed. Dead bodies reached through towards him, and Billy realised he was cornered.

His pulse raced. His hands shook. "George! Get your arse out here."

The lower window smashed. For a moment, the internal chicken-wire enforcement held strong, preventing the glass from falling free, but an onslaught of swipes and kicks from the corpses soon popped it from the frame. Further limbs reached in, and a hundred dead fingers stretched to grab their prey.

"George." Quick breaths dried Billy's mouth. He tried to swallow but his tongue stuck to the ridge.

From the cells, a shadow danced in the doorway light. Billy halted and stilled, too nervous to breathe, and prayed these things hadn't already gotten inside.

The shadow neared the doorway. To Billy's relief, George appeared, rubbing his stomach and not noticing a button had popped from his shirt.

A quick glance to Heaven to thank God, and Billy banged on the security partition to gain his sergeant's attention.

George looked up and frowned when he saw Billy. "Where in the hell have you been? I've been calling—" He stopped the moment he saw the disfigured arms reaching in through the main door.

"What the...?"

"Never mind that, just get this door open."

"I can't." George hurried to the counter and pressed the door release. It buzzed, but the door didn't budge. "The quake must have shorted something out. It won't open."

"Shit." Billy turned back to the zombies. "They're coming in. What do I do?"

"Try kicking the door in"

"This door's made not to be broken into."

"What's the alternative?"

George was right. Billy was cornered, and the front door didn't look like it would hold out much longer. He twisted the handle one last time in the hope the release had worked. The brass knob rattled under his grip, but the door didn't open and Billy punched it in frustration.

"Okay, stand back," he said to George, who promptly backed away.

Billy held either side of the doorframe, and kicked. The heel of his boot connected just right of the door handle, causing tiny wooden fragments to ping free. The door shuddered, but its refusal to open enraged Billy further. He planted a second kick. Then a third, and a fourth, each strike hammering harder and faster than the last, until they resembled nothing but frenzied movement. He heard the wood pulse and crack, until it finally splintered from the frame and burst open.

Billy hurried inside, slamming the door shut behind him, and raced to the metal filing cabinet. "Quick, help me move this."

George did as he was told, his bulk squashing against the cabinet when he leaned in and pushed. Papers and files weighed down every drawer, and the cabinet screeched across the linoleum floor. The noise seemed to heighten the zombies' desire to get through the door even more.

When the filing cabinet finally blocked the doorway, Billy stood back, wiped his brow, and took a deep breath. "That should hold them off."

"Hold what off? What in the hell are those things?"

"I think they are dead people."

"Dead people. Like at the hospital?" George's eyes widened. He looked around the office. "And how the hell are we supposed to get out?"

Behind Billy, the main door burst apart and several zombies pushed and stumbled into the waiting room. "Well, it sure ain't gonna be that way."

Billy ran his fingers through his hair and searched around the office. It had not fared well against the quake: paperwork littered the floor; chairs lay overturned. The toppled water cooler swam in a puddle of its own liquid.

Then it hit him. "Where's Eliza?"

George froze for a second. His shoulders tightened, and he averted Billy's gaze. "She's gone."

"Gone? Gone where?"

"I went to the toilet. When I came back she was gone."

"You gotta be kidding me. George, she'll die out there on her own. What's the matter with you?"

"Hey, remember who you're talking too." George straightened his uniform, no longer looking away. "I am your sergeant."

"I don't give a rat's arse about rank at the moment. You should have stopped her."

"How? Tie her to the chair?"

Billy pulled open his desk drawer and rummaged through the mess inside. When he couldn't find the keys he wanted, he slammed the drawer shut and pulled out a lower one.

"Shit!" He glanced towards George. Police headquarters had supplied the station with a little electric car a few months back. Apart from moving it round to the back of the station so nobody could see it, the thing had never been used. Billy argued it was so slow it would be quicker to walk. George couldn't even squeeze behind the steering wheel, and nineteen-year-old Eddie the probationer said he wouldn't be seen dead in it. "Where're the keys to the hybrid?"

"We still got that thing?"

"There." Billy spied them hooked on the key rack.

"Will it even work?" George asked.

"Should do. It's been on charge for ten weeks." Billy grabbed Eddie's belt from the back of his chair.

"What're you doing with that?"

Billy removed the Taser and Asp, and slid them into his own holster. Then he grabbed a radio from its dock and hurried to the back door. "I'll be on this. Grab every weapon we have in here."

"Where are you going?" George followed.

Billy hit the security bar and pushed the door open. Outside, the living dead trudged the car park. In the far corner, the little hybrid nestled in bay two.

George came up behind him. "Holy crap."

Two zombies stopped and glanced towards them. They groaned, causing two other monsters to look up.

"Shit." Billy pushed George back inside the station and closed the door.

"What in the hell are they?" George asked.

"I already told you."

"The dead don't come back to life."

"Well, tonight it seems they do." Billy sidestepped him and ran back into the main office. "We need to get to that hybrid."

"How are you going to do that? Those things are everywhere."

The filing cabinet inched forward, and the main security door edged open. Billy drew his Taser and backed away.

"What're you going to do with that?" George said.

"If they come through that door..." Billy never finished his sentence. He heard George mutter a short prayer and unbutton the clip on his belt.

"George," Billy glanced over his shoulder. Sweat dripped from George's forehead; dark patches stained the shirt around his armpits. "Aim for the head."

"What?"

Billy shrugged. "It works in the films."

"You think these are zombies?"

Billy didn't answer. He turned back towards the door and saw a grey, vein-covered arm reach through and push the filing cabinet out of the way. It toppled over, drawers sliding open and sending papers scattering across the floor. The security door jutted open, and a female zombie – similar in looks to Billy's old history teacher – squeezed through. Billy fired the Taser, and the dart hit the centre of her forehead. Her arms stiffened, and her body shook for a full minute while the voltage paralysed her. She fell to her knees, still no expression in her eyes, and remained there until the electric current ceased and she collapsed face down on the floor. He'd hated the old crone back in school.

"Make it count, George." Billy replaced the charge and aimed towards the door.

A second zombie, this time an older man, climbed in. George stepped forward, the Taser unsteady in his hands. He fired. The dart embedded in the zombie's cheekbone, the high voltage shaking the man more vigorously than the woman before him. His jaw fell free and swung from the left side of his face.

"His head, George," Billy said.

"I did hit his head."

Billy motioned towards his own forehead. "Don't you watch zombie films? Hit the brain."

"You mean that crap actually works?"

Honestly? Billy had no idea whether it worked or not. All he knew was that when the voltage from George's Taser stopped flowing, the dead man came for them again. Billy fired, hitting him right between the eyes. Like the woman, the zombie fell to his knees. He shook for a moment, and then collapsed in a heap. Another zombie edged through the gap. George reloaded and fired. The projectile hit its head, and like the two before him, he dropped to the floor.

"At least we know this works," Billy said, reloading.

"Yeah, but we don't have many charges."

"How many we got?"

George took two charges from his drawer and put them on the desk.

"Is that it?"

"We used all the others pissing about out back, remember?"

Two more zombies climbed through the door and clambered over the cabinet.

"Best save them, then." Billy holstered his Taser. He grabbed his Asp, extended it with a swift flick, and charged. Just like he would when teeing off with his three-iron, he belted the head of the nearest zombie. He heard the skull crack, and the dead man fell to the floor. Billy turned to the second zombie, and just like the first time, he whacked the Asp towards the head.

"We need to get this door barricaded again." Billy grabbed the side of the filing cabinet, and George hurried to help him. "And that desk. Slide it in front."

The table legs ground and juddered across the floor, the rubber pads leaving four perfectly straight black lines. "Hopefully that'll hold them off long enough."

"Long enough for what?" George was sweating like a pig.

Billy glanced at the window. Outside, the station entrance was awash with the walking dead. "We need to cause a distraction, something loud. Draw everything to that area."

"Then what?"

"Then we leg it out back to the hybrid."

"You still going with that plan?"

"It's the only one I got."

"It's suicide."

"So is staying here. That door isn't going to hold them back for long. What're you going to do when they get in here?"

George chewed on his lower lip. "What do you have in mind?"

"Those rolls of firecrackers you confiscated from the Webster boys last week. Where'd you put them?"

"Bottom drawer of my desk. Why?"

Billy pulled open the drawer and there they were – a whole bag of them. He held them up to George, and smiled. "Because these are going to be our distraction."

George didn't look happy. "Why don't we just lock ourselves in the cells and wait for help to arrive?"

"What help? These things are everywhere."

"But they won't get in the cells."

"They will get in, and then you'll die."

"Arnold Schwarzenegger himself couldn't get in those cells without a key."

"And what if help never comes? How long do you think you'll survive in there without food and water?"

"A damn sight longer than I will out there."

Billy stopped talking. Nerves had gotten the better of the sergeant, and who could blame him? George's shoulders sagged in defeat. "Okay. Let's light these things and get the hell out of here."

Billy pushed a coat stand out of his way, retrieved his lighter, and opened the window. He lit a couple of fireworks and threw them as far as he could. Small flames fizzed from the wick, and then a succession of loud cracks and pops echoed through the air. The zombies turned from the station entrance and shuffled towards it. Billy lit another, dropped it in the bag, and threw the lot outside. The noise roared, and he was sure the zombies out back would have heard. He closed the window and hurried towards the back door, with George following close behind. "Right. You ready?"

George nodded, but it was obvious he wasn't ready. He, like Billy, was scared to death.

Billy opened the door. Zombies trudged towards the far end of the building, the sound of firecrackers much louder than he could have ever hoped. He glanced at George and nodded the all-clear, and quietly stepped out.

The hybrid sat in the far corner of the yard, partly covered by overgrown brambles the council had promised to cut back months ago but as yet hadn't. "Okay, c'mon."

"You sure it's safe?"

"Yes, I'm—"

A corpse stepped out from behind the open door, mouth snarling, saliva frothing from the corners of its lips. It grabbed Billy's shoulder and pulled him closer, dead eyes filled with bloodthirsty hunger.

George edged away, stumbling over the step. He scrambled back inside the station and slammed the door shut, leaving Billy outside to fend for himself.

"George!"

But George was gone.

Billy jerked his shoulder free, but the zombie's bony fingers clasped tighter around his shirt. He pulled and struggled, but the monster refused to release him. His uniform ripped at the seam, exposing his bare shoulder, and the zombie surged forward with lips parted and ready to bite. Billy rammed his Taser against the side of the dead man's head, and fifty thousand volts of electricity pummelled into the zombie's ear canal. Smoke poured from its nasal cavity, and for ten seconds the monster convulsed. Finally, it slumped to the floor, knocking over a dustbin as it fell. Rubbish spewed across the tarmac, and the lid rolled a good ten metres until it collided into the side of the station. Several zombies looked back at the clatter, and saw Billy. In unison, they turned and began to shuffle their way back. Billy fumbled to reload the Taser, but he was out of charges. He threw the useless gun at the nearing crowd, a pathetic attempt to halt them, and raced for the station's back door. "George, open the damn door."

The zombies closed in on him.

"George, open this fucking door."

But George never appeared.

"George! George!" Billy whacked his fists against cold metal until his palms bruised.

Behind him, the dead lumbered nearer. He turned, his back pressed against the door, his path to the hybrid now blocked. He gripped the Asp, ready to swing at anything that came within a metre of touching him, and stepped forward. The direct route across the yard looked to be his best chance at reaching the little car alive. Three further steps and he swung at the first zombie, breaking its neck, but unsuccessful in killing it. Billy swung again, and this time the zombie's skull cracked open like a broken egg. Two more steps and

Billy whacked a second head, this time the single strike putting the zombie down. A third head, and a fourth. More zombies surrounded him, and for every one he killed, three more closed in. One reached for his hair, and Billy drilled the Asp into its eye socket. The zombie stilled almost instantaneously, and only dropped to the floor after Billy pulled the baton free. Congealed blood dripped from the Asp, but Billy continued to swing and smash it into every skull that crossed his path. A zombie clawed at his arm, another at his leg. Billy whipped the Asp around and stabbed it down through the body at his feet.

Billy was losing this battle.

CHAPTER FORTY-NINE

The clamps chafed Eliza's ankles, and the short chain connecting them only allowed her to take small and unsteady steps.

"Faster." Mr. McKenzie took a torch from its holder and nudged Eliza towards a narrow passageway.

"I can't. The chains..."

Mr. McKenzie tutted. He pulled a key from his trouser pocket and bent down. "If you try and run, I will cripple you. Do you understand?"

Eliza nodded. She heard McKenzie curse as he tried to get the key in the lock, and then the shackles around her feet were gone.

McKenzie stood in front of her. "Remember what I said, girl. Now walk."

The beginning of the tunnel glowed under the flickering light, causing the stone walls to dance before her eyes. Eliza shook her head and tried to clear her vision, but whatever her father had drugged her with had numbed her senses and showed little sign of wearing off. The stone walls soon disappeared into a pit of darkness, but Mr. McKenzie's footsteps still echoed behind her.

A sea breeze howled through the gangway like a tiny tornado, and Eliza pushed her hair from her face. Another wave of nausea swept over her and she stopped, reaching for the wall for support.

"What's wrong?" Mr. McKenzie said.

"I feel sick. What did my father make me drink?"

Mr. McKenzie chuckled. "Just something to stop you using that mind magic on us. Now keep moving."

One narrow corridor after another, until the sound of the ocean echoed around her and the hard rock beneath her feet softened. Had she reached Readymoney Cove? Her feet sank into the wet sand and she stumbled, her tortured body too numb to hold her up any longer. She fell forward, and her face hit the sand with a hard slap.

"Oh no you don't. We're nearly there."

Not far from where Eliza lay, she heard the waves roll across the shore. She tried to focus, but her hampered vision was no match for the dark evening.

"Come on. I said get up. I ain't carrying you."

"I can't." Eliza grabbed a handful of sand.

Mr. McKenzie hooked his arms around her waist and winched up her limp body. Eliza didn't fight him, not even when she noticed a darkness blacker than the night itself swelling behind him. Then, alongside it, another Shadow grew. Eliza froze. The Shadow had found her. She opened her mouth to scream a warning, then realised the Shadow's timing could not have been more perfect. She felt the sand slipping between her fingers, and sprayed it out like a fan across Mr. McKenzie face. He cursed, his hands coming to his face. This was Eliza's chance. Around her, the all-too-familiar objects morphed into one Shadow.

Eliza shook her head, trying to clear her thoughts, and then ran as fast as she could.

CHAPTER FIFTY

Teeth chomped towards Billy's arm.

Another mouth swooped down upon his neck.

Billy twisted his upper body, elbowing the zombie away from his collar before turning on the second one. He wrapped his bicep around its neck, locked his arm, and squeezed. To his surprise, the corpse's head popped clean off its shoulders.

Two more carcasses attacked from the front. Billy turned to run, but three more blocked his retreat. Billy skidded to a stop, his police shoes sliding on the gravel. He swallowed and tried to catch his breath. With five against one, he was clearly outnumbered. Still, he raised his Asp and readied himself to fight.

Holding position, he waited for the monsters to shuffle in a little closer and circle him. Then he spun on his heel, and whirled the Asp. It breezed past the first two zombies, and narrowly missed the third by inches. It never reached the fourth. Instead, it collided straight into the palm of a hand and stopped dead.

Billy glanced up at the person standing before him. Timberlands and baseball cap, just as he had seen at Eliza's house. He took a breath, and swallowed. "Roman?"

Roman released the Asp. "Behind you."

Billy turned, but Roman moved quicker. His fist demolished the first skull, and penetrated the second as though he were punching through paper. Without looking, he swung back, pushed Billy to one side, and ripped the head off a third zombie. He wiped the goo from his hand and turned back to Billy. "You'll have to move quicker than that if you want to stay alive."

"Where the hell'd you come from?"

"Let's leave the explanations until later, shall we?"

Blood trickled from Billy's shoulder, and suddenly he had a new focus. "Shit. They've bit me. I've been fucking bitten."

"You'll live."

"But I've been bitten."

Roman looked him in the eye. "And you will live. They are the un-dead. That's all."

Billy straightened. The Asp felt heavy in his hand, and he tightened his grip. "Who the hell are you?"

But something behind Billy now held Roman's attention.

Billy turned. In the centre of the car park, through the darkness of night, a Shadow rose from the ground. "What now?"

"Do you have a way out of here?"

Billy pulled the car keys from his pocket and nodded towards the hybrid.

"Good. Then go."

"But my sergeant is still inside."

"With Eliza?"

"What? No. Eliza's gone."

"Gone? Shit." Roman stared at the Shadow, then towards the hybrid. "Get to the car."

"But George..."

"You go back in there after him, you will die."

Billy didn't move, and it was Roman who forced him towards the car. Billy squeezed behind the steering wheel, watching the Shadow grow to well over six feet. "What the hell is that thing?"

Roman opened the passenger door and jumped in beside him. "It's come for Eliza. She must be here."

"George said she left."

"Then it doesn't make sense."

The Shadow engulfed the little hybrid, cutting them off from the rest of the car park. The vehicle rocked side to side, and the back window smashed in.

"Jesus Christ, do something."

Billy turned the key and the engine sparked to life.

The Shadow swept into the car and the back seat darkened. Slowly, the view in the rear-view mirror disappeared from Billy's sight and the darkness surrounded him, wrapping round his neck and squeezing his throat so tight that he felt the blood vessels in his eyes bulge. The Shadow tried to pull him over the driver's seat, but Billy grasped hold of the steering wheel. The pressure around his neck intensified, and his grip slipped from the wheel. Then, the Shadow was inside his mouth. Billy thrashed, his body arching towards the ceiling. He heard Roman shout something about having Eliza's blood on his clothes, and then felt his police shirt being ripped from his body. The Shadow retreated from his mouth, and the hold around his throat loosened. Billy slumped back into the seat, coughing and spluttering, his hands at his throat, trying to massage some air back into his lungs. He whipped around to check the back of the car, but the Shadow was gone, and outside Roman was charging across the car park at top speed, tossing the shirt as far as he could throw it. The Shadow followed it, pouncing where the garment landed.

Roman raced back towards the car. "Drive!"

Billy did.

CHAPTER FIFTY-ONE

Pain arched throughout Eliza's body as she fled Mr. McKenzie and the Shadow.

The soft sand crumbled beneath her weight, making each hampered step more difficult than the last. She felt the surf splash across her bare feet and soak the hem of the gown. Waves crashed against her legs, their coldness disorienting her further. Behind, the irate voice of Mr. McKenzie yelled her name. Eliza glanced over her shoulder, but darkness eclipsed the beach, just as it had the sun. She couldn't see the Shadow, but she knew it was there...somewhere, ready to attack.

Freezing water rose higher around her legs the further in she waded. Past her ankles, around her calves. Waves lapped her knees, her thighs, around her waist. She had no idea where she was going, or how the hell she intended to get to dry land again.

Something clenched her ankle, hard and tight, and before she could stop it, a fearful cry left her throat.

She tugged her leg in a bid to free it, but the clasp tightened and pulled her beneath the ocean surface. Salt water flooded her mouth and nostrils and she coughed, swallowing more water. Her flailing arms reached the surface again, and the night air hit her face just long enough to allow for a single gasp for breath before the ocean pulled her under once more. Water stung her eyes, and pockets of air escaped her lips until her lungs emptied. She kicked, but her robe entwined her legs like ivy, its heavy material weighing her down and making her fight for oxygen that much harder.

The grasp around her ankle tightened. Desperate, Eliza kicked again, clawing for the surface until she was released. Then, cold air hit her skin. The ocean mist rolled into her ears and up her nose. She spluttered, treading water as best she could, allowing the waves to carry her to shore until she felt the sandy bed beneath her feet once again. She hovered for a while, the water sloshing just beneath her jawline, and coughed the remainder of the sea from her throat.

"Eliza." Mr. McKenzie called her name like a father would his child. "I can hear you out there, girl."

Mr. McKenzie was on the beach; if she could see him, maybe he could see her. Her fate boiled down to one thing: How did she want to die? She waited, too frightened to move, and yet aware that something, probably the Shadow, was in the water waiting to drown her.

"Eliza?" Mr. McKenzie called again.

Eliza contemplated her dilemma. If she continued to shore, the promise of further torture and eventual death awaited her at the hands of her father. But if she stayed put, then what? Something below the water had already attacked her. Eliza ducked lower, the water bobbing under the tip of her nose. A wave rolled in behind her and broke, engulfing her entire body. Her head disappeared beneath the water, and again the sea attempted to take her. The wave passed, and Eliza found the surface again. But gone was the evening freshness she'd breathed before. Now, a decayed stench filled her nostrils. She coughed the last of the salty water from her throat, and parted her wet hair.

Something moved on the surface beside her, and the rancid smell grew stronger. Eliza rubbed the water from her eyes. Whatever it was, it didn't look like the Shadow. She backed away, the tips of her toes struggling to keep contact with the seabed. The shape followed her, pale and gaunt, until a man looked her in the eye.

He lifted out of the water, a shredded shirt hanging from his shoulders, a faded skull and crossbones evident on his upper arm, and stopped in front of her. One side of his face had been eaten away by the inhabitants of the sea, the remaining skin whiter than snow itself. Seaweed tangled his black hair, and a small crab scampered from the socket of his missing eye and fell onto his shoulder.

The zombie pirate moved closer.

Eliza waded back.

He reached for her.

She ducked his hand.

Beneath the water, something different reclaimed their hold around her ankles. Eliza screamed, but the pirate's bony fingers grabbed her face, cutting short her cry for help. His skeleton teeth chomped towards her while, below the water, something clawed up her body and bit into her thigh. Eliza screamed and water flooded her mouth, washing to the back of her throat. Her body jerked in response, and like a frenzied dog she fought for the surface. Salty water flooded her lungs. Her chest tightened. Weightlessness took over, and other than the rabid jerks from the zombie pirates clinging to her, she felt peace.

Then cold.

CHAPTER FIFTY-TWO

Headlights lit up the road like a flare brightening a stormy night.

Mile after mile, the hybrid police car navigated the chasms and raced through the tunnel of trees, leaving their ashen trunks to disappear into the darkened forest.

"Anything out there?"

Roman shook his head. But then again, with the speed the cop drove, he'd be lucky to see anything that wasn't a blur. He reckoned another half mile until they'd hit the main road and open fields – then he'd be able to see more clearly. That's when he'd make the cop pull over.

"You sure?"

"I'm sure." He wasn't.

Billy punched his foot on the brake. Tyres screeched, and the car skidded to a halt in the middle of the road.

A little premature for Roman's liking. "Is something wrong?"

Engine still running, Billy twisted to face him. "What in hell was all that back there?"

Roman sighed. "What bit?"

"What bit? Dead people were trying to eat me. A bloody Shadow tried to choke me. I want to know what the hell is going on!"

Roman sighed for a second time. He had neither the time nor the inclination to explain this whole story again. He turned to the window. Outside, tree tops swayed, the storm not letting up.

"Hey, I'm talking to you."

Roman turned and gave what he considered one of his more hardened glares.

Billy whacked the steering wheel, and saliva spat from his mouth when he spoke. He didn't seem put off. "What the fuck is happening?"

The cop was beginning to irritate Roman. If it wasn't for the want of needing a car... "It's all because of your sister."

"Eliza? Why?"

"Look, I don't have time—"

"Tell me, goddamn it."

Roman scanned the area outside. Still no sign of trouble. "She's to be sacrificed."

"She already told me that shit. It didn't wash with me then, and it doesn't wash with me now."

"And that's the attitude that will get her killed." Roman looked at Billy. "She's to be crucified."

"Why? Who by?"

"That old guy who works for your father."

"Davis? He's like a hundred and ten."

"Yeah, well, it seems he wants to live a little bit longer."

"You're wrong. He practically raised Eliza. She's like a daughter to him."

"Believe it, don't believe it. I don't care. He's going to kill her."

"By sacrificing her? You're insane."

"Maybe. But it's the truth."

"I don't even know why I'm having this conversation with you." Billy pushed the stick into first gear. "I'm taking you over to Liskeard. You can spend the night in their cells while I go look for her on my own."

"Hey." Roman slammed the gear back into neutral, and the engine stalled. "You know what you've seen tonight, right? That ain't shit I made up. That Shadow? That's been sent to kill your sister before the old man can get to her. And why? Because the old man's managed to gather all four pieces of the True Cross, and now he's re-creating the Crucifixion. Eliza's blood is going to open the Gateway to Heaven. The Shadow needs to stop that from happening."

"By killing Eliza?"

Roman clenched his jaw.

"So what are the dead people trying to do? Hitch a ride up?'

"Now you're beginning to annoy me." Roman forced his building anger to calm. "Every time the old man puts a piece of the Cross together, history starts to repeat itself."

"You're referring to the Crucifixion?"

"You've seen the moon, the storms, the quake. The dead are just another duplicated event." Roman removed his hand from the gearstick. "You want to help Eliza? Then we need to stop the old man."

Billy stared at him. Behind his eyes, Roman saw the cogs turn as he digested the information. "Is this happening everywhere?"

Roman shook his head. "Just within a certain distance of Eliza."

"So you know where she is?"

Roman glanced out the side window again. Still no sign of zombies or the Shadow, but he didn't want to stay put for too long. "I wouldn't be *here* if I knew where she was."

Billy glared at him. "Who the hell are you?"

"Does it matter?"

Billy's eyes widened, and Roman watched his hands tighten around the steering wheel. The cop's next words came through taut lips. "What's your involvement in all this? What's in it for you?"

"Who said I'm involved?"

"You kidnapped Eliza."

"Kidnapped is a little strong."

"I know you're involved."

"This conversation is tiresome." Roman cast another quick glance at the forest outside. "Are you going to drive?"

"Answer my goddamn question."

Roman took a deep breath. It occurred to him to ditch Billy and steal the car. It wouldn't be that hard, after all. But he needed the cop. Brother or no brother, when the time came he may need a diversion – that was, if he ever found Eliza. "I'm trying to save her."

CHAPTER FIFTY-THREE

Water spurted from Eliza's mouth.

She opened her eyes. Above her, nothing but a dark, starless sky. The cool night swept across her wet body and involuntary spasms took hold, but all she could do was lie there and shiver.

The imposing bulk of Mr. McKenzie leaned over her, blocking the moon from her view. Water dripped from his drenched hair and splashed onto her face. "You stupid little brat."

"Where's the Shadow?"

"Around. It can't find you now."

"Why?"

"You're freezing cold... So is your blood." He hoisted her off the sand and threw her over his shoulder. One arm locked around her thigh, and Eliza hung there, her hands brushing against his arse as he walked.

Half a dozen mutilated corpses littered the sand behind them, their heads smashed in, similar to that of

Jason Devlin in the hospital morgue. Eliza remembered them biting her legs, but either due to shock or the fact she was freezing to death, she could feel nothing anymore. Waves rolled across the sand and filled her captor's footprints before washing back out to sea, and the strangest thought struck her that on any other day, it would be a beautiful thing to watch. But not tonight. Tonight, she was being taken to her death. She felt Mr. McKenzie's arm disappear from around her thighs, and his shoulder tensed as he pulled himself up a step. Eliza's body slipped off his shoulder, but Mr. McKenzie grabbed her waist and secured her back against his neck.

Step by step, he carried her up the carved stone stairway. Below, the sand drifted further away until the distance made her head spin. Again, Eliza's body started to slide off Mr. McKenzie's shoulder. There was nothing but the dead of night and a whopping long drop below her, and she grabbed the leather belt securing his trousers, closed her eyes, and hung on for dear life.

"You can walk from here," Mr. McKenzie said when they reached the top.

Eliza's feet touched the ground. Blood rushed from her head, and for a second she felt even more lightheaded than when in the tunnels.

"Careful." Mr. McKenzie pulled her away from the cliff edge. "Now go that way. Towards the light."

Eliza glanced up. Through spotted vision she saw a flickering glow in the darkness some distance away. This was it.

Loose gravel replaced dirt and mud, and she slipped several times. The light grew nearer and the pathway narrowed, the overgrown foliage eventually thinning out to unveil an old, rusty handrail. Three stone steps led up towards a crumbling archway, and Eliza stopped. She glanced up at the ruins of the derelict tower, a place where she'd played with Billy as a child. So this was where she was going to die?

Beneath her wet robe, she felt trickles of blood start to flow from her thigh.

"Keep moving," Mr. McKenzie said, shoving her into a circular room, each quarter lit by a torch flame.

A timber frame shaped like a cross lay in the centre of the floor, a small sign written in Latin nailed to the top of it. Behind it, two men she didn't recognise hung from wooden poles. Light glowed across their dirt-smeared skin and unwashed hair. The nearest one glanced up, clearly struggling to focus, and unsure of his surroundings. Horror filled his eyes when he spotted Eliza.

A man stepped into the doorway, the flicker of light behind him silhouetting his shape perfectly. Even donned in the long cloak and hood, Eliza could still tell it was her father.

"Where the hell have you been?" James asked Mr. McKenzie.

"She—"

"Never mind. We don't have long." He rubbed his hands together like an excited child on Christmas morning. "Get that robe off her, and turn her around."

He picked up the leather whip he'd used on her earlier, but Mr. McKenzie interjected. "I don't think you should do that anymore."

"Oh? And why would that be?"

"The blood, her blood." Mr. McKenzie glanced around. "I thought the Shadow was a myth..."

"What Shadow?"

"From God."

"What are you talking about? I've never heard of this entity."

"Most haven't, but it came looking for her. Down on the beach—"

A darkened shape crawled from the edges of the tower and crept across the floor.

Mr. McKenzie noticed. "It's here," he said, releasing Eliza and grabbing a torch from the wall.

James backed away towards the door. "What does it want?"

"To kill your daughter, and stop you from opening the Gateway."

"Can you stop it?"

Mr. McKenzie smiled. "Aye, that I can."

The Shadow rolled to the middle of the room, where it swelled to a size much larger than the one Eliza had seen in her house. She closed her eyes, accepting her fate. With her senses dulled, she had no chance of beating it, just as Mr. McKenzie had no chance of beating it. At least the Shadow would kill her much more quickly than her father.

Mr. McKenzie stepped forward, the torch held at arm's length in front of him until it hovered inches from the dark mist. Taking a deep breath, he took one last step forward and waved the flame through the Shadow like a child writing his name with a sparkler. The amber fire zigzagged its way left and right. To Eliza's astonishment, the Shadow caught fire, glowing embers fizzling and crackling like lit gunpowder until all that was left was a mass of ash floating in the air.

He'd killed the Shadow? As easy as that?

"Is it dead?" James called from the stone archway.

"Yes." McKenzie glanced up at the sky. "One thing Heaven and its inhabitants up there can't stand, and that's Hell's fire."

James entered the room, the whip heavy in his hand and ready to use again. "How did you learn that?"

Mr. McKenzie dropped the torch and untied Eliza's hands. "Everything has an answer. You just need to know where to look for it." He pulled the belt free from her waist and the wet robe fell around Eliza's feet, leaving her standing in nothing but her soaked and sand-covered underwear.

Immediately, Eliza edged away from her father.

James smiled at her. "Now, where were we? Oh yes." He raised the whip.

"No, please. You're my father..."

James lashed the whip, striking Eliza across the thighs and hacking through her flesh like a garden strimmer. She cried out, clasping the severed flesh, and hardly noticing Mr. McKenzie spin her around until the second lash cracked across her shoulder blades. Eliza wanted to fight her neighbour's hold, but all she could do was scream in pain. The third lash landed across the base of her spine and she collapsed to her knees, begging for mercy, praying unconsciousness would come for her. Another lash against her skin jarred her back to full consciousness in an explosion of agony. She fell completely to the floor. Her eyes closed, and her senses dulled again.

Another strike. Another agonising eruption. Her eyes shot open. A blurred glance at the blood-splattered dirt around her, and then darkness once more. The pain slipped from her mind, and in the distance she heard a voice shout for her to wake. The Shadow was supposed to have killed her. She'd wanted it to kill her. But instead, it had been defeated – and so easily, at that.

A fiery irritation burst into her nasal cavity. Her eyes opened and her lungs hastened, pumping out breath after rapid breath. She flinched away from the smell, but a hand clamped the back of her head and the rancid odour found her again. Mr. McKenzie leered down at her. In his hand, he held a small bottle. He stuck it under her nose again, and the pungent aroma attacked her nostrils like acid. Eliza tried to knock the bottle away, but Mr. McKenzie laughed and shoved it closer.

Eliza gagged. Her arms flailed. Her heartbeat raced, and images of Mr. McKenzie flying back away from her and smashing against the far wall raced through her mind.

"Get her to the Cross," James said.

Mr. McKenzie dragged Eliza to her feet.

Then the movie reel inside Eliza's head came to life, just as it had every other time before. Mr. McKenzie catapulted away from her. Not as vigorously as she'd visualised – he didn't even reach the wall, falling short by three or four metres.

Surprise marred his expression, and he leapt to his feet. "The ammonia's aroused her senses."

"Then force some more drugs down her throat before she's time to do any more damage."

Mr. McKenzie grabbed Eliza by the arms and dragged her across the dirt. Eliza screamed, imagining a torch flame hoisting from its iron holder and hurling towards her father.

It did just that. James saw it coming, and ducked. The torch crashed into the wall behind him and landed on the floor, the flame extinguishing in the dirt.

"Hurry, she's getting stronger," James said.

Mr. McKenzie slammed Eliza down on to the wooden frame and pinned her. Eliza writhed beneath his body weight, then visualised the whip wrapping his neck and tightening until every blood vessel in his face burst. The whip floated from the floor as if on invisible wires. It coiled Mr. McKenzie's neck, who promptly released Eliza and tried to loosen it.

"Don't release her," James said. "Hold her."

Mr. McKenzie grabbed Eliza again. His face reddened and his eyes bulged. Slight breaths wheezed from his throat as the whip continued to strangle him, but he didn't release his hold on her. James stepped into view, the water bottle in his hand. Eliza glanced around, looking for anything to knock him off balance, but he already had his hand clenched around her jaw. She tried to shake free, but his grip only tightened, and she felt the open bottle forced between her lips. Water swirled across her tongue and around her mouth, but as quickly as it entered, she spat it out, spraying her father's face. His nostrils flared, and he tightened his grip, pressing his fingers into the hollows of her cheeks. Her lips parted, and more water sloshed into her mouth, this time slipping straight to the back of her throat. Eliza gagged and tried to straighten her head, but her father held on even tighter. More water entered, and then the bottle disappeared and her father's empty hand pressed down and covered her mouth. Mr. McKenzie's grip loosened, and Eliza broke free, clawing at her father's fingers. Water filled her mouth, and she struggled to keep it from slipping down her throat. She reached out and scratched at her father's face, her nails drawing blood. But her father fought her attack and pinched her nostrils shut.

"Now swallow before I'm really forced to hurt you." He pressed her lips harder together.

Eliza couldn't breathe. She gagged and reached out again, pressing against her father's chest, trying to push him away from her.

A crooked smile curled the corners of James' mouth. "You stupid girl. Just swallow before you pass out."

Liquid filled Eliza's throat. Instinctively, she coughed as her body tried to reject it. No air could escape her mouth, and the water at last slipped from her oesophagus down into her stomach. Her choking intensified. She saw the whip fall from around Mr. McKenzie's throat and heard him gasp new air into his lungs. Her vision blurred, and images swayed before her eyes as the drugs took effect. Her hands flopped beside her, too heavy to lift again, and she knew she'd blown her last chance to escape.

"Stretch her out. I've wasted enough time," James said, standing.

Mr. McKenzie extended Eliza's right arm across the length of timber.

"Now, hold her still." James knelt beside his daughter, placed a nail against her skin, and raised a mallet above his head.

"Why?" The word whispered past Eliza's lips.

"Because it's both our destinies." And James brought the hammer down, impaling the nail into her wrist.

Eliza screamed, her torso arching from the wood. James whacked the nail again and again, and Eliza's body contorted with each agonising scream until nausea blocked her airway.

"Get her other wrist," James said, stepping over her and kneeling beside her other hand.

Eliza curled away, but Mr. McKenzie extended her left arm, stretching her upper body across the top of the Cross.

"No more," Eliza begged.

James' eyes widened with sadistic pleasure, and he brought the mallet down upon the second nail. Eliza's body jerked and convulsed, and she cried out for mercy.

"She's gonna bite her tongue off," Mr. McKenzie said.

James wasn't listening. He banged the nail again, ramming it down into the wood.

CHAPTER FIFTY-FOUR

Billy whacked the steering wheel.

Thanks to the Shadow he was shirtless, freezing, and not one icon on the dash illuminated as to why the hybrid refused to start. He pumped the accelerator a couple more times, and turned the key. The full beam activated, and the tiny engine roared to life. Billy relaxed back in the car, allowing himself two seconds to rejoice in this break of luck. In the rear-view mirror, the brake lights illuminated the darkness.

"You should never have stopped the bloody car in the first place," Roman said.

"Fuck you." Billy pushed the gear stick into first, lifted his foot from the brake, and punched the accelerator. The little yellow car shot forward, four thousand rev's rumbling through the engine before he slammed the gear stick down into second.

"What the...?" Billy eased his foot from the accelerator.

In the light of the full beam, a strange mist swept across the road ahead of him. Billy leaned forward, his chin brushing the top of the steering wheel, and wiped the windshield.

"It's outside," Roman said, also wiping his window.

The hybrid continued forward, although at a much slower pace, and the mist engulfed the car like a cloud, tiny particles of grit hitting the windows. Billy wound down the window a couple of inches, and a shower of sand rushed in. He spat the grit from his mouth and fumbled to reclose the window.

"Shit. Davis must have already started the ceremony."

Billy glanced at Roman. "You mean he's started to kill Eliza?"

A figure ran into view, and Billy slammed on the brakes. The wheels locked. The car skidded into the person, knocking him into the air like a bowling pin. The car continued on several feet before it finally stopped, and the engine stalled.

Billy gripped the steering wheel. His body shook, and for several seconds he found himself incapable of reacting. He repositioned the rear-view mirror. The body lay in the middle of the road behind him, face down and unmoving.

"Shit." Billy raced through his options. He couldn't radio for help because the police station had been taken over by zombies.

He reached for the door handle but Roman pulled it shut. "What the fuck are you doing?"

"I've just hit someone."

"You've just hit someone who's already dead."

Billy checked his rear-view mirror. The body still wasn't moving.

"You open that door and you're going to bring a shit-storm down on us."

Billy looked at him. "What if he isn't dead?"

"And what about your sister? You get out of this car and I guarantee she will be."

Roman was right. Billy knew it. He turned the key. The car groaned.

Shapes began to materialise from the sandstorm, arms outstretched and heading straight towards the moan of the hybrid engine.

"I'd get this thing started if I were you," Roman said.

Hordes of zombies emerged into view, way more than had been at the police station, with more gathering by the second.

"Hurry up."

A zombie, wearing nothing but a pair of boxer shorts, climbed onto the hybrid's bonnet. A child appeared at the back of the car and thumped the window with slow, clumsy punches. A woman dressed in a blue baby-doll nightdress slobbered across the passenger's window. Roman responded by winding it down and allowing the woman to lean inside.

"Are you insane?" Billy turned the key again.

"Relax." Roman grabbed the woman's hair and, holding her head steady, wound the window tight. The glass inched upwards into her neck, and a black substance dripped from her throat. The zombie gurgled a cry, but one last crank of the handle and the woman's head popped free. Roman lifted her head out of his lap, and shook the sand from her hair.

"What are you doing?" Billy said. "Get rid of it."

They heard glass smashing behind them, and Billy turned in his seat to see the young child climb in through the back window. Blonde ringlets bounced around her face, and navy blue ribbons decorated her pink lace dress. She looked almost angelic.

Roman threw the severed head behind him and knocked the little girl clean out of the car.

This shit can't be real. Billy turned the key. The engine sparked to life, and he whacked the gearstick into first. Through the sandstorm, in the glow of taillights, Billy watched the little child roll across the tarmac and disappear into the darkness.

A smug smile creased the corners of Roman's mouth. "Drive through them."

Billy punched his foot down on the accelerator and sped forward into the crowd of zombies. Bodies bounced across the hybrid's bonnet, face after face hitting the windscreen, some women, some men, and others whose gender were totally indecipherable. One – a man wearing paint-covered boots and grubby clothes – held tight to the wipers. His lips curled open, saliva dripping over plaque-covered teeth. Billy swerved the car across the road, trying to shake him off, but the man clung tight, his face pressed against the glass, which only emphasised the light-blue veins beneath his skin. The engine screamed for second gear, but Billy ignored it. He flicked a button, and the wipers swished across the window, skimming the man's nose repeatedly until he slipped from the bonnet and rolled onto the tarmac. Only then did Billy manoeuvre the gear stick into third, bypassing second altogether, and give a sideways glance towards Roman.

"Okay. I'm impressed."

"Damn right you're impressed. Fucking Zombies."

"They're not zombies. They are just the undead."

"Whatever." Billy rotated the steering wheel left, and the car swerved into a lane too narrow for two-way traffic.

"Where're you going?" Roman secured his seatbelt.

"You want Eliza, right?"

"I thought you didn't know where she was."

"I don't." Billy pushed the gear stick into fourth. "But she isn't at the police station and she isn't with you."

"So?"

Car tyres squealed as Billy rounded a corner. "So, we're going to Fowey."

"You think she's at your father's house?"

"It's the only other place I can think of." Billy whacked the gear into fifth.

"Your father isn't even in the country."

"Which is perfect for Davis."

Roman leaned on the dash. "Then you're going the wrong way. The ferry's quicker."

"Even if this was a normal functioning night, the ferry wouldn't be running at this hour."

"Where's the river's narrowest point?"

Billy half laughed. "Seriously? You wanna swim to Fowey?"

Irritation clouded Roman's eyes, and he turned his attention back towards the road. "I thought you wanted to save your sister."

"And you think swimming the river will help do that? You're out of your mind."

He heard Roman sigh, and waited for an answer. It never came.

"We're fifteen miles away from Fowey by road. Trust me. It's way quicker in the long run."

"I don't think so."

"Look, I have no reason to trust you, and if I still had a police station, you'd be locked away in a cell right now. I have no idea why you want to help Eliza, and right now I don't care. This is my goddamn car, and I'm telling you the quickest route is by road."

CHAPTER FIFTY-FIVE

"Get the crown," James yelled to Mr. McKenzie over the storm.

Dust and sand rose off the ground to join the gust, swirling higher and higher into the air. The wind tore through Eliza's hair, the grit scratching her skin. She cried out, begging her father to end the nightmare. James lifted a crown woven entirely of thorn branches and placed it on Eliza's head. He surveyed her for a second, his eyes sparkling with excitement, then pressed the barb into her skull. Inch-long spikes pushed through Eliza's brunette hair and pierced deep into her skin. Blood trickled into her eyes and down her neck, and a shriek screamed past her lips, but anything more required effort and energy, and she had neither.

"There." James stood back, seemingly to admire his work. "Now you look like your distant ancestor before you."

Eliza didn't respond, her eyes half-closed. She wanted nothing other than freedom from the pain. She wanted to die.

James slapped her across the face. "This is an honour. You should be proud of what you are about to achieve." He gripped the crown and wiggled it, as if checking it was secure.

Eliza winced, and felt further blood trail her face.

"Now get this thing upright and planted in the ground," James said to Mr. McKenzie, pointing to the Cross.

Eliza felt her father's breath warming her neck. "You're going to like this, my dear."

CHAPTER FIFTY-SIX

The yellow hybrid sped around the fountain and pulled to a stop outside James Hamilton's home.

"Hurry," Roman said, jumping from the car and fighting the ferocity of the storm between him and the front door. "We have to stop Davis before he opens the Gateway."

"You mean before he kills Eliza, right?" Billy raced up the steps behind him.

"If we stop him opening the Gateway, we stop him killing Eliza."

They rushed into the house, gales and debris gushing in behind them.

"This way," Roman said, leaving the door open and taking off along the corridor. He stopped in front of two oak doors and tried the handles. The room was locked. "Stand back."

He backed up and mounted a firm kick against the panelled wood. The doors smashed open, and he strode inside. The room was empty. "There's a secret door in the bookshelf over here."

Roman began to yank random books from the shelves, only stopping when Billy made no attempt to help. "Don't just stand there."

"I'd help if I knew what the hell you were doing."

"One of these books is the release mechanism."

Billy started towards the shelf. Book after book flew over Roman's shoulder until...

Click.

Roman paused. "That's it."

The shelf swung inwards.

"How on earth do you know about this?"

Roman headed into the tunnel. "I saw the old man come through it."

When he didn't hear Billy's footsteps following, he turned. "What's wrong? Scared of the dark?"

Billy stood in the doorway, his expression stone-like. He raised his hands in surrender, an odd motion given what they were doing. Then, he twisted slightly to reveal Davis, a sword in his hand, its tip pressed into the upper part of his back.

For a split second, Davis' disbelief at seeing Roman alive betrayed him. "You heal quicker than I gave you credit for."

"Surprised?" Roman said.

"Disappointed." Davis moved the sword to Billy's shoulder, resting its edge against the side of his neck.

"Are we really going to play this game?" Roman said.

"What game's that?"

"Oh, the one where I ask where the girl is, and you reply that you don't know."

Davis smiled. "No. She's here."

Billy glanced at Roman. "Looks like I was right."

Roman forced a smile. "Yeah, you called it."

"Unfortunately," Davis said, "you're too late."

"I don't think so." Roman paced back towards the door. "If we were too late, you wouldn't be here."

Davis pointed his index finger at Roman and grinned. Instantly, Roman cried out. His leg crippled beneath him and he fell to his knees.

Roman clasped his shin and felt the bone protruding out beneath his trousers. He took a breath and re-stood, holding the wall for support. He needed to buy time for his leg to heal. "How many times do I have to say it? You can't stop me."

Davis' index finger extended and again Roman cried out. This time, he clasped his arm. Heavy breaths exhaled wild and quick. "You can't kill me, you fool."

"No, but I can kill him." Davis gripped the sword with both hands. "You, I just need to keep away from the girl."

With a flat palm, Billy twisted and pushed the sword up off his shoulder. He dropped into a lunge and the blade scraped his ear, immediately drawing blood. Billy grabbed Davis' wrist and locked his hand. The heavy sword dropped to the floor, the clang of steel vibrating for several seconds. He pulled Davis close. "Where is Eliza?"

Roman watched, hardly impressed at the simple move or the fact Billy had just defeated a man of such advanced age.

Davis laughed. Not a flicker of emotion crossed his eyes.

"I want to know where Eliza is."

Davis laughed harder.

"All these years... She thought you were her friend. I thought you were my friend."

"She's nothing more than a vessel." Davis raised his index finger.

Billy clenched his fist. He punched Davis square on the jaw. "You piece of shit."

Davis' legs buckled beneath him, and he fell to the floor.

Billy grabbed him by his tie. "Tell me where she is."

"It's her destiny to die."

Billy eyed the old man. Then he punched him again.

"Wait," Roman hobbled inside the library. He knelt beside Davis and grabbed his hand. With the old man's fingers clenched in his palm, he squeezed until he felt every one of the bones break.

The old man cried out, but Roman continued to squeeze. Giving one last twist, he grabbed what little tuft of hair was left on the old man's head and yanked it back until he could see every bloodstained tooth in his mouth. "Try and break me now, you little fuck."

Davis chuckled through his tears. "You know nothing."

"That's it. I've had enough." Billy pushed Roman aside. He reclaimed his hold on the butler's tie. "Last chance. Where's Eliza?"

"Fulfilling her destiny."

Billy punched Davis, over and over until Roman pulled him away. Davis' body spilled across the floor, unconscious – maybe even dead.

Roman picked up the sword. He handed it to Billy. "Feel better?"

Billy felt his ear, checked out the blood on his fingertips, and took the sword. "We still don't know where Eliza is."

The sound of the ocean raced through the passageway, bringing with it sand-filled gusts. "I'd say she's somewhere in there, wouldn't you?" Roman hobbled back into the tunnel. He shielded his eyes, and followed the torch-lined stones until he found the small room at the far end of the tunnel. His leg ached like hell but, although not as quick as he'd like, at least it was healing.

"I've lived here nearly all my life," Billy said. "What the hell is this place?"

Empty crates and straw covered the floor. Iron shackles bolted to the far wall lay unlocked and open. Roman stepped forward. On the floor, Eliza's clothes lay discarded and shredded. "He's used the cat o' nine tails."

Billy took Eliza's torn shirt and held it out. "Whoa. There's blood on this. We have to find her. Now."

Roman agreed. "Okay, he'd have to construct the Cross outside, right?"

"How the hell would I know?"

"There's another passageway back there."

"So?"

"So, this sea breeze is coming from somewhere." Roman passed to leave, but Billy stopped him. "You're perspiring. You okay?"

"I've just had my arm and my leg broken. Of course I'm perspiring."

"Then I need to know you're in this to save Eliza, and not for your own gain."

"I am in this for my own gain. But I also don't want the girl to die."

Billy wavered, but dropped his arm and let Roman pass.

The wind howled through the corridor, and sand stung Roman's skin, invading his nose and drying his throat. He spat the grit from his mouth, and tucked in close to the side of the tunnel as he stumbled his way through the dark. "We killed Davis, so the storm should be easing by now."

"What does it mean that it's not?"

"It means we have to hurry."

The further they walked, the more ferocious the weather became. Cold air dropped to almost freezing, and the darkness made the wet, uneven floor hard to navigate.

Roman slipped and cursed at the pain in his leg, but continued onwards, battling against the elements. An iron gate swung open, and he felt his boots sink into the soft sand. "We're on the beach. Stay close to me." He waded through the water, the ice-cold almost blotting out the pain, and limped out into the open. Sand swirled through the air, hitting him like tiny razor blades.

"I don't see her," Billy shouted.

Roman didn't see Eliza either.

The faint outline of Billy brushed past him and stopped three feet ahead. He faced away, looking off towards the darkened cliffs. "I know where she is."

"Where?"

Billy pointed towards the top of the cliffs. "Up there."

Roman looked up. Nothing. Only darkness merged with darkness. "Are you sure?"

But Billy had started off towards the cliffs.

Roman waded through the ocean after him. Freezing water lapped past his thighs, past his hips, around his stomach. Where the hell was the cop leading him? The water level rose up his body with every step he took.

"Up here," he heard Billy call out.

Stone steps emerged through the night. Billy had already climbed the first couple, his pale, bare back the only visible thing left to see. Roman grabbed the iron railing and hauled himself out of the water. "How'd you know about this place?"

"Eliza and I played here as kids. There's an old ruin up there."

Roman followed him to the top of the cliff. The sandstorm was ferocious as ever, and Roman nearly didn't see the decrepit tower standing proud in the distance. Inside, shadows danced underneath flame light and cries for help echoed from within, but they were not from Eliza. Roman raced to the entrance, hugging the shadows of the stone walls. Two wooden poles stood erect a couple of metres apart, a male body tied to each. Probably thieves or beggars as history dictated, but nevertheless, sacrificed men. Between them, the True Cross, with Eliza hanging from it like Jesus Christ himself, her scrawny arms stretched to their limit, nail rods puncturing her wrists. Her head lolled on her right shoulder, her face covered by a mess of auburn hair. If it hadn't been for the lack of the Gateway, Roman would have sworn she was dead already. Bile caught in his throat and he swallowed it back. How could he have played a part in this? Maybe he did deserve to spend the rest of his days in Purgatory.

Billy came up behind him, Davis' sword still in his hand. "What's going on? Is Eliza in there?"

Roman held back. "Something's not right. Davis would need to be here when the Gateway opened." Roman glanced back through the opening. Mr. McKenzie knelt in the far corner, a sword embedded into the dirt beside him, his head tilted, his gaze locked on the floor.

From a darkened area of the room the flame light didn't quite reach, a cloaked figure stepped up to the Cross, a dagger gripped between his fingers. He paced the dirt. "Not long now," he said, rubbing his hands together.

No sooner had the words left his lips then the wind died.

"The eye of the storm," James said. "This is the moment I've been waiting for."

"That's my father's voice." Billy scrambled for a better view, but Roman held him back.

James held the dagger out in front of him, an admiring look in his eye. The men either side of Eliza began to wrestle the ropes binding their wrists. James stood centre of the poles, and turned to Mr. McKenzie. "Remove their tops."

Mr. McKenzie grabbed the tramp's grotty shirttail. With one swift slice of his sword, the front severed and parted. Old skin clung around the man's rib cage. Excess skin, from an age of starvation, sagged around his stomach. Frayed string belted the waist of his trousers. He murmured an objection at the act about to happen, but his voice was weak and barely audible. Mr. McKenzie turned the sword to the second man, cutting through the wool of his cable sweater in a downward motion. Halfway down, he stopped, embedded the blade back into the dirt, and yanked the remainder of the jumper apart.

"What's he doing?" Billy clawed past Roman again, this time getting a look inside the tower. His eyes widened at the horror, and he launched himself forward.

Roman hauled him back and forced him against the wall as best as his broken body would allow. "We're gonna save her, but just wait."

"He's going to kill them?" Billy tried to get back up, but Roman bit back the pain and held him down. "Game's over if we run into a trap. You got me?"

Billy reluctantly nodded.

Slowly, Roman lifted his weight off and, when he was certain Billy wasn't about to bolt, he turned back to the tower. There didn't seem to be anybody else inside.

"Stop this," the thief pleaded with James.

James raised the dagger horizontally until the tip rested against the prisoner's chest. Roman heard the fear inside the vagrant's voice as he begged for his life. It was in him, too. Eliza's own father planned to sacrifice her. And Roman had ignorantly played his part, too well. He glanced again at Eliza nailed to the wood he himself had found, and bile rose in his throat. What had he done? What had he become? What would his Jane think of him now?

He turned to Billy. "Okay. Go."

Billy leapt from the floor and charged the small tower. "Dad!"

CHAPTER FIFTY-SEVEN

James froze.

The shocked expression on his face when he saw Billy enter, sword in hand and anger burning in his eyes, said it all.

Roman hung back and watched from the shadows of the doorway. Hard as he tried not to, his gaze found Eliza. Blood trickled from her hairline, reddening her already bloodied body, the same body Roman had held in his arms and carried from the hospital twenty-four hours earlier. She stared at her father, her eyes filled with fear, and Roman buried the overwhelming urge to rush to her. He felt his leg and immediately the dull ache screamed in pain. *Damn it.* Both his arm and leg were not healing as fast as he was used to. Whatever voodoo shit Davis had used when breaking them was slowing his recovery now.

He turned his attention back to Billy. Apart from their father, the only other adversary seemed to be the old guy who, unfortunately for Roman, was built like a brick shit house. Still, his odds could be a hell of a lot worse than two on two. One thing was for sure; whether be took on the old guy or father, this was one battle Roman was going to struggle through.

"What the hell are you doing, Dad?" Billy raised the sword and edged to Eliza's side.

Mr. McKenzie grabbed his sword from the dirt and moved to intervene, but James motioned for him to stay put. He lowered the dagger from the thief and seemed to take several seconds before he regained his composure. "I must admit, son, you weren't the one I expected to come save her."

Billy ignored him, his sword still pointed towards McKenzie. He pulled at the rope that bound Eliza's ankles. Secured tight. "Eliza, can you hear me?"

Eliza looked down at him, but the couple of words she spoke were no more than a whisper.

McKenzie edged in closer and Billy turned on him. "Drop the sword."

"You must be joking, boy."

Billy glanced at his dad. "Tell him to drop the sword."

"You haven't really thought this through, have you, son?"

Now Billy wavered. He pulled on the rope again, a sudden urgency to his movement, and looked up at Eliza when it still wouldn't unravel. "I'm going to get you out of here, you hear me?"

"And how do you plan on doing that? You're outnumbered." McKenzie slowly circled Billy. Now the two men had him cornered.

Roman watched the realisation dawn on Billy. His look of fear turned to defeat and then defiance, and a sudden admiration for the cop swelled inside Roman. The guy certainly wasn't going to go down without a fight.

Billy pivoted the sword from left to right, unsure at whom to point it.

"You can't take us both down, Billy." McKenzie moved nearer.

Billy twisted the sword in his direction. "I'm warning you. Stay back."

"Kill him, and I kill you," James said from behind.

Billy spun on his heel, the sword turning with him.

It was a classic move and one that was inevitable. Mr. McKenzie seized his chance. He lunged forward. In one swift motion, he smashed his sword handle against Billy's temple. Billy fell and sprawled across the dirt, his own sword sliding a few feet from his grasp. He reached for it but McKenzie grabbed his feet and dragged him away. Billy's fingers clawed the dirt but Mr. McKenzie was upon him. He had Billy's face in the dirt and his arm twisted halfway up his back before Billy knew what had happened.

"You got no business being here, boy." As a show of power, Mr. McKenzie forced Billy's arm higher.

Billy winced. He lifted his head what little he could and glared at his dad. "For fuck's sake. What's wrong with you?"

James glanced back at the dishevelled thief hanging before him. "I thought that was obvious, son."

"You need to let them all go."

"Is that request coming from my son or the police?"

"Jesus Christ, does it matter?"

James shrugged. "May have had more sway coming from a professional body."

Billy struggled to free himself, but Mr. McKenzie held tight. "Fine, then I am ordering you as the police."

James laughed. "And I promise to take it under advisement."

"Under advisement? Eliza's strung up like Jesus-bloody-Christ himself. She's going to die if we don't help her."

"You misunderstand me. I do honestly feel a little guilty about doing this to her, son." James glanced across to Eliza and his face took on a look of admiration. He turned back to Billy and smiled. "But sacrifices have to be made. She is my key into Heaven."

"You're insane if you think I'm going to let you kill her."

"You're hardly in a position to stop me."

"Then take me."

A smirk found James' lips. "You?"

"Yes. If you need a sacrifice in this demented plan of yours, for fuck's sake use me."

James rubbed his chin. Even if Billy couldn't see it, Roman could. The guy was just playing with his son. "Interesting idea. But I think I'll stick with the girl. You just don't have what it takes inside you to open the Gateway."

Billy struggled further – all to no avail. "Christ, Dad. Please don't do this."

James lifted the dagger back towards the thief. The dagger gouged the thief's chest. The man lifted his head and his screams filled the night. His body stiffened and veins bulged in his neck to the point of bursting. Blood trickled from the corner of his mouth and only then did James pull the dagger free. The life in the thief's eyes died. His head lolled forward, and any fool could see what Roman sensed – that the man was dead.

Shock greyed Billy's face. "You have to stop this."

James smiled. "Everything I have done has come from generations of planning."

"This madness is barbaric. You're barbaric."

"I am dying, son, and I have no intention of spending my afterlife in Hell." James stepped past Eliza and stood before the second thief.

The man began to cry out, offering money and anything else James desired if only he'd let him live.

"If you take one more step, I swear I will kill you where you stand." Billy stretched for his sword once again, but his reach fell short by a foot or two.

"You won't kill me. I'm your father."

"Maybe he wouldn't," Roman limped through the doorway, his right arm held close to his side. His time to heal had just been cut short. "But I'd have no hesitation whatsoever."

James paused. His gaze found Roman. "Ah, you must be the elusive Roman. Now you, I *was* expecting." He clasped the dagger with both hands and smiled.

James raised the dagger and just like he had with his first victim, he placed its tip against the man's chest. He glanced over his shoulder towards his son.

Roman hobbled forward. The attempt to stop Hamilton killing the poor bugger that hung on the pole was nothing more than wasted energy on a futile gesture. His injured leg slowed him, and he never reached Hamilton in time.

McKenzie stood and pressed the tip of the sword against the back of Billy's neck. Roman saw and halted. He needed a plan, and quick.

James smiled. Just like the first man, he plunged the dagger into the thief's chest. The man's savage cries died quickly and within seconds, his body hung limp on the pole.

James wiped the blade down his robe then looked at his daughter. Eliza struggled, but it was short-lived. She looked drained of energy and ready to die.

Shit. "Wait." Roman limped forward.

"Stay where you are or I'll kill the cop," McKenzie said.

Billy craned his neck. When he spoke, it was directed at McKenzie. "For Christ's sake, you were Eliza's neighbour."

"Neighbour?" Roman's interest was piqued. Suddenly he had a plan to get the sword away from Billy. "No relation to a bad Dolly Parton lookalike by any chance – like, say, your wife?"

Mr. McKenzie halted. Now it was he who looked unnerved. It took a full minute before the confused look on his face was replaced with concern. "What have you done?"

"Me? Nothing. She accidently fell on a knife and split her jugular wide open."

"You're lying." Now Mr. McKenzie had the sword trained inches from Roman's abdomen.

Roman held up three fingers. "Scouts honour."

"She's dead?"

"Well if she ain't, she's definitely going to be a lighter shade of white now."

"It doesn't matter, McKenzie," James interrupted. "You can be with her again."

Anger filled Mr. McKenzie's eyes. He glared at Roman. "I'm going to kill you."

"McKenzie," James said, but Mr. McKenzie wasn't listening. He stepped away from Billy, his glare fixed on Roman. "I'm going to gut you until your insides spill across the floor."

Now Billy crawled for the sword. "McKenzie!"

Mr. McKenzie turned in time to block the blade that Billy reigned down upon him.

Billy sidestepped, raising Davis' sword again, and in unison, the two men circled each other. McKenzie launched his attack and Billy responded, the clang of steel upon steel deafening.

Roman looked at Hamilton. Now it was just the two of them.

James rushed towards Eliza.

Roman hobbled to intervene.

Hamilton was quicker. He held the dagger centimeters from Eliza's neck and almost dared Roman to continue forward.

The urge to rush to her side and pull her from harm's way was immense for Roman...but stupid. He stopped just feet from Eliza's body. "Her blood is all over the Cross. You don't need to kill her. You never needed to do any of this."

"Ah, but I do." James pushed the matted auburn hair away from Eliza's neck.

"Damn it. All you needed was a little of her blood."

"I need her to die."

Roman glanced at Eliza, and her eyes met his with a look of painful bewilderment at the predicament she found herself in. "I'm begging you. Don't do this."

James grinned. His lust for wanting to get to Heaven couldn't be bartered with. Evil filled his eyes, and Roman's heart sank. James pressed the dagger against his daughter's throat.

Roman limped another step closer. His heart raced. He didn't need his senses as a Reaper to know Eliza was close to death. "Let the girl go and I'll let you go to Heaven and do whatever the fuck you want to up there."

"Her blood has already been spilt on the Cross. Whether I kill her or not, she will die. It's just a matter of time."

"Then put the knife down and let her go."

James smiled, but his eyes remained cold. "I can't do that."

"Then you leave me no choice." Roman raised his hand.

"You're no longer a Reaper, and I'd hazard a guess that my soul hasn't been earmarked for the taking. Kill me like this and you're signing your own death warrant."

Roman clenched his fist, his power taking hold of James' heart. "Trust me, it'll be worth it."

James' face drained to almost grey and he clasped his chest. His face creased with pain and he collapsed to his knees. "They'll find you, like they did the last time," he gasped.

"Maybe."

"And Eliza's life is worth that much to you?"

Roman thought of Jane, and wondered if she and their son waited for him in Heaven. All he had to do was release Hamilton and he'd be able to find out. He glanced at Eliza, her head slouched to her shoulder, her eyes closed. This girl had been a pain in his backside the last couple of days, but life without her? Well, that suddenly wasn't an option. Roman twisted his fist, his body rigid with anger. "Hell yes, she's worth everything."

James collapsed to his knees. Roman had not taken a life as a Reaper for centuries, and it felt good using his power again. But taking Hamilton's soul in this way would reveal his whereabouts to those who hunted him. And if they found him, they'd take him back to Purgatory. Flashes of his past spotted his vision. Bellowing cries deafened his ears and images of harrowing torture filled his head. He couldn't go through with it. He couldn't go back to that hellhole of a prison. He unclenched his fist, defeated, and concentrated on not collapsing under the exertion. He wanted to kill Hamilton, but he couldn't go back to the place he'd evaded for so long.

"You had me worried for a moment." Rattled breaths wheezed inside James chest and, although he struggled to breathe, he smiled. "I thought you were going to kill me."

He struggled to his feet, his attention once again firmly set on Eliza. "But Davis told me you were an egocentric bastard."

Roman dashed forward. Pain erupted down his arm. His knee buckled beneath him, but determination kept him moving forward.

James sliced the blade towards Eliza's throat, but this time Roman reached him. He stretched out his arm. The dagger sliced his wrist and Roman felt his veins sever. Blood painted his skin within seconds. James swiped the dagger towards Eliza again, but Roman blocked the blade.

"Did Davis also tell you I'm unpredictable?"

James' eyes widened.

"Thought not." Roman twisted Hamilton's wrist until it pointed towards its bearer. In one swift motion, Roman forced pressure behind James' elbow, and stabbed the blade into the man's abdomen.

James dropped to his knees and clasped the wound, but the blood already seeped through his fingers. He glanced up at Roman. "You stupid idiot. Good luck when they find you."

"Research your history, mate. There's nothing in the rule book about killing you like any other human being."

Behind him, Billy clashed swords with McKenzie like an expert and looked to be winning his fight. But it was a fight that Roman needed to be over. He pulled the dagger from James. Roman's vision spotted, and he glanced at his wrist again. Way too much blood. He gave himself minutes before he passed out and probably died before the wound could heal – and he didn't have time to waste on dying. He refocused on Billy, flicked the dagger into the air, and caught the cold steel between his fingers. With lightning speed, he launched it towards Mr. McKenzie. The blade passed by Billy and embedded McKenzie between the shoulder blades. McKenzie stopped mid sword swing and he fell forward against the stone wall.

Billy paused, sword raised above his head. He glanced at Roman, an element of contempt in his eyes that it had not been he who'd won the fight. Nausea overwhelmed Roman, and he turned and vomited.

"You okay?"

But Roman had moved on. He reached up, cradling Eliza's face in his hands, and soon Billy was beside him, both men tugging to free the nails that pinned her wrists. Billy's spike slithered easily from the wood, and Eliza's body swung to the left, her impaled right wrist the only thing keeping her from dropping to the floor. Roman's nail wouldn't budge, and he had no choice but to slide her wrist over the end of it. Eliza fell from the Cross, and Roman caught her body in his arms, falling to the ground with her. "Billy, grab that robe."

Billy did. "Is she dead?" He covered her nakedness.

"No." Her breathing was slow. Roman brushed the blood-soaked hair from her face and her eyes opened, taking a while to focus on him. He repositioned himself beside her, still holding her in his arms. "It's okay, you're safe."

Behind him, Roman heard James crawl to his feet.

"She's dying. It's only a matter of time," James said, his face already pale from his blood loss. He picked up Mr. McKenzie's sword, and stumbled to the corner of the tower.

Hamilton was right. Roman could feel the life draining from Eliza's body with every second that passed.

Thunder roared across the night, and light swirled in the sky above him like poured cream in stirred coffee.

"Looks like I win. And you lose." Amusement licked at James' words.

Roman glanced down at Eliza.

A faint smiled creased the corner of her lips. "I want to go home," she whispered.

Roman pulled her close.

Her eyes slowly closed, and Roman felt her body go limp.

Billy saw. He raced to Eliza, but Roman shook his head. She was gone.

A lightning bolt cracked through the darkness, and a ray of beautiful white light shone down directly over the Cross.

Crippled and dying, Roman glanced at his bloody wrist. Anger bubbled inside him. Throughout his life, love had only ever found him a couple of times. Once, when his brother brought home his new wife; and two days ago, when he first saw Eliza at the train station. He stood, dizziness instantly taking him, and limped towards the Cross. "You forget one thing, Hamilton."

James staggered towards the light, a look of delight twinkling in his slowly dying eyes.

"A Reaper chooses the soul's destination to the afterlife." Blood dripped from Roman's wound, running the length of his arm. He glanced at Eliza, her dead body motionless and finally at peace, and grit his teeth. "And yours definitely isn't going up."

Guilt and sorrow raced Roman's veins. He could easily jump into the light and be with his beloved Jane. But he didn't. He slapped his bloodied palm against the weathered timber, the purity of Eliza's blood now contaminated by his.

He wanted vengeance.

The ray of light started to grey, darker and darker, until it turned blacker than coal itself. It whirled like a tornado, churning the ground and overturning everything in sight. The sky crackled, and thunder boomed down past the clouds.

"He's getting away," Billy shouted above the noise.

"He's not getting away with anything," Roman said. "I'm sending him somewhere where he'll never get away from it."

But Billy raced towards the darkness, the sword outstretched and reaching for his father.

"Billy, don't!" But Roman couldn't stop him.

Billy lunged for his father. The sword ran through his torso and Billy took him down to the ground...and into the pit of the dark tornado.

For a second or two, Roman heard their screams. Then their voices drifted away. When the black light dispersed, both Billy and James had vanished.

The winds grew more ferocious. Roman's broken body collapsed beside Eliza's and he hugged her into his chest to shield her body from further torture. The wind howled around them, and piece by piece he heard the True Cross splinter apart. He didn't look up, and instead clung to Eliza as he waited for the storm around them to die.

When he finally opened his eyes, moonlight flooded the sky. The True Cross was gone, along with the two bodies that had hung from the wooden poles. McKenzie remained in a heap, the dagger still embedded in his back.

Roman cupped Eliza's face, tilting her head so he could see her one last time. Blood smeared her skin, and anger surged throughout his body unlike anything he'd ever known. Tears burned his eyes, and he grabbed the crown of thorns from her head and pulled it free from her tangled hair.

"I'll make this right," he said, throwing the artefact across the tower.

Then, he glanced up towards Heaven.

And screamed.

CHAPTER FIFTY-EIGHT

Heaven did not respond.

But then, Roman hadn't expected it to. Heaven hadn't helped when he'd asked for Jane's life to be returned to him, and he knew it wouldn't help now.

He glanced down at Eliza, the seconds ticking away before he lost this window of opportunity and was forced to live with yet another bad decision for the rest of his days. Eliza deserved to live. He'd hidden as a coward for far too long. Now he needed to do what was right – no matter what consequences he was about to bring down on himself.

McKenzie lay facedown in the dirt, and Roman sensed that death hadn't taken him yet. Well, he'd just have to help death along a little. He got to his feet, unsteady and wondering if he had the strength to pull off what he was about to do. Not just the physical strength, but mentally as well. Pulling a soul back from the afterlife would be like hanging a neon sign above his head. Purgatory would know his whereabouts almost immediately and he reckoned he'd have little over half an hour before they sent the Sheriff for him.

Nevertheless, he limped across the tower and grabbed hold of McKenzie's arms. His body was like dragging a dead weight across the dirt, and Roman stopped midway to catch his breath and alleviate the pain in his leg. He glanced at Eliza, detecting nothing but coldness inside her heart. It was his fault. Anger rose within him and he grit his teeth. When the frustrated yell left his lips, he did nothing to stop it. Every painful step he dragged McKenzie was comeuppance for his part in Eliza's death. And everything he suffered from here on out, he deserved.

He flopped McKenzie beside Eliza and pulled the dagger from his back. When he rolled him over, McKenzie's eyes were open. He stared at Roman, almost as if he knew what was about to happen.

"You know someone needs to take her place, right?"

McKenzie's eyes widened.

Yeah, he knew alright.

Roman turned to Eliza. His energy was waning. He could feel it inside: the usual rush of adrenaline was drying up. He needed to do this now, before it was too late. He pulled down her robe, revealing skin stained red by her own blood. She didn't move or protest the action, and not a single acknowledgement of pain or discomfort crossed her face. Roman grit his teeth, pressed his hand against her chest, and sighed. He had to stay focused.

He glanced back at McKenzie. Gone was the thug prepared to do anything for his diabolical employer. Now all that remained was a weak and dying man full of so much fear and dread at the anticipation of what was going to happen, he'd lost control of his bladder. Roman wanted to smile, to believe the man before him deserved this comeuppance, but the truth was, Roman didn't truly believe it. He just knew that Eliza didn't deserve it more.

Roman moved his other hand to McKenzie's chest, his broken arm shaking under the movement. Around him the tower blurred, and light-headedness took over. A blue light emanated from his hand and warmed his palm, its light glowing brighter and brighter until it formed the perfect sphere. McKenzie's body went as rigid as an ironing board. His face paled and shadows darkened his aging skin. Faint whispers begged for mercy, but Roman closed his eyes.

Still, Eliza remained motionless; her struggle would come soon enough, when the discomfort hit. Roman blocked the thoughts from his mind and drew a deep breath. This was going to hurt all three of them.

He swallowed, preparing himself for the agonising pain that would certainly consume his broken arm, and punched his fist into McKenzie's chest. McKenzie's gurgled cries confirmed he was inside, and only then did Roman reopen his eyes. No broken skin and no blood shed, and when Roman located and clasped the man's heart, he found it surprisingly warm and beating strong. Roman tightened his fist and twisted. McKenzie's arms shook and his bloodshot eyes bulged.

Roman turned to Eliza. He wanted to promise her it wouldn't be painful, but the truth was it was going to hurt like hell. He wanted to apologise for the pain, but the agony he was about to inflict was unforgivable. Gently, slowly, he pressed his hand against her chest, his fingertips soaking in the softness of her skin until they were inside her. The holes that pierced her hairline vanished. Bruises faded beneath blood-dried skin. Roman felt everything, all the pain Eliza had suffered before she died: every kick, every punch, every lash of the whip. He waited for her to gasp the first breath of her next life cycle, which she did with a short intake of air. Her eyes widened and she cried out as he wrapped his fingers around her heart, and immediately her arms pushed and clawed at him. Her body arched and contorted, and she tried to roll away. Behind him, he heard loose stones rattle from the walls – her doing, not his. The dagger catapulted towards him and he ducked from its path, hearing it smash into the opposite wall.

"Eliza. Stop." Roman pressed harder, holding her in place. Pain boiled inside his head, and the tower darkened from his sight until he saw nothing but a blue glow explode from McKenzie's body and cross to Eliza's.

Eliza screamed, and her body thrashed beneath him. The pain inside Roman's head boiled hotter than a crematorium furnace, and he bit down, the taste of his own blood filling his mouth. Now rage consumed him, and he squeezed McKenzie's heart until he felt it harden like a rock. Spasms dominated the whole of the man's body, and he writhed uncontrollably until the last of his dying screams gurgled from his throat and Roman felt his heart crush into powder and syphon between his fingers. He withdrew his hand and stared at McKenzie. Pain contorted his face. His open eyes stared directly towards the sky, confusion and fear still clouding them. He was dead.

Eliza's eyes, however, were closed, and her motionless body didn't move, not even when Roman slipped his hand from her. He collapsed back on his arse, watching her chest rise and fall with each shallow breath. He watched nearly two dozen of them before she finally moved and sat up. She peered down towards her chest and trailed her fingertips across the red imprint of Roman's hand. When she finally raised her head and glanced around the tower, it was as though she were seeing it for the first time.

Roman cradled his broken arm and waited for her search to reach him. It located McKenzie first. A brief frown lightly creased the ridge of her nose, and the faintest of smiles flickered in the corners of her mouth. An oddity Roman didn't expect from her. Finally, she looked away, continuing to scan the area until she saw him sitting, breathless, only metres away from her.

Shock replaced the smile. She scampered away to the far wall and stared at him. A green tint lightened her usually dark-brown eyes, and then it was gone. In the flash of an eye, the worrying look fell from her face. Her eyes darkened to their normal colour, and she placed her hand on her chest once again. "Is he dead?"

Roman looked at McKenzie, his body riddled with pain and already stiffening.

"That thing you did to him...to me. Is that what killed him?"

Roman nodded.

"Am I going to die as well?"

"No. I did it to save you."

"I feel different."

"Trust me, you are the same as you were before." Roman clawed himself to his feet.

Now she was scanning the tower again, this time with more urgency. "Where's Billy?"

Roman clenched his jaw. He glanced at the patch of dirt where Billy had vanished into the dark light. Eventually he'd have to tell her what happened, but not right now. "We need to go."

"Not until you tell me where my brother is."

Roman limped towards the tower entrance. He'd done what he needed to do, and now he needed to get as far from here as he could. He needed to hide once again.

"Where are you going? Is my brother alright?" Eliza was on her feet. She blocked his path.

Roman cradled his broken arm to his chest. He thought about lying and telling her what she wanted to hear. Instead, he sidestepped her and headed through the doorway. "Billy's dead."

Behind him, he heard her muffled sobs. He didn't want to turn around. If he did, he'd see her gazing at him with that pleading look upon her face, and he'd crumble. *Fuck*. Roman turned to face her.

Moonlight rolled across the stone walls like a morning mist, its blue haze sucking away what little colour remained in her face. Shadows darkened beneath her eyes and hollowed out her cheeks. The robe no longer covered her, exposing her semi-naked body. Her whole demeanour took on that of a haunted skeleton.

She said nothing, her brown eyes glistening behind her tears.

Roman forced his gaze from her. He grabbed the robe from the floor and wrapped it around her shoulders. "Eliza, I need to go. Some people...they're coming for me—"

She stared at him, acknowledging his words with a slight nod. Then she collapsed.

Roman caught her and lowered her to the floor. He couldn't leave her, but he couldn't stay either. Every second that ticked by was one less second he put between himself and Purgatory.

He hugged her shaking body, the strawberry scent still lingering in her hair even after all she'd been through. Then he released her and got to his feet once more.

He hobbled through the tower entrance, and this time he didn't look back.

RESURRECTION

Read on for an extract from the next Hunted thriller
in the series

DONNA COLLINS

CHAPTER ONE

SATURDAY
The Chamber, Purgatory

Not even the lad's screams could cover the sound of his arms being dislocated from his shoulders.

The Sheriff cranked the handle again. The already-taut rope pulled further, and the gurgled cries the Sheriff loved to hear spat from the young lad's throat.

Shame. The boy passed out before his pelvis had a chance to splinter apart.

The Sheriff slapped him across the face. The lad's head just whipped from left to right, then lulled against his dislodged shoulder. He wasn't going to give anything more tonight – and that infuriated the Sheriff. He hadn't frequented this chamber in little over six months. His involvement with the rack had been even longer than that. And now the eagerly anticipated build-up of brutalising this peasant for the best part of the night left him feeling deflated and unfulfilled. He'd have to choose his next victim more carefully, and make him pay in spades.

Behind him, he heard one of his aids approach.

The Sheriff glanced once more at the lad lying stretched on the rack, his head of orange hair hardly discernible beneath the clotted blood, his skin lacerated and shredded from the whipping the Sheriff had administered earlier that afternoon. It would be an age before the Sheriff's main duties of overseeing these torture chambers would allow him the time to come down and indulge again.

Damn it. Humans just weren't as strong as they used to be.

The aid nervously cleared his throat.

The Sheriff sighed. "You'd better have something worthy to report."

"Sir, we've located prisoner 4429."

The Sheriff lost interest in the red-haired lad. He spun towards the aid, unconcerned if his sudden elation and sadistic delight were obvious. "It's about time. Where is he?"

"England. South"

"Be more specific."

"Somewhere around the Cornwall area."

Disappointment momentarily quenched the Sheriff's joy. He inhaled. Held it. Drummed his long fingernails against his leg. Exhaled. "I can't fetch him from *somewhere*. I need an exact location."

"I'll get one for you straight away."

"I don't want you to get it – I want to you to already have it before you come here and disturb me." The Sheriff's fingers paused drumming. He glanced at the pathetic red-haired boy and thought back to better times, when his prisoners could handle hours of torture before they finally died. He grabbed the rack handle and twisted. He didn't stop until the young lad's body completely severed apart. The bloody sight failed to calm the building rage he felt. He noticed the aid. "You're still standing there, which would suggest to me that you now have the location."

The aid's eyes widened with fear. He cleared his throat. "No."

"Then why are you standing there?"

"I have the men ready to move upon your command."

"Without a location?"

"I'll get it now, Sir." He bowed. Turned. Scampered to the doorway.

"And tell the men to stand down. I will do this capture myself."

"But, Sir, the support of your men is a requirement."

The Sheriff reached the aid in two long strides. He slapped him across the face. Watched the disfigured skin redden almost immediately. "Your job is not to preach the law. Your job is to get me the exact location before I slaughter you."

The aid bowed again. He backed away as quickly as he could, and made haste. The Sheriff waited until his scampering footsteps disappeared down the passageway. Then he sighed. He was surrounded by nothing but incompetent fools.

He turned his thoughts to prisoner 4429. The same sadistic delight returned. It would do him good returning the escapee back to Purgatory. He had, after all, been one of the Sheriff's unapologetic pleasures back in the day. Not his most favourite victim, mind you, but the man could suck up pain like nobody else. It would be a pleasure to hunt him down and bring him back to the fold.

It would be just like the good old days.

CHAPTER TWO

St. Catherine's Castle, Fowey, Cornwall

Eliza drew her knees to her chest and rocked like a small child.

Coldness had battled its way through the velvet robe that wrapped her semi-nakedness, and her body shook under the attack. A tear rolled down her cheek, but instead of giving in to the many more that wanted to follow, she wiped it away.

Her father had vanished.

Her brother had died.

Her neighbour had been murdered.

And herself? Well, she'd been strung up on a crucifix and sacrificed like the Messiah himself.

It was a colossal, disturbing mess, and she understood none of it.

Well, apart from the fact that she now watched the one man irrefutably stuck in the center of it all limp away from her.

Not that Roman – the man she watched walk away now – had been the one to sacrifice her. No. That small feat belonged to her own dear, psychotic father. Roman had in fact saved her from that outcome. But, he was the one man alive who knew how to help her now.

Eliza shook her head. Had it really only been two days since Roman first walked into her life? Two days ago that he'd first stopped the Shadow from choking her to death. A Shadow that, according to Roman, had been sent by God himself, because her blood happened to be the key into Heaven.

She wanted to laugh.

How absurd did all that sound? Even just thinking it?

In fact, just believing what she'd lived through in the last forty-eight hours was enough to convince her that a nut home was where she really needed to be.

She continued to watch Roman. The man had saved her, kidnapped her, drugged her... Jesus, he was more screwed up than her. And yet, deep down inside, she felt sorrow at the prospect of never seeing him again. Maybe she did need that nut hospital.

She pulled the robe tighter around herself. She had a choice to make, and very little time to make it. First choice – the better choice – was to remain crumpled on the dirt and allow Roman to disappear from her life forever. After all, danger followed the man around like a virus. To even consider her second choice, and follow him, would be rubber stamping her own death warrant for sure.

Besides, she hated Roman... Didn't she?

She'd spent the best part of two days trying to flee him. Now she was finally rid of him, was she actually considering following him again? What in the hell was wrong with her?

She slowly got to her feet. Around her, the inside of the tower looked ransacked. The Cross her father had assembled no longer dominated the centre of the area. Just like her brother and father, it had vanished into thin air. Her neighbour, Mr. McKenzie, on the other hand, lay flat out on his back. His eyes were open, and fear seemed to distort the whole of his face. Eliza turned away. She desperately wanted to believe he deserved whatever Roman had done to him, but wouldn't that make her just as bad as he?

She glanced towards the tower exit. Roman continued to limp away, but he moved slowly, and hadn't made much progress.

The earlier rain had ceased, and the wind had died to little more than a light breeze. Still, the previous weather had left its mark. Water trickled over rocks and raced towards the cliff steps, leaving a muddy and slippery bog in its wake that looked to test Roman's balance to the limit. He certainly hadn't walked away from this mess unscathed.

She wished him gone – she truly did. But the truth was, she owed it to her brother, Billy, to call Roman back... Roman was the only person alive who knew what had happened here tonight; he was the only one who could find Billy. The only one who could save him. And Roman owed her.

Eliza's first step towards him was unsteady. Stones and storm-shredded foliage tore at her bare feet. When she reached the exit archway, she leaned against it for support and took a deep breath. She thought about calling out after him, but somehow she sensed he already knew she was there.

She pushed herself away from the stone wall and continued on. Strength slowly found her, and her steps grew into strides. She expected him to stop and wait, but he didn't even look back. Anger bubbled to the surface. When she finally reached him, she grabbed his arm. It wasn't hard to spin him to face her.

"Eliza, I don't have time to deal with shit from you."

For a brief second, Roman's gaze met hers. Was that sympathy she saw there? Bizarre really; Roman didn't do sympathy. He tried to pull from her grip, but he was weak. Weaker than she'd ever seen him before.

She tightened her hold. "What in hell's wrong with you? Why didn't you wait for me back there?"

"Let go of my arm."

"Not until you tell me what went on here tonight. Where's my brother?"

"Dead. But I told you that already."

She resisted the pain the words struck in her heart, clinging instead to a knowledge she still couldn't define. Didn't understand. "You're wrong," she said.

"See, now that right there's your problem." Roman shrugged free. "You always think you're right."

"But you saved me?"

"Yeah. So?"

"So, you're the only one who can help me find my brother."

"You're delusional."

"You owe me."

Roman chuckled. "Owe you? For what? Ruining my life?"

"Your life? I died. My brother is gone."

Roman turned from her and limped to the edge of the cliff, where stone steps led down to the beach.

"You kidnapped me," she continued, undeterred. "You tied me up. You drugged me. You bloody stuffed me in the smallest car boot in the world—"

"And, boy oh boy, do I wish I had it here again now." He reached for the rusty handrail.

"You'll never make it down those steps alone." Roman's irritated sigh didn't stop her. "If you help me, I'll help you."

His jaw tensed. "I don't need your help."

"That's one hell of a drop to the beach."

Roman paused. He glanced up, and Eliza expected to see his blue eyes twinkle the way they had when he'd arrived at her door the day before. Instead, they remained dull and grey. In fact, she saw nothing but hatred inside them.

"And just how are you going to help me? What, you going to sling me over your shoulder and carry me down?"

Eliza stared at him. "What the hell's gotten into you?

"I don't like being blackmailed."

"I'm not blackmailing you. Just proposing a business arrangement."

Roman scoffed. "That's the sort of crap your father would say."

Eliza slapped him across the face. His legs seemed to buckle and, for the briefest moment, she thought he was going to fall. She went to reach for him, but his hand tightened around the handrail and he steadied himself. The hatred in his eyes deepened. His lips pursed tight and, although she was sure he had a barrage full of obscenities to throw at her, he remained quiet.

"What is wrong with you? Why are you so weak?" she asked.

"You're why I'm so weak."

"Me?"

"What? You think dragging a soul back from the dead is easy?"

Eliza took a deep breath. Where had the man who'd begged her father to spare her life vanished to? "What have I done to suddenly make you hate me so much?"

Roman's face softened slightly. Again, he looked as if to speak, but chose to remain quiet.

Eliza placed her hand on his shoulder – a show that she didn't judge him. And she certainly didn't want to argue. "What happened here after I died?"

"You lived again."

"That tells me nothing."

"Well, that's all you're getting."

"I just want my brother back."

"And I want to get the hell out of here…without you." He turned from her and hopped down onto the step.

"Please. I'm begging you. Help me find him."

"No." He hopped another step. His shoulders tensed, and he stopped for a second.

Eliza stepped down behind him. Her robe tangled around her ankles and she scooped it up. She manoeuvred herself beside him and propped his arm around her shoulder. To her surprise, he didn't fight her intervention.

"You helping me changes nothing."

Eliza chose not to answer.

The previous rainfall still gathered in pools on the uneven steps, and Eliza wasn't entirely convinced they were the easiest choice to go with. If she was being totally honest with herself, she expected the pair of them to have slipped and fallen way before reaching the fourth step. She was pleasantly surprised when they both still held strong by the sixth.

She glanced at Roman. Pain creased his face with every step he hobbled down. He paused for a moment and drew a deep breath.

"Are you okay?"

"Just get me the hell down." He lowered another step.

It took a good ten minutes to finally reach the bottom, and regardless of the obvious excruciating pain that consumed him, Roman looked exhilarated when his feet hit the surf and sunk into the sand.

Eliza mirrored his relief with a short intake of breath. But, the comfort of the tide quickly turned cold, soaking her bare feet and freezing her body to the core. The cold had the same effect on Roman. Within seconds, his teeth chattered together, and shivers rocked his whole body. Hell, her medical training as a nurse told her he'd probably pass out before he made it back to her father's house, and there was no way in hell she could drag him up to her father's house. She released her grip on the robe, watched its hem fan across the surface of the water, and repositioned herself under his arm. He didn't give one of his bad-tempered rejections as she'd expected. Instead, like before, he swallowed what was probably his pride and allowed her to take as much of his weight as she could handle.

They made it to the cave, the ocean air pushing and urging them through the tunnels, and it wasn't long before the dull flicker of torches lit the main corridor that led to the library. The bookcase remained ajar, and Eliza pushed it open.

She spotted Davis's highly polished shoes first, and then the butler himself. He lay on his back, his eyes wide open, his face twisted in pain. "What did you do to Davis?"

For a brief moment, Roman's gaze froze on her. A flicker of disbelief betrayed his eyes, and then anger reignited them. He removed his arm from around her shoulders. "Why is it you see a dead body and immediately ask what *I* did?"

Eliza stared at him. "You seem to kill a lot of people."

"Yeah, well, this one was on your brother."

"Billy did this?"

"He hit him."

Eliza knelt beside the old man and checked for a pulse. "And that killed him?"

Roman shot her a look. "The heart attack afterwards killed him." He hobbled towards the library door.

"And what about my father? He couldn't have just vanished into thin air."

"Wanna bet?"

"Did you kill him?"

Roman looked at her. "Contrary to what you clearly believe, I haven't killed everybody I've ever met."

"Then where'd he go?"

"Heaven."

"Really?"

Roman rolled his eyes.

Eliza's patience hit the boiling point. "Where the hell are they?"

Roman sighed. He looked fed up to his back teeth with this conversation. "I altered the pathway to Heaven."

"Altered it? To where?"

"Purgatory."

"Purgatory?"

"Yes."

"What's Purgatory?"

"You really don't know much of your history, do you?" Roman rolled his eyes again, a mannerism that was beginning to aggravate Eliza. "Every soul has to be processed and go through a kind of inventory stock-take."

"So you can get Billy back? Like you did me?"

"It's not that simple."

"But you got me back—"

"There are only five routes for a soul to take. First and foremost, you have to die. Then, your soul is registered. After that, it remains in a sort of waiting room until its number comes up. That's when you find out if you're heading to Heaven, Hell, being Reincarnated, or just getting a second chance with your own life with the good old Resurrection card. I just pulled you back out before the powers that be had time to place you."

"I don't understand."

"You were destined for Heaven. I sensed that much. By bringing you back, your soul had to be replaced... Keep the waiting room's stock-take balanced."

"With Mr. McKenzie?"

"With Mr. McKenzie."

"So, he went to Heaven?"

"It is a slight drawback, I admit."

"But he did so much wrong."

"Would you have preferred it to be you?"

Eliza stared at him. "How could evil like Mr. McKenzie even be allowed in Heaven?"

"Does it really matter?"

No. In the big scheme of things, it didn't matter one bit. "What about Billy? We can still save him, right?"

Roman shook his head again. "Your father and Billy didn't die in the conventional sense. They physically entered Purgatory. They completely bypassed the whole waiting room process. Their presence will do more than unbalance things. Purgatory will be in chaos, and they'll be hunted down."

Eliza paused. She wanted to know exactly what Roman meant by that, but was too afraid to ask. "You said there were five choices."

Roman swallowed. He shifted position. "Nobody speaks of the fifth path – and for good reason."

Eliza didn't say anything, dread building in her chest as she waited for his next words.

Finally, he continued. "When a soul doesn't fit any of the first four choices, it's thrown into the depths of Purgatory itself, and tortured for all eternity."

"And this is where Billy will be sent?"

"No. This is where Billy is. I told you, I altered the path."

Eliza stared at him through glazed eyes. "He's being tortured?"

Roman looked away.

"But he has to be caught first, right?"

"Your father and Billy will stick out like two sore thumbs. Trust me. They've been caught."

"Then they can escape? I mean, we know where he is. We can get him out."

Roman turned back to her. "Your optimism is misplaced and stupid. This place is reserved for the worst of the worst. Once you're sent there, you never get out."

Eliza digested his words, her tears ready to overflow. Instead, she blinked them back. "If nobody speaks about this place, how do you know it really exists? How did you know to send them there?"

"Have you forgotten I'm a Reaper? And I wasn't sending *them* there. I sent your father there. Billy should not have been in that light."

"But how can you be so sure? Maybe you made a mistake. Maybe Billy can escape."

Roman looked her in the eyes. For a moment he seemed to contemplate whether to actually answer. Finally, he said, "I know, because I've been there."

He turned from her and walked into the corridor.

"Where are you going?" she demanded.

"Away."

"Away where?"

"Away anywhere."

Within seconds, Eliza was behind him, the damn robe wrapping her legs and nearly tripping her. "You need a hospital."

"I'll be fine."

"What about Billy?"

Roman paused. "Are you deaf?"

He turned to face her, his broken arm cradled against his chest. "What part of 'your brother's dead' do you not understand? How many times do I have to say it before it registers inside that head of yours?"

"I was dead."

"And, if you carry on, you're gonna be again – very soon."

Eliza ignored his idle threat. "You're a reaper. That means you have the ability to bring people back. To bring *him* back."

Roman clasped her by the shoulders. His hands trembled. He stared at her, just as he had in the cabin after he'd taken her from the hospital. But even then, when she'd thought him a psychopathic killer, there had been warmth in his eyes. Right now, there was only desperation. "You're stupid and deluded."

Fury at his lack of remorse flooded Eliza's veins. "And you're an arsehole." She pushed his hands from her shoulders, unbothered if he collapsed, and glared at him.

He turned to leave, but Eliza blocked his path. "I'm not done with you yet."

"But I'm done with you, and this fucking place."

The movie reel inside her head began to play. Unwelcomed, this time. She desperately tried to shut it off. She didn't want to hurt anyone else. Nevertheless, the table lamp behind Roman – and the table it sat on – started to rattle violently.

Roman steadied himself against the wall. He shifted his weight from his injured leg. "Is your telekinetic party trick supposed to scare me?"

"Why not? It scares the hell out of me." A picture left the wall and flew across the hallway.

Eliza's heart raced. Now her irritation matched his. "You're going to get Billy back, you hear?"

"Or what, Eliza? It's death by oil painting?" Roman side stepped her and hobbled along the corridor.

An ornament catapulted towards him. He ducked and watched it smash into the wall.

He straightened, his face doing its best to hide the pain that obviously crippled him. "You think you're the only one who's lost someone? We all lose people, Eliza. We all make sacrifices. You need to grow up and live with yours."

"And what sacrifices are you living with? Who, other than yourself, have you ever put first?"

Roman stared at her. When he spoke, his voice didn't convey the anger that remained in his eyes. "You."

She hadn't expected that answer. In fact, she hadn't expected any answer. The furniture stilled, and the movie reel faded.

"I sacrificed being with my son and his mother because I chose to save you instead."

Eliza remained silent. She didn't know what to say. Thank you? Somehow it sounded more patronizing than sincere.

"And now I wish I hadn't."

"You bastard." The words left her lips before she had a chance to stop them.

"Probably, but I'm a bastard who's now outta here."

"No." Eliza pulled him back. "You need to help me get my brother back first."

Roman stumbled. His knees shook under the pressure to remain standing, and he leaned against the wall again for support. "I'm getting fucked off with this demanding shit of yours."

But he didn't straighten. He bent over and just stared at his boots like they were a safe haven to hide. When he finally glanced up, the colour had drained from his face.

"Roman, you are not well. You need to rest."

"I don't have time to rest."

"Then tell me how I can get my brother back."

"I told you, Billy is dead." His hands slipped down the wall, no longer able to hold his pathetic body up. He fell to the floor and sprawled across the marble tiles. When he tried to get back up, his body shook, his arms unable to hold his own weight.

Sweat and blood soaked his jumper, and when his eyes met hers, fear was the only thing she saw.

His last words were little more than a whisper. "Don't let them take me back."